2

S0-BND-387

# THE DRUM CONCERTO

Other Books by EMILY KATHARINE HARRIS

◀ POETRY ▶

SAINTLY MILK TO BETTER WINE

CARNIVAL WOODS (With Ellen Tifft)

A GYPSY SOLD ME HEATHER

WALK CHANT

# The Drum Concerto

## STORIES BY EMILY KATHARINE HARRIS

MIDDLEBURY COLLEGE LIBRARY

◫ IRIS PRESS ◫

3/1980
am. Lit

PS
3558
A6445
D7

IRIS PRESS, Publisher
27 Chestnut Street
Binghamton, New York 13905

© 1979 by Emily Katharine Harris

All rights reserved

Printed in the United States of America

LIBRARY OF CONGRESS CATALOGING IN PUBLICATION DATA

Harris, Emily Katharine, Date—
    The drum concerto.
    I. Title.
PZ4.H31354Dr  [PS3558.A6445]   813′.5′4   78-31137
ISBN 0-916078-05-1

This project is supported by a grant from
the National Endowment for the Arts in
Washington, D. C., a federal agency.

On the cover and title page are reproductions
of a painting by the author.

# ACKNOWLEDGMENTS

The following four stories were first published in *The Anglo-Welsh Review*:

"Providence," Volume 13, Number 32 (Winter 1963);
"The Steps in the Dance," Volume 23, Number 52 (Summer 1974);
"Goodbye to Two People," Volume 14, Number 34 (Winter 1964-65);
"The Legend of Gray Mountain," Volume 16, Number 37 (Spring 1967).

The following two stories were first published in *Antaeus*:

"Regan the East," 4 (Winter 1971);
"We Laughed Till We Cried Till We Laughed," 13/14 (Spring/Summer 1974).

"The Happy Couple" was first published in *Heirs*, Volume 6, Number 1 (Winter 1975/1976).

We thank the editors of the journals cited above for permission to reprint these stories. In some cases they have been slightly revised.

FOR ELLEN TIFFT

# CONTENTS

# INTRODUCTION

READING CONTEMPORARY fiction is usually an exercise in déjà vu—not only has someone done it before and done it better, but dozens are doing the same thing, with slight variations, at the present moment. Consequently, the pleasure of discovering a new writer clears the lenses and makes one adjust one's sense of the world surrounding us. In the work of Emily Katharine Harris, it turns out to be a multiple correction. She focusses her keen, intense, narrative eye on one kind of material and then the opposite extreme. From one story to the next she introduces us to mental patients and mandarins, those who are engaged in the struggle for equilibrium and those who are blessed with the "grasping imagination" which masters the circumstances around them. Concomitantly, her settings range from sleazy motels, sordid bars, to the most elegant interiors. In the former, she sometimes reminds me of the kind of loneliness and terror Edward Hopper can evoke, and in the latter there is a late, tentative modulation of Henry James. It is as though an elegant-souled person had been subjected to so much metamorphic circumstance that she has been forced to become a quick-change artist.

Consequently, the reading of *The Drum Concerto* is somewhat of a staccato experience, and some readers may not be able to make the constant adjustments of sympathy and understanding which are required. They will prefer the longer, more sustained, pieces which calibrate their effects exquisitely, and it must be admitted that, on the whole, these are the most successful. But they will perhaps miss the full rhythm of the book which insists that existence is blatant with antinomies. It is as though the author were turning restlessly here and there from one kind of life to another—if one will not yield meaning, the other might. In this sense, the entire collection seems to be a search for health and wholeness. There is not much resolution, the endings of the stories are generally muted and inconclusive, but in the obsessive gathering of a wide variety of experience, there is at least an implied hope and a tough-minded resistence to the dissolution of herself and others.

On her deathbed, Gertrude Stein was asked, "What is the

answer?"—and she replied, "What is the question?" Emily Katharine Harris asks as many questions as anyone could desire, or handle, and in this strategy, often employed with a mordant wit, she puts off the dark day when we close our minds on too little too soon. There may be a touch of the macabre in a dance of so many interrogative gestures, intense and vital though they are, but at least they provide a widening circle, a ceremony, around the mysteries of the spirit.

*Charles Edward Eaton*
WOODBURY, CONNECTICUT
1979

THIS IS A WORK OF THE IMAGINATION
AND ANY RESEMBLANCE TO PERSONS LIVING OR
DEAD IS PURELY COINCIDENTAL.

# REGAN THE EAST

ESTUS AND I rented the Bonney-Gere House at East Tonbridge the summer of 1956; that is ten years ago but I remember it perfectly. It has colored my thinking, my painting, my life with Estus and with everyone I meet, every act, thought and even my dreams.

Last night as the city seared through the rainy streets I sat before an unlit fire—unlit because I was so intent on my thoughts motion was forgotten, and even Estus comes and goes in the room without any response from me. Tonight as we drank a bottle of Suragni he brought from Algiers after his visit last fall he said he had grown to love silence. And I was happy because a quiet silence between people is a fine and lovely thing.

Last night, for what reason I don't know, I sank into a wondering, marveling, querying three hours pondering on the summer, with Estus, at East Tonbridge, where the tall elms and bulging old apple trees shaded high grass; the past stood over the town and Estus was the whole of it, to me.

Very much because of Regan.

Estus and I met in Istanbul the summer of 1955, at Ben Loman's hotel by the bay. I heard about the hotel by chance from some quite desperate looking men who stopped by my table on the boat on the way. Whatever their past, a drink seemed to be what they wanted, that, and to reach Istanbul in a hurry. Along with talk hinging amazingly on types of cattle and cattle dogs came out the information about a small hotel on the bay and Ben Loman, who owned it. Perhaps it was because I was charmed by the warm brown eyes of the younger of the two men—his name was Guy Something Italian—and his attentiveness to my emptying glass. I went on a long devious sort of walk to find the hotel, and stayed there the full month I was in the plaintive and beautiful-of-blues city.

Estus came a week later; I first saw him on his small cluttered balcony next to mine one evening when I was frankly longing to talk to someone about Tanglewood or Mount Washington, or, though I do not like them, a hot dog.

I had walked out onto my balcony for a cigarette and drink before I went out into the city looking for dinner. The room beside mine had been empty and I rather liked that and felt the vast view was mine alone. It surprised me utterly to see a tall man, his back to me, standing among the vivid cheap ashtrays and other objects Ben liked to put around his boarders' quarters; the man held a small flute in his hands and did not move, if he heard me. My God, if he blows on that all the time, I thought. But he merely smoothed it in his long hands and watched the water and the ships. Once he sighed, I thought partly in fatigue, partly at the stupendous width of the view. Not good to interrupt, I decided, and withdrew to my room. He would have known I was there by the penetrating Turkish tobacco in my Eccos; I admired the fact that he did not rush into an introduction. In fact I thought how good not to have to bother at all, however long we both stayed.

And we were never formally introduced; on the next evening at midnight when I had returned from a long walk with my cousin, Custanza, passing through that week, he stood on his balcony in nothing but a pair of gray slacks. This time he turned his head and looked at me briefly, silently. I, the same. And at the same minute we smiled.

That was the beginning; and how much, how much was left unsaid of love; Estus, you fine, you temperate, you of the large thoughts, I am happy I learned my lesson from Regan. I did learn it, at last.

We returned via Greece and Dubrovnik at the end of the month to find a place to live and a place where I could paint. Estus was deeply involved in memoirs of the Italian battles he had fought in during the war and we drove from the city often to find a house in the country. Money was no problem for either of us; it was simple, when we came on the Bonney-Gere House, to walk once around it, to look briefly at the cool sparsely furnished rooms, and to contract to move in then.

It was June; for one day there was to be a wedding there for a young relative of the owner, Mrs. Hadley Spear; we said we would turn it all over to her and leave for a week but she said with typical New England practicality that the arrangements would be simple; they would move the furniture out of the dining room, that looked over at the Gunshaw Hills, place nothing in the room but rows of cedars, and of course a white satin cushion for the couple to kneel on.

So, simply, the wedding took place. It was on that day I met Regan Bergman.

She was later than the other guests and came alone, wearing a sari of scarlet and gold, with her thick blond hair hanging blown around her shoulders. She was barefoot and held a small gibbon by the hand. The gibbon behaved well at the wedding, contenting herself with toying with Regan's hair from her seat on her shoulder. All the guests stood during the short and lovely ceremony and I could examine Regan's features from where I stood. She perhaps could have been Jewish but although she had a handsomely beaked nose I thought not. Her front upper teeth were of the sort that protruded but attractively, giving her jaw line a special fineness. Her eyes were large, gray and dreamy and thoughtful in turn. She would gaze around quite frankly and look at the other guests as she willed during the service, unabashed to meet eyes staring back at her.

After the ceremony we all moved about the garden eating the rather sparse refreshments Mrs. Sears saw fit to serve; we briefly were introduced to guests, among them Regan who seemed friendly and remote at the same time; then she walked directly to a stocky young man with a cold face and thin lips and said "Roger, you'd better come to supper tonight; Sandor will be there." She searched his face with a smile. Roger blushed and bent to caress the gibbon.

"I guess I can come," he muttered. "How do you do," he said stiffly to the gibbon. Regan moved away to go and walk by herself through the rose arbor. Completely unselfconscious she was singing La Damoiselle Elue, in a low voice but passionately; looking at the red-cheeked linen-and-seersucker-dressed New Englanders that made up the main part of the gathering I could see that she had arranged things so that she would get the most out of the afternoon.

Estus told me something about her afterwards. He had been drawn aside after the wedding by Frieda Brooks who found Regan too fey, too precious, and commented at length acidly about her. Regan, when she was not traveling the length and breadth of the globe, lived with her aunt, who was generally known as Mrs. Wycherly but who had been married to a count; a small woman with a cast in one dark brown eye, she wore shantung in black or navy blue and no jewelry at any time; her hair was jet black and pulled back into a severe bun. Her teeth were her best point but they were rarely seen in a smile; the Countess never smiled even when confronted with a superb joke told in good taste by a man she favored. She would, at such a time, cock her head and an eyebrow, look at the floor and say "Ah." Her relationships with her niece were cool and distant; both went their proper way in and out of the large gray mansard house on Old Windsor Road; the servants, most of them European, ministered skillfully and allowed no amusement to penetrate their expressions in Miss Regan's presence. Frieda told Estus that Regan had a constant claque, a stream of young, medium and elderly men calling on her, and they often stayed a week uninvited.

I was interested in the girl—she must have been my age but she seemed somewhat younger, or ageless, rather; and thought of putting her, or her essence, in some way into a painting; one morning at eight o'clock I walked over to Old Windsor Road, sure that Regan would be up early.

She was up and I found her halfway up the huge stairway in a chiffon ball gown; she had not been to bed at all; she was looking upwards whistling and speaking in a language I thought must be Oriental. To my delight a scarlet bird with long curving tail feathers flew down from somewhere above and alighted on her shoulder. Calmly then she looked at me and said "Let's get some yogurt and go out by the pond." The bird caressing her hair, she led me through several large cool rooms into the butler's pantry where two short dark hairy men were washing a mass of thin china, and on to the buttery. I expected the usual commercial pots of stamped yogurt, but Regan lifted out a large white crock and dipped out two soup dishes for us. In a huge basin beside this were bright orange peach slices; she heaped some on our yogurt and we walked out the back door and into the kitchen garden.

"Oh," she said absently, "this is Karanye." She indicated the bird, who was greatly excited at being out of doors. "He's from Thailand. His lady friend is Filla; she's blue. She stays in front of my mirror or Celeste's"—I gathered this was Mrs. Wycherly—"and looks at herself, doesn't she, sweet one," she said to the bird. Rose briars and coarse hay pulled at Regan's dress but we went swiftly through a pasture to the small perfect pond surrounded with clipped lawns and groupings of cedars and apple trees. We sat down.

I told her that Estus sent greetings.

"Ah, Estus—he looks marvelously Scottish," Regan said. She had not begun to eat but was delicately dissecting a cornflower. "And he's yours, and you're his. In that pure house—all so pure," she said dreamily. She looked at me with her firm jaw lighted by the sun. "I think you should leave each other before you get too bound up," she commented, surprising me with this personal remark. "Yes," she mused as she laid the flower in the grass and continued to look at it. "People will try to make it all regular; but by the time they succeed in doing that I hope I shall be in Ottawa," she added somewhat vaguely. I somehow felt one did not quiz a person like Regan. She added "I know some people there."

The bird circled us, making a raw peeping sound, and came to rest on my shoulder. In the early morning sun it gave me a wonderful feeling of closeness to some far-off place where meals were not punctual, worship took any form, most things were acceptable to most people, and to one who did not demand a clear outline for life it was beautiful. With Karanye caressing my cheek my mind wandered to this place where ultimates rested gently on a tough and tender people. Suddenly my painting and its exigencies receded; or, rather, took on a new sort of beckoning overtone, as if saying it could be a farther, stronger, lovelier statement in this other world.

I thought briefly of the people Regan knew in Ottawa; all I knew was that they would not be the customary articulate organized well clothed Northerners who are the ones other Northerners know and visit briefly, in Ottawa.

Regan said thoughtfully "These people have a farm. They're Indian. I go there off and on, to talk to the children." She stirred her untouched yogurt and set it down once more. "There are seven of them, all ages."

The days don't wear on her, I suddenly observed inside my mind, of Regan. She's something of a saint, a child, one of those children of nature that light like butterflies on life. A lovely one; I thought of the Blessed Damoiselle under the rose arbor. If it should rain, she was a part of the downpour; if there was blood, much blood, she would accept it as perfect poetry as she would a storm. I wondered how death would affect her. "I am just now painting a picture of a suicide," I said. I felt the morning sun beating on me; Karanye took flight, swooped once brilliantly over the water and returned to Regan's knee. I was not diverted; my suicide haunted me. Creepingly I began to feel I had been disloyal to him. I had killed him; I had conceived and then killed him. He lay endlessly fatigued, endlessly rejected, endlessly unfulfilled on a big canvas, in pale convincing colors. He seemed, at that moment, to call me. A sudden perspiration covered me and I hastily stood, picking up my bowl as I did so. Unquestioningly Regan, looking into her bird's eye and talking to him, stood also, and we walked back to the great house. We left our food in the spotless, huge bare kitchen and I told Regan I must go back to my suicide; "suddenly," I put it.

"Yes," she said, pausing in the hall, her mouth open as if in mid-thought. "Most do go back, don't they; but I would just let them have the beauty of death."

"Ah, Regan," I sighed, and could smile, for then. "Goodbye for this morning," I added, and left her standing, again, on the stairs, calling for Karanye's wife.

The door to our house was open; I entered it clogged, choked with the many things I wanted to say. Estus was sitting on a windowsill eating a plate of eggs. I could not speak. I was so happy he was there, with eggs, in a morning light; was happy I could go to my suicide and feel unspeakable, unfathomably terrible about him, I was glad to find an Ecco lying on the table and to light it and savor its taste; I was infinitely glad to be committed, involved, standing over perhaps some terrible pit, some hell, holding my life up from it, loving Estus, requiring, getting, cursing, reaching, estimating, judging, yes, judging to the point of hate, if necessary.

To Estus I said, after a peaceful silence in which I could hear one thrush call, "I know what sort of thing to put on the face of my dead man." There was another silence. Then Estus said quietly "I believe you could put the right face on him," and I told him I would go immediately and work. He nodded, looking at me. He set his plate on the table and stood leaning on his hands, not looking at me. "I brought a speçial bottle of Raki from Crete, last time; let's drink."

We stood the plain dusty bottle on the stove as we drank and the thrush called in the deep woods; plainly the face of my suicide showed before me: that of a man who would not be involved.

So began a summer of hard and soft facts, decisions, mocking and seriousness, mastery, partial mastery, waiting, working. I think I heard that Regan left her aunt's suddenly in the company of a Nigerian; then someone said she was in Calcutta.

Estus and I wonder somewhat more about a lot of other people.

# WE LAUGHED TILL WE
# CRIED TILL WE LAUGHED

I WAS just leaving Mrs. Ballou's on Pearl Street to walk home in the February twilight. Mrs. Ballou—Mrs. Fern Hazlett Ballou—who gave piano lessons in the drag-your-fingers-up-the-keyboard-before-you-start type jazz, stood by the orange varnish woodwork at Number 4237, holding her orchid shrug closely under her raddled throat as she pressed me hurriedly into the weather. It was cold and Mrs. Ballou's house had depressed me. Mr. Ballou sat as always in an overstuffed chair in the dining room, his bare feet with long grainy toenails on a newspaper, gently breaking wind all afternoon. Mrs. Ballou, a warty growth on one eyelid, had played a rendition of "When the Red Red Robin," and then had sunk her skinny tall frame on to the chair beside mine while I played "Tiptoe Through The Tulips," imitating her as best I could with waggles of my head and much throwing of my hands and arms dizzily around. I had not mastered the secret smile she held on her face throughout. I was only thirteen and aware I was plain and awkward. Mother said I would lengthen out and be like my father, who was dead; she said I'd be a knockout like all Swedes.

All I knew, playing sweatily, grimily in the overheated room with the air full of gases from Mr. Ballou's sickness, was that I had on a Kelly green stringy hair ribbon, I wasn't much good at anything, and I had no belt to my dark green second-hand coat. It was all awful.

Outside Mrs. Ballou's, edging over the freezing slush in my old crepe-soled moccasins, my knees bare, I glanced up at the car making its way towards me along the dirty sloping street; it was a big low-slung, rattling, dirty and rusty bright blue and slunk along like a friendly tart. It was Mother's car.

My throat gulped; pure joy. Behind the V in the dirty windshield was Mother, sitting low, her frizzled hair sticking out, her small brown eyes behind the glasses peering, looking for me.

All thought of the bad air and childless hollow ways of the Ballous left me. Hope of pancakes or enchiladas in our jammed small kitchen rose within me. The car slid to a stop by the curb. Mother had on a terrible old brown and yellow plaid jacket. A bright green unpressed skirt hung over her thin thighs. One foot in a spotted beige moccasin shoe pressed the brake; the other, bare, rested comfortably on the cluttered floor. She leaned over to yank the door shut beside me as if I were still small. She twitched at the piece of striped yard goods covering a rip in my side of the seat.

"Nair-now," she said, smiling at me and clasping my cold wrist with a stubby strong hand. "Let's go eat out. Let's go to Harry's and have hamburgers." She ground the gears warmly and we spun down the hell of Pearl Street and into the spitting traffic of South Thayer.

"Pancakes," I said, all joy. I loved going to Harry's Lunch. It was warm and cheerful and Mother gave off some quality of ladyness that kept the overcoated men away. I think it was because she sang the Greek national anthem with Harry himself and then topped that with a pagan prayer in Greek. All the men sensed it was a prayer, and Harry saluted her with one boiled hairy hand with tears in his eyes and served us—her—humbly, instead of having Claire do it.

Once installed at Harry's, in a neon-lit booth on the comfortable seats, Mother blew her nose on her napkin and then without looking up took a piece of paper out of her big red cracked handbag. She began to write in her messy writing.

"I think you need a skirt," she said, writing. "How bout a new pull-over, too?" She jotted a list: "New—hair—ribbon—shoes." She looked at me.

"I gave you a comb; use it," she said, not knowing or caring that her hair looked like a collection of mattress stuffing in a high wind. "Yes, Harry," she said coolly, reaching for a greasy menu. "We would like pancakes—buckwheat, I think." That "I think" got Harry all over again; he was dying to lean his fists on the table but didn't dare.

"Okay! Yoh!" he said forcefully. He looked at me, unseeing, and back at Mother. "Buckwheat, the bes'," he echoed, and went immediately behind the counter to throw the ingredients together, glancing off and on at Mother under his sweated beetling brows.

"Mother," I said tentatively.

"What, dear," she said, looking over the second cigarette she was lighting. She looked at me steadily from behind her horn rims that tipped slightly up on the left.

"Mother, I hate to say this—but Mrs. Ballou's—smells. I mean really smells." I stopped, staring down at my fingerprints on my water glass. I frowned and went on, "I mean, it makes me want to throw up. And his toenails—."

"Just tot it up to experience, Kitty," Mother said, staring across the room. "Now, I find these things disgusting too but they're here—even Christ had to use the pot, I imagine," she added and inhaled with enjoyment. Her focus lengthened and I knew the signs of her becoming fascinated with someone across the room.

"The man with the bunch of grapes on his face—he really is quite handsome on the side that doesn't have it," she said dreamily, ashes falling generously into her lap. She leaned out a little.

"Mo-ther," I whispered, agonized. I hated deformity; I lay in bed and feared that I would be paralyzed all over and wet my bed; I feared I would go blind and fall down a manhole into the sewage and rats and drown; I feared too I would lose my arms and never do anything but sit in whatever awful chair was Kitty's Chair where my toenails would grow like Mr. Ballou's and no one would admire me. I longed to be admired but could see no reason why I should be; I had wavy unshaped short-long black hair jammed back with a ribbon; Mother made most of my clothes with the best will in the world, staying up late nights enjoying working on a strident plaid or dull brown pattern for me, proud, with sweat on her upper lip, threads on her lap and love in her eyes.

"Here, lambie," she would say, throwing it in a ball to me across the room and turning to fold up the remnants which she never used. She also loved to have Laura Whipple give her Marguerite's out-grown clothes for me. I couldn't see why because Marguerite was large and sly and I thought bourgeois; but they were rich. One time three dresses came my way from her: a large-flowered red and white linen, a navy blue princess style and a white linen with pleats and an embroidered bunch of cherries on the shoulder. I hated them because they were castoffs and wore them negligently, using the skirt folds to hold hot things and throwing them into my chair when I took them off. I preferred my clothes, made by Mother.

I looked for someone to admire me but it was hopeless. It was my constant search as I butted, dreamed and worried my way to school and Mrs. Ballou's. Mrs. Ballou had been my idea: I saw myself another Judy Garland only better, capturing the hearts of America as I molded the music, my lovely and intelligent face on the silver screen endearing me to all.

"Hey!" Mother was saying. "Eat." She warmly buttered her pancakes, poured syrup and wedged a large forkful into her mouth. Suddenly she lurched forward and blew the mouthful on her plate. "Any other damned fool woulda burned their mouth," she said smiling, tears in her eyes. She paused. "Now, you eat *all* yours. You don't eat enough. Have a butterscotch sundae, after," she suggested. She looked back at me to enjoy again the moment she had spat out her food and we laughed till we cried. Then, in silence and pleasure, we started to eat the pancakes, their smell mingling with tobacco, soap, syrup and wet wool.

"Ah," Mother sighed. "My shoes are off somewhere under the table; I must look, in a few minutes—." Her voice trailed off as she looked up and focused on someone behind me. "By golly, it's Helen!" I turned and saw with happiness Mother's sister Helen walking towards our booth. I clumsily got out of it somehow, and waited for her to clasp me to her. I recalled Mother telling me how taken Helen was with me at four; I had had a rosebud mouth and sang *Au Clair de la Lune* to them—the dear thing I used to be, I thought. Ah, Aunt Helen, admire me. . . .

She wore an expensive fawn cashmere coat with a neat collar under her neat, chic, waved hair, and an expensive small hat. Her large lips and spreading nose were composed and expertly made up; her glasses were clean, sparkling and smart. In neatly gloved hands—the gloves were the palest pink, and kid, I knew—she carried a large smart plain handbag with a dangling gold chain for the gloves, and on her lapel was a big diamond H. She wafted operatic perfume all around her; her profusion of white folded teeth gleamed and her glasses sparkled as her cold glove touched my wrist and she pressed the side of her hat to my cheek.

"Dear little Kitty," she said in her phony Virginia accent, already moving towards Mother. Mother got up and embraced her and they played a silent secret game of Pease-Porridge-Hot and then laughed merrily. "I recognized your car from the taxi, Honey."

"Well, are you through?" she said, still standing. Mother had sat down and moved over to make room for her.

"Oh. Don't you want to eat?" Mother asked her, brushing her ashes from the seat.

"I had bushels on the train," Aunt Helen said, staring through her glasses at our stacks of wheatcakes. "C'mon, le's go home and talk, out of this—place," she said, and jiggled her eyebrows at me. Somehow I knew, sadly, that this was a gesture she would have made to whoever sat near; she always, I remembered, had to be funny.

Mother and Aunt Helen preceded me out of the cafeteria and I looked down briefly at Aunt Helen's tiny trim ankles in dainty fur-edged boots. Mother's old shoes were whole but her legs were spattered with slush. A taxi waited outside.

"He has ma bag, honey," Aunt Helen said. "Here, sweetheart, give him this." She held out a new five-dollar bill to me.

"Do I give it—all—to him?" I said, looking at Mother.

"Here, sweetie, give," Aunt Helen said impatiently and took the money back. She stood a yard away from the cab on a dry clear spot. The driver leaned out the window, his breath rushing. "Want me?" he asked, tired.

"No, suh, I want my bag," Aunt Helen said, twitching the bill. A colored man went by, brushing her slightly, his dark hanging coat spattered and torn. Aunt Helen turned to Mother and made a deft vaudeville gesture as if she would break into a buck and wing. I looked at Mother, who was standing hugging her arms in her jacket and her red bag hung open. She tilted her head on one side with an absent-minded smile, looking at me.

The driver paid, we walked to our old dirty big car and all got in the front seat.

"Ah'm plumb tuckered, Peg," Aunt Helen said to Mother. "Ah, I'd love a cup of tea. Make me one, sugar?"

"Yup. Sure," Mother said, squinting through the sleet that had begun to fall. She swung our rattling car in a swooping slipping arc.

All the way home Aunt Helen reminisced about Lucie, about Baird, Amy Bee, someone named Quent, Jack, Ollie and Dot. She did not look at me or talk to me.

At home in our green shabby bungalow on Third Street, Mother and I went stumbling around in the dark turning on lights and worrying about no heat. Aunt Helen undid her coat but kept it on. She took off her hat and ran a comb through her beautiful hair.

"Les see if you're tall as my Suzy Belle," Aunt Helen said to me, holding out a peremptory arm in front of the mirror. Glad of attention and aware that I was dumb, I went to stand beside her. She put a perfumed cool arm about me and surveyed us in the dim mirror over the untidy cold fireplace full of half-buried butts. I saw my white anxious face and stringy hair beside Aunt Helen's tall, groomed figure. She looked at me briefly.

"Well, you're gettin' there," was all she said, her arm dropping from me, "Suzy Belle's my li'l light o' my life," Aunt Helen called to Mother, who was in the kitchen trying to make the stove work. I knew Suzy Belle was Aunt Helen's one other niece, who lived in Virginia near her.

With a clank Mother put down whatever implement she was trying to work with. "Kitty, come here, for heaven's sake," she said loudly. I went to the kitchen.

"Lambie pie, you start the stove. Somehow it'll work for you," she said. "Tea," she said under her breath and slammed a pan down.

"What, hon?" Aunt Helen called dreamily. I worked on the stove and a small jet of flame appeared. "There," I said, going proudly to Aunt Helen in the other room. "You can have tea shortly, madam," I said, being theatrical. I thought I was rather good.

"Don't talk like your father, hon," Aunt Helen said, her mouth drawing into a line. "Never could stand that man."

Mother appeared with tea for Aunt Helen and sat down with a cigarette. She looked at me with a worried smile.

"Why don't you play something while I fix Helen a bite," she said, ashes dropping into her crushed lap. She wore a dirty apron of a hideous design.

"No, you play," I said, somehow realizing it was hopeless to try to win over this smooth aunt. "I'll make her something, something quite good."

I walked through the garish dining room where the only nice things were two still lifes on the brown wall-paper done by Mother during the week we had taken in Harwichport two summers before; one hung crooked, the one of tiger lilies; I straightened it, pushed a maroon and black sweater of mine out of sight in a drawer, and went to the kitchen where I began preparations for baking powder biscuits. I thought those, and some cold salami, and a glass of milk would be very nice for a guest. I waited for the piano to sound with Mother's spotty renderings of Chopin and Scarlatti; or perhaps *Der Erlkönig*, that I loved.

Aunt Helen came, once, curiously, to the door. She stood leaning on the jamb in a beige wool and pearls, her large lips pursed, her hungry eyes watching what I did. Then she went silently away; I could hear low voices in the living room. They seemed to be intense about something.

Just as I had put the food on the green tray with our one slightly rumpled Italian place mat, I saw Aunt Helen in her coat go and stand in the hall.

"All right, go on and go," I heard Mother say.

"Ah'm goin, Peg, ah'm goin," Aunt Helen said. "You and Kitty can live like this but ah cayan't, honey chile. Well, boompety-boom," she said. I stared over the tray in the kitchen doorway.

The door closed on her. Mother came into the dining room; her face was not red but her features looked hurt. I slammed the tray onto the dining table and dashed to the front door. I wrenched it open and yelled out thinly, "Don't you ever come here more, you fiend!" to Aunt Helen's slim back going on down the street. She did not turn.

Cold but happy, I shut the door. Mother was fingering some ugly black material at the dining table.

"We didn't get to finish our pancakes, Mother," I said. I stood looking at her, stricken with concern for her.

"Ah, pee on her," Mother said suddenly. "Kitty, she was always like that—." She sat down happily, lighting a cigarette, ready to reminisce.

"Here. Now, eat," I said, putting the tray with its heavy biscuits and strong meat in front of her.

"Yes," Mother said, warming to the thought of food. She buttered a biscuit, crumbs raining everywhere. "Lambie, get my bag, it's on the ice box. I want that shopping list for your skirt and all."

I went to find it, happy, and old.

# THE HAPPY COUPLE

RYMAN JOHN Puckey sat contentedly at the wheel of his new Chrysler waiting for his wife who was buying fish. The fact that she so often bought fish did not disturb him particularly; all their married forty-three years she had fed him with much fish, pudding, consommé and many overcooked domesticated pale dishes, but she had such a queenly air of not seeing what she ate that he was proud of the way she did things.

Ah, Marianna, he sighed humorously to himself as he spied her toque moving above a coffee-colored Ford towards where he sat. Her glasses flashed as she crossed the street majestically and her beige cotton gloves held the small flat package of the fish.

She stopped as usual outside the car door waiting for him to open it; he rolled from his comfortable seat and went around courteously to help her in. This he had always done, knowing most men never did; but he was of the school that preferred women who liked to be served; some things were reserved for men to do, some for women only, like making all the fringed shades in the dining room windows hang even or picking off the dead fern fronds in the hall.

Marianna sat erectly beside him and said, "I look at all those dead fishes and always think of an old teacher I had in Sunday school. She looked just like them . . . smelled, too, as I recall . . . MmmmHmm."

Ryman started the car and pulled out into the line of traffic not paying too much attention to the other cars. One of them blared his horn; Ryman rolled down the window to say, into the other car, "Shut up." He laughed and drove calmly and very slowly along Mygatt Street past the bakery and Humbert's Restaurant. "We'll have to go there again sometime," he said, gesturing. Marianna said, "Any time you wish." She did not look at him; she never looked directly at anyone she was with. She did her looking when they were involved elsewhere in the room. She had a very good notion of how her husband looked at all times. Many took him for a Roman Catholic priest because of his weight, his large amount of snowy hair and his ripe red face; also he always wore luminous black clothes and a black tie and could frequently be seen out for lunch with some of the true members of the cloth. He usually picked up the tab for these lunches, not wanting to owe Catholics anything since he was a Baptist himself; but he was proud of the number of Catholic friends he had; acquaintances, really; he and Marianna had no friends, only acquaintances. But the tenor of their life did not require friends and the others filled in the little silences very well.

They turned into Baldwin Street and off that into Alice; they arrived at their drive just as the mailman dropped something into their box. Calmly they went to the side door, unlocked it and entered the square cream-colored house. Marianna took off her maroon coat and blue scarf and the toque, neatly putting them in the hall closet, the door of which she closed firmly. Then she took the mail—one letter—out of the box and went to her desk to find the letter opener.

"It's from Adele," she said to Ryman who was buffing his shoes with a sheepskin polisher, his coat still on.

She read. "Wants us to come and take her out today," she told him.

"Mmh," he said, buffing heartily. "Well, we can, why not, poor devil." He stood looking down at his shoes proudly and then put the buffer in the drawer of the dresser in one corner of the hall.

Marianna laid the letter on the dresser and took the fish to the kitchen where she put it into the refrigerator. Not bothering with an apron and not concerned that she was wearing her best boucle dress and the earrings Ryman had bought for her last birthday, clusters of brilliant fake jewelry which, with the plenitude of rouge she wore always made her look very festive, she began to make junket, neatly boiling just enough milk and arranging four dessert saucers on the working counter. It took her fifteen minutes before they all stood neatly filled waiting to jell.

Ryman, still in his coat, came into the kitchen, the newspaper in his hands. He was reading one of the back pages. "Think I'll take a run down to Solomon's," he said. "Says they've got those three way lamps in again we wanted. And I think I'll go to Rosen's and get some sort of overnight bag for Adele. We don't want people to think we don't care what she carries her things in. Certainly no more paper bags."

Marianna stepped around the spotless bare kitchen watering her philodendron and feeding two monstrous gold fish that swam in a bowl over the sink. She liked her kitchen almost as much as she liked the dining room with the lace tablecloth always on the table and the large photograph of Ryman on the sideboard. She admired the effect of halo the photographer had included behind his big and impressive head; no doubt he thought he was immortalizing one of the divine calling; Ryman let him think it as usual and was happy.

"So goodbye," he called to her as he went out the side door.

Marianna did not answer; she never spoke if the utterance was to be something trite. She was not cold; she simply would not waste words.

She got out Adele's letter again and reread it in the living room, sitting down at last. She was accustomed to Adele's shocking letters from the institution where she lived; even Adele's reproaches as to the way they had deprived her in her upbringing she took calmly; she did not approve of undisciplined letter writing and when the first outpourings arrived she burned them, after Ryman had pored over them.

She paused to reread one sentence Adele had underlined: I will not NOT no no no Marry Roger Singleton and no one can MAKE me . . .

Why this fixation on Roger Singleton, the simpleton, she asked herself. I never said she should marry Roger or anyone else. If she wants to stay single in that place her whole life I can't help it.

She set the letter aside and went upstairs looking for an emery board. She sat at her dressing table and carefully groomed her already neat nails. She added a coat of pink polish and thought a bit longer about Adele and Roger. Knowing that this kind of thinking never got anywhere she dismissed the subject and turned her attention to choosing clothes to go to the cleaner, both hers and her husband's. Soon she had a heavy armful laid out on the bed for Ryman to take away. She felt tidy and clean when she finished and decided to fill in the rest of the time while Ryman was out with a short stroll around the block. Another woman would have planned to include dropping in at a friend's but Marianna needed no one but Ryman and needed him only as a focal point for the pale meals she made and ate so coolly.

She knew that Adele's room was neat; she always cleaned there when she cleaned the guest room and theirs; all of Adele's things were stored in labeled boxes in the attic; she kept out two or three books to make the room a little less bare but she knew Adele never read them; they would always be in the bookends she had set them in. She had enjoyed *The Rosary* as a girl; why shouldn't Adele enjoy it; Shelley was a favorite with everyone, so that too was there; the third book was Showerman's *Eternal Rome*, a solid book that should help anyone with flighty thoughts. She knew it steadied her a great deal just to see it in its place.

Another woman in Marianna's position would have been impatient for her husband's return but Marianna knew in good time they would reach the hospital and their unpleasant daughter and get in all the visiting they could tolerate; perhaps Adele would have overnight permission to come home with them and she resigned herself to this, counting on Ryman's serenity and booming laughter to keep things on a fairly even keel. Ryman was far less bothered by the whole situation than most people would have been, probably because Adele was adopted and it surely was not their fault she had become ill three years before at the age of seventeen. Marianna decided against the walk around the block and went to the kitchen to see what could be found for a light supper with the fish. Actually there was not enough of it for three; she meditated for a few minutes on casseroles. Adele only picked at her food so she need not be overly concerned with the meal. She too felt calmly cheated that the girl they had taken in at the age of six had turned out so badly but life went on; she and Ryman were serene and compatible throughout the simple days; they never argued and the house was quiet and comfortable without Adele's troubled presence.

The side door closed; Ryman was home. She went from the kitchen to greet him; he held a blue plastic overnight case in his hand and had just set down a compact cream-colored lamp.

"Rightyo," he said. The case had a tag that read $3.98; the lamp, he pointed out to her, was ten dollars on sale and well worth it, he thought, for reading the newspaper, for instance.

"When would you like to leave for Adele," she asked him, picking dead fern fronds from the plant.

"Right away, why not," he answered, picking up his black hat which he had left behind while on his errands.

Marianna put on the scarf again carefully and her coat and the toque, took out a small rouge case from the dresser and renewed her bright color. They went out to the car ticking in the spring heat, in the driveway.

Ryman turned on the radio to some schmaltz and hummed as it played. He drove quickly and they were soon on the drive leading to the hospital; it stipulated fifteen miles an hour but Ryman serenely took the hill at forty-five. They passed a sad file of female patients out walking with two attendants; all stared hungrily at them and at their speed.

They parked outside the main building where Adele was housed and went in to the large dark hall off which was the ward they wanted. The door was open and they passed into a high ceilinged corridor where two steel engravings of Roman battles hung.

Mrs. Meehan was on duty, starched and efficient and giving off a smell of cheap pink perfume; as soon as she saw the Puckeys she bawled "ADELE! Adele PUCKEY!" Then she said to them in a normal voice "Nice day," and went on with a list.

Adele appeared in a doorway and walked toward her parents with a large paper bag on one arm. She hurried toward Ryman as she drew nearer and said in a whisper, "Wait till I tell you the latest!"

16 □

"Here," Marianna said, turning to Ryman for the suitcase. "Here—put your things in this."

Adele got all the contents of the bag out on Mrs. Meehan's desk and started to shove them into the suitcase untidily. Mrs. Meehan said impatiently, "Now your mother wouldn't pack like that—here—let me do that." Seriously she repacked the clothes and several comic books with them; she briefly looked at them and shook her head at the Puckeys.

"Sign here, please," she said, sliding a sheet of paper across the desk to them.

The three went out into the March sun.

As soon as they were in the car Adele said, "Marianna, you wouldn't believe what goes on in this place. In the bed next to mine last night two women got in together and were making out—what do you think of that?"

"I don't know. I might like it," Marianna said, looking out the window at the bare fields and tall elms.

"Marianna. You're as stinking as they are. Ryman, what would you do?"

"Me? Never thought about it. Turn over and go to sleep and forget about it." Ryman made a smooth turn off the hospital grounds and picked up speed. He turned up the music and hummed with it. "Spending the night with us?" he asked Adele.

"No—those clothes I want to put away—they told me to take them home; I can stay for supper. But, honestly, I get scared—these people are just not good for me." Adele went on, enjoying feeling upset and featuring herself. She lit a long cigarette and smoked untidily all the way home, flicking the ashes on the floor. Marianna said nothing.

They drove into the small yard and got out, Ryman with the suitcase, Marianna stopping to scrape a small amount of gravel from the drive with her narrow polished shoe.

"Well. What'll we do?" Ryman asked them once they were inside.

"I want to talk to you. I want you to get me out of there," Adele said hysterically. Her face was garishly made up, her lipstick did not follow the lines of her pulpy thick mouth, her eye make-up looked gummy and her hair was dirty and uncombed.

They moved into the living room and sat, a large space of brown patterned rug between all of them; the shades were half drawn and the room poorly lit.

"Marcy Delaney has cancer and won't let them operate on her," Adele went on, smoking again. "She has this big red thing on her front; I saw it when she was washing; Jesus, I felt like throwing up."

"Adele. You are going to see many remarkable things in that institution," Marianna said with deliberation. "You must realize that the people you describe cannot live outside of that place for the very reasons you are complaining about to us. They are not socially adjusted; they don't do the right thing at the right time so they must stay where they cannot harm others or themselves. Probably some quite funny things happen," she added ruminatively.

"Like what? Like what?" Adele jumped up. "Nothing is funny. Oh. I went to a Jerry Lewis movie the other afternoon and that was funny as hell; I'm in love with him," she said coyly to her father. "You love me, don't you, Ryman John Puckey? You have to. I've got you, and I've got Norman over at the store—he loves me; but not my own mother. No, no, no—never her..." Adele flopped down again on the sofa and took a massive drag on her cigarette.

"Now, now," Ryman said peaceably. "How would you like a Pepsi?" He got up. "I'll get us all one," he said, going out to the kitchen. Adele got up suddenly and followed him. In the kitchen she stage whispered to him, "Get me out of there, Ryman John Puckey. I know my mother put me there and you want me home, your only daughter—I'm young and lovely and ought to get married and Jerry Lewis is just my type, I just know; we could have a reception here and it'd be fun and you could perform the ceremony—I've told everybody you're a Catholic priest so you could."

Ryman got three cold cans of soft drink from the clean refrigerator and handed one to Adele. She wrenched the metal top off and drank a long swallow, her eyes hotly on Ryman.

"Well. Sit down," he said, pulling out a kitchen chair for her and then sitting himself. "You look very pretty today," he said after a pause in which her eyes were glued on him.

"So it's okay if I get married?" she went on, sitting on the edge of her chair. "I can marry Jerry Lewis, once I meet him, or I can marry Norm. Oh, Norm's nice; he works in the laundry. I love Norm. He buys me a coke any time I want one," she went on further. She suddenly scratched her groin and stood up, setting the unfinished drink on the stove. "Let's eat and get that over with," she said impatiently, going to the sink and turning on the water which she watched minutely and then turned off, leaving the spigot dripping.

Marianna came to the door. "I'll fix something," she said remotely, not looking at anyone. She moved majestically around the room preparing a simple sparse supper of soup, the two pieces of fish and the junket. She added a plate of ginger snaps. Adele had left the room. Ryman went to call her, could find her nowhere and went outside. He came around to the front of the house where he saw Adele talking to Walt, the policeman on the beat. He heard her say urgently to him, "Here he comes—DO SOMETHING!!"

Walt looked at him sheepishly and said to Adele, "I expect your supper should be ready—and I'll look into this, uh, matter you describe, Adele..." He walked on down the block and Adele stood petulantly on the sidewalk.

"He's going to get you and Marianna for locking me up, that's what we were talking about ha ha," she said defiantly.

"Come and eat, Adele," Ryman said, reaching for her arm which she yanked away. "Well, come on, anyway. We all got to eat," he said. He was hungry himself for all meals; one of his chief pleasures was to take Marianna in the new car and go as far as a neighboring town looking for places to eat. They all appealed to him, diners with home fries and eggs, old inns with dry meat and very small pieces of cheese, small roadside places with their good hamburgers, the classy places he went to with the Catholic brethren where they ate lobster.

In silence, in the kitchen, they sat down and chewed the food. Adele was a messy eater and smeared food and lipstick all over her water glass; she was jumpy and scratched a good deal. She was through picking at her food before they were and got up and took a comic book from her case, leaving it open on the sofa. She sat crouched on the edge reading avidly until they joined her. Ryman turned on the television to a quiz show which he and Marianna watched with concentration for an hour; Adele went on with her comic books. She got through them very quickly and when she had looked at them all she threw them violently one by one out into the hall. Marianna went to pick them up; Ryman said, "How about a little ride in the car before we go back?"

Marianna removed the clothes from the suitcase, closed it and placed the comic books in a neat pile on top. Adele, now absentminded and docile, followed them out to the car. As they drove through the supper-time sunshine around the neighborhood she said suddenly, "I think I'll be a nun. Norm would hate that, ooh he'd miss me I KNOW he would...." Her thoughts seemed to stay on the subject until they drew up at her building at the hospital three-quarters of an hour later.

Ryman and Marianna took her back to the ward, now dimly lit with dusty ceiling lights; a toothy black girl stood twisting her skirt in her fingers watching Adele return. Adele paid no attention to her and did not say goodbye to her parents. They went out the door to their car and got in in a silence.

On the way down the hill Ryman turned the music back on and said, "Let's go get some pie at Bus Horigan's. I'd like something hearty now that she isn't with us any more tonight, poor devil...."

"Yes, I could eat a little something," Marianna said, nodding, and a vision of a tasty sandwich came temptingly to her.

"Rightyo," Ryman said, gunning the motor heartily toward the restaurant.

# THE TART'S DEMON

BARTER BILLINGS, the horrid old man, finally moved out of our boarding house. The family that got him was an Italian one up the street who had a puffed-looking house with white asbestos shingles and hot red trim. He won't like it there and they will hate him.

He was a legacy Mrs. Meehan got when she took over the house. Mr. Billings was to stay on, having been boarded with the previous owners. He had two closet-size adjoining rooms in the rear on the second floor. They overlooked the back yard where the dogs barked, where the incinerator was, and the sandpile, and the parking lots of our house and the one next door.

Since he had nothing to do he helled around annoying everyone; he could also be a dear old duffer type too. A real gasser with a stock of remarks like "he wun't," "I cal'late," and "there's a sucker born every minute," a fact he would announce importantly on the stairs as you passed him.

I was prepared to like this old fellow. He got his own meals, I thought, and had a handsome well-shaped head, a lot of snow white hair; also he owned and rode a new lightweight English motorcycle, wearing a white linen cap, black suit and spats. Once he put a rose on my dresser while I was taking a bath, and a little later in the season he showed up with a whole bunch of them, all colors.

One time he intercepted me on the way down the dark hall to get the mop with a jolly invitation worded like this: "Hey, I bet you never seen a refrigerator like this!"—cried out with the buoyancy of Tom Swift summoning his best chum on a challenging summer morning. I went down the hall to his room, not at all wanting to see one, and he proudly opened the door of a midget refrigerator in which were two hot dogs, wrapped, a cloudy container of water, and a saucer of ugly jelly.

"J'ever see anything like that," he laughed, slamming the room door resoundingly. "Works entirely without electricity. Whole motor's contained in that compartment there. I never had a breakdown. Have a chair." With whizzing speed he yanked one around facing his Morris chair and as I lowered myself he tossed the refrigerator door shut and also sat down, bursting into talk. With hands crossed on stomach and his feet in their old leather slippers also crossed he told me all about the food he would and would not eat. "I like Swift and Company," he said. "Boy I'd like to eat Swift's and nothin else. A nice slice of ham, or chicken. I wun't touch chicken packed by anyone else. The missus don't give a hoot ner a holler if she eats horse meat. One reason I moved right out of my own home."

This was the first I'd heard of it.

"Got so noisy over there I come over here to live, not that this is so quiet, neither. That old bitch—" he gestured towards the downstairs—"Yellin her head off at Aunt Sally and the kids screechin in the back yard—holy Joe, I can't hardly stand it."

I could tell by the seat he had in his chair that he was on his best-loved subject. The floor model gas heater was nearly knocking me out but I stayed put. He turned his pasty but rather handsome old face to me. "Know why I moved out on the missus; she's got her goddam brother livin right in the other half of the house; he never was no good. He always will be broke. Noisiest cuss you ever had near you. I left," he said with pride. While he chatted I took a look at his rooms, about what would be used in a big house for servants or storage. They were drab and stuffy but he did have a comfortable bed which looked as if he slept on top of the covers, and an expensive complicated shortwave radio. In his kitchen were just the heater, a cream-colored table, a hot plate and the refrigerator. He had his food brought him mostly by his elderly wife who worked all day on tailoring, our landlady told me later. He was wearing his spottiest light gray trousers and his hair was tousled.

Now he was telling me about the *Reader's Digest*. He swore by it and got all his medical knowledge from it. "But that old fool downstairs"—again the landlady—"when I told her she ought to paint that kid's tonsils with what it says in here she just said she'd see. Hell, she'll see plenty, she'll see a dead boy, that's what she'll see. Oh, this is a great magazine," he went on. "Did you see that article on jets? I'm keepin that one, by golly. Goin to cut it out today."

I got up. He looked at me surprised. I said I had to go and clean my room. A mean look came into his eye as he said "Now, you ain't just makin an excuse," and then smiled as if I knew his bark was worse than his bite. I thanked him and said I'd enjoyed the visit. "Wait," he said, lowering his voice. "Whaddya think of the crew we got livin here? Lousy I say. You like 'em?" I smiled and said I didn't really know them. "Gee, lady, that Mrs. Meehan, she's the worst stinkin pill." Foreseeing more of the same I edged out the door, thanking him again. He was disappointed at losing his audience but he cried "Come any time. Like to have some one to talk to!" I felt sorry for him as I heard him shut his door, closing out all the noise I was going to make cleaning my room.

There was a section of the long dark back hall, at right angles to it, that was partitioned off to make a sort of room. It was right next to Mr. Billings'. By hanging two cheap cotton and rayon bed spreads of old apricot and a dull green over a rope the piece of hall with one dark window high up and the kitchen stairs dropping away in the gloom of the small space became a bedroom for Aunt Sally, the elderly deaf mute who was sister-in-law to Mrs. Meehan and did all the worst drudgery. She was stumpy and short and evidently lived on charity. Her hair was quite short and a pinkish brown; from time to time she curled it and then let it go for weeks, wisping and childlike. A bobby pin smacked it down close to her forehead. She had a red, ravaged, innocent face which broke into a violent smile when she saw anyone she knew, and she would nod, gesture and breathily mouth something. Her clothes were hand-me-downs; in winter she wore for best a blue and white cotton with a large pattern, with dark twisted stockings and castoff Spectator pumps. In the daytime she had another dress, a faded drooping apron and cracked spotted black shoes which pattered like a child's on the linoleum that was everywhere in the house. As she walked she wove from side to side in the hall and her arms idly slapped her hips. She once was married but whoever he was died within a year of the wedding. Now she made her life around the TV set, the housework, and brief encounters with the boarders. She was very good at sign language and could read and write. She knew and could convey all the gossip with amazing speed.

In this temporary and horrible cover she slept; a bed and bureau were wedged behind the spreads and the room was always filled with what looked like junk from waste baskets; she often could be seen bending over them with concentration.

In spite of the dazed and miserable look she often wore she was at times gay and vivacious. She tyrannized over the small white short-haired household mongrel, who loved her, and she often stumped importantly onto the front porch and called in an unvibrant tone, like sound under water, to order him back across the street. She also ordered the landlady's grandchildren around but they ignored her. It was excruciatingly sad to run into her on a rainy drab Sunday, the boarding house dark and empty, and see her hyper-cheerful sign language indicating, with false broad smiles, that the family, Mrs. Meehan, any sons and daughters and in-laws, and Mrs. Meehan's friend, Mr. Savory, who did all her husbandly chores, had all gone down to the farm for Sunday dinner, but she wasn't invited. As usual she would wind up the pantomime with a noisy flop of her stubby red hands against her solid hips, to say to hell with them all, and vanish aimlessly up the dim hall. The boarders would all be out somewhere and she would either work alone in the kitchen or sit squinting in the half light of the dining room over a box of letter paper, writing.

The boarders treated her with tolerance, taking in her violent, grinned communications with the barest interest. Occasionally they gave her a small present or old clothes, and some remembered her at Christmas time with cards though the turnover in the house was great; an average stay was three months. The boarders looked like owners of diners or shoe salesmen, with mail forwarded from places like Kansas, Southern California and Atlantic City; these people had almost no belongings and wore spotty, unpressed clothes; they sat on the metal porch chairs in the lovely late summer evening light tensely, responding to the small town serenity but pathetically insecure.

Mr. Billings treated the mute alternately with familiar hilarity and cold brutality. If it were nice and sunny and he had been digesting well he might be seen going eagerly through the house looking for Aunt Sally with a bunch of roses from his house over on the next street, at the same time too distributing flowers to favored boarders, never mind how he was depleting his wife's rose garden. Another time, though, if he had nothing to do, it was raining and he couldn't be tinkering with his motorcycle, he could be heard yelling at her to get some mess cleaned up and hurry up about it, she was a goddam mute and who did she think she was. She could read lips and never missed any of what was said to her. Treatment like this fired her up and she made her one sound in protest, a toneless terrible cry of "hhhfffffvvvv," repeated with gestures. Her revenge on him was to stop one of the boarders in the hall, tap them, point to his door, shake her head with a sly grin and twirl a finger beside her ear. Then the gesture that she always wound up her conversations with, arms outflung, indicating I'm through with it all, the hell with that, it beats me, etc.

When the warm weather came this year and the boarding house windows were opened all over the neighborhood, and the sounds of the yards came in the windows, the noise of the children playing in the yard under Mr. Billings' window infuriated him. He would take his screen in and lean out and holler at them in language fit for an abattoir, not even seeing their pale, serious, appalled little faces, and he went on and on. Naturally when he backed in again and a moment or two passed the children had adopted the new words and screeched them ever louder and louder around the yard as their daring bolstered one another. Mrs. Meehan did not hear of this immediately, and when she did she reacted in a surprisingly mild way, biding her time smoulderingly but in silence, merely muttering as she battered the mop through the dark upper hall outside his room "Ole devil, I'll fix you, you!" And when he complained to her she hinted strongly that he could leave any time as far as she was concerned.

One day in a mischievous mood he borrowed a water pistol from one of the children and took it off craftily to his room. He kept it until one day the children made noise in the yard again and Aunt Sally also was in the yard emptying the garbage. Quietly removing the screen he yelled, in incredible language, at the children to keep quiet, and squirted them with the water from the pistol. Then he refilled it and squirted the mute all over the back of her dress and told her to get the hell in the house. Mrs. Meehan was in the kitchen, however, this time, and in a flash, or as soon as the children and Aunt Sally told on him, she was upstairs, in his room, shaking in a towering rage, snatching up the pistol, the water glass, and ripping the bedclothes off his bed, saying quiveringly he never once made it decent and this time he could if he dropped dead doing it and she for one wouldn't mind the least bit.

She slammed out of his room after warning him, breathless with anger, that any more of that and he'd leave inside fifteen minutes.

In addition to feeling proprietary about everything in the house, ordering people not to use the bathroom at his end of the house, sassing everyone coming along the walk from behind the plant stand on the porch, tormenting the dog, racketing up the street on his motorcycle and smelling up the second floor of the house with a faulty gas heater, he formed a great and consuming hatred for a pathetic, harmless roomer in the neighboring boarding house. Privately she was called "The Tart" by the people around because that is what she looked like; an old woman of over sixty who tried to look young with a bleached pageboy bob, a redly rouged mask of a face and Hollywood clothes of the champagne-color and fox fur variety. She had decided to learn to drive late in life, had bought a purplish 1935 Chevrolet, and although nearly stone deaf, was practising driving. At first, unfortunately, she practised in the various parking lots near our house, running helplessly over bushes, thudding into the old garages in the alley, or shooting in uncontrolled horse-powered silence, riding on the foot clutch, right out into traffic and across the street into whatever was there. She maddened Mr. Billings as she patiently raced the engine by the quarter hour; and since she was deaf he could not make her hear his obscenities. He took to calling the police and reporting her. Once or twice they investigated the situation but found nothing to pinch The Tart on. Mr. Billings had to resort to getting in her way when he could on his motorcycle and gesturing threateningly at her.

The thing that finally took Mr. Billings out of Mrs. Meehan's boarding house was almost inevitable.

Because of his glowing hatred for The Tart and his contempt for her activities in her tub of a car, he drew closer and closer to her on the days she tried driving. From yelling epithets at her from the porch and yard he moved out onto the walk; from there he strolled one day right up to her closed window.

Gesturing at her to roll it down, which she did as I watched from my open front window, Mr. Billings hollered at her at length. I heard "goddam woman" and "think you're doing." Then to my amazement he jerked the car door open on her side and manhandled her out. There and then he began to shake her, her fox fur lolling and her stiff bleached curls snapping to and fro. She could now hear him, since he was yelling right at her, and she realized that she was in the grip of a deadly enemy. Raddled cheeks wobbling, large painted mouth open in one long scream, she pounded the old man in the face and about the shoulders as a small crowd gathered from neighboring houses. At first the onlookers stood by inactive, savoring the ruckus; finally Mrs. Meehan, broom in hand, hurried from our house and over to the miserable pair. She wrenched them apart.

"I seen you, you bastard," she screeched at Mr. Billings. "You laid hands on her, I seen you lay hands on her." She gave him a thump. "You all right honey?" she said to The Tart who was weeping largely against the bosom of a sympathetic stranger. Mrs. Meehan turned back to Mr. Billings. "You get to hell out a my house as of right now and I'll be glad to be rid a ya," she hollered at him.

"I ditn mean no harm," The Tart wailed.

The crowd stood glued to the spot to see who would leave first. It was Mr. Billings, rubbing his bruises and beet red, turning to go, shaking with anger; the others aided The Tart in stowing her car away and reassured her. Mrs. Meehan with her broom followed Mr. Billings to the house, railing at him.

A nephew of Mr. Billings, heavy and sweaty, arrived soon after to move his refrigerator and other heavy things out to an orange trailer; there was nothing to signal the actual final departure of Mr. Billings himself except the mute's expressive cry of "Hhhffffvvvvhh!" as he slammed the screen door for the last time.

# PROVIDENCE

IT WAS hot; the sun bleached the soft asphalt to no-color and the elms hung ochre and wilted. Laura continued to pedal her bicycle doggedly along the smoother part of the road and tried to keep up with her companion bicycling strongly on ahead.

By a shady stone wall he paused to let Laura catch up, his long legs straddling his bicycle easily. He tightened the straps holding his pack to the rear of his bicycle with a gesture and waited. She came to a stop beside him.

"How I'd like some beer!" she said, resting limply on her saddle. She was well made without being husky and she was very brown. Her hair hung casually, blown by her ride.

"Beer isn't good for you on a trip," John said, looking at a torn place in his shoe. "Orange juice would be better."

"Beer, I'd like," Laura said stubbornly. "I could die for a glass."

"You'd be a fine one in the desert," John said. His craggy brown face was preoccupied. Laura knew he was remembering. He had told her a good bit about the geology expedition in Israel and the one before in Iraq and she knew this bicycle trip was only a stop-gap attempt to use up his tremendous energy some way until the time came that he could go off on another venture. She felt useless and small compared to the big trips, the big preparations, the big goals, the big bravery of John and the rest of the men.

"How far is it to Providence?" she asked him.

"We ought to be there now; in fact I think these houses are out-skirts," he said. "Let's get going, girl." He rolled off smoothly, leaving her to come along behind. Then he slowed and they rode along side by side, silent in the heat.

The straggling houses became more frequent; the road became a street. It was an unattractive, typical New England city approach, unplanned and anticlimactic. In the yard of a geranium-green bungalow a man in a sport shirt that stuck to him held a small, knobby dog, petting it, his white face following the two on their bicycles emptily. Farther along the street a group was gathered around an old maroon Buick eating ice-cream bars; the radio in the car boomed rock-and-roll. John and Laura bicycled past quickly. John did not pay any attention to the group. Laura glanced at them with a shy smile so that one of the men whistled. She hoped John noticed.

Soon they came to solid rows of stores and the first traffic light; the town became a city. There was a strong smell from the docks and at a corner John stopped, looking around him. "I think we go down here—this should take us to the waterfront," he said. His brown hair hung in a lock over his high forehead and even in the heat he looked handsome, Laura thought as she drew up beside him.

"You look very handsome," she said, conscious of her own hot, blown look and the torn sleeve of her shirt. John glanced at her quickly, very pleased.

"Your shirt's ripped," he commented, looking her up and down. It was hard for Laura at times like this to remember hours on the living room couch or in John's car when he pressed her to him and in monosyllables made her feel he loved her as she loved him.

Agilely John swung off his bicycle and with a graceful motion lifted it and its load up on to the side walk. "Let's go in here and get something," he said, indicating a drug store. Laura could picture him leading the explorers of his group on the mountains of Alaska or the deserts of the Middle East with just such briefly-made decisions— "Let's take that crevasse," or "The rest of you stay here and I and So-and-So will go on ahead," she could picture him saying. How she admired him. She followed him through the acid screen door into the store. They sat on stools by the counter and John ordered two milk shakes. As they drank them he examined a map; Laura watched his big brown hands turning it over and drank her milk shake in a misery of inadequacy. She wished she were tall and glamorous and had a string of degrees in brilliant languages and difficult sciences. She wished she were Norwegian and had been raised by a lama in Tibet; she wished she could go on one of John's rock-climbing expeditions and save his life with a brilliant decision high on a difficult traverse; she wished she were not earnest and earthbound and was a thrilling contralto and could spellbind John.

"When we leave Providence we'd better go this way toward Fall River," John said, pointing on the map. "We can sleep along the way at some tourist place—there's a lot of 'em." He folded the map and put it in his pocket. "Ready?"

They went out again into the heat and bicycled slowly over the cobbled streets. It was the oldest section of the city; small shacks with

Pepsi-Cola medallions nailed on them sold fish and chips; cheap asbestos shingling in greens and pinks covered the frames of two-hundred-year-old houses built close together; warehouses and garages, cheap restaurants and grim bars lined the dirty street.

But as they rode and the water appeared molten ahead Laura saw a church between two abandoned houses. It was old and made of brick and appeared closed. Nevertheless she slowed and stopped in front of it.

"John," she called. He stopped and looked back. "I want to go in there," she said, pointing to the church. He wheeled his bicycle back to her, frowning a little.

"Why?" he asked, looking at it. "Looks shut up to me."

"Come on," she said, going over to the church and leaning her bicycle on the grimy bricks.

"Someone'll steal the bikes," John said.

"Come on," she insisted. The staid old building drew her; she had to go in. She tried the cracked door; it opened. John followed her. Inside it was dark in spite of four stained glass windows. But their soft light gleamed on a lovely altar, in front of which flickered the white, delicate flame of the small candle in the sanctuary lamp. The silence was complete and it was cool. Laura genuflected beside a pew and sat down. John joined her and they sat quietly. The walls and ceiling around the altar broken with heavy beams were painted a soft scarlet. The altar was gold and lacy. On it were four unlit candles and a wilted bouquet. The rood screen supported a large, beautifully carved Crucifixion group softly lighted. Laura found the silence and the altar, empty of activity, moving to the point of tears. She looked at John but his face was inscrutable; in the twilight he was handsome as he had never been before. They had never gone to church together; John never went. As Laura looked at the sorrowful Crucifixion scene before her she thought how free of trouble her life was; she wished for an opportunity to do something for the strange and strong man on the cross before her. At last John looked at her with raised eyebrows and they rose and left the velvety interior.

"Phoo. Hot out here," John said.

"Did you like the church?" Laura asked, still under the spell of the mystery behind her.

"Nice," he said absently. "Small, though." He wheeled his bicycle to the street and started to get on.

Until now they had seen only a fat middleaged woman in green with a bag of groceries and two lounging men on the steps of one of the saloons. Now they became aware of a procession coming up the street. As it drew nearer they saw that it was a funeral. They stood where they were to watch it pass; they had never seen one like it. A group of perhaps fifteen men and women and several half-grown children moved along the street on foot behind a hand-drawn cart supporting the coffin. All of the people wore black except the children who were nondescript and plain. All were very poor and the saddest evidence of this was the quality of the bouquet on the coffin made of thin sprays of gladiolas in crimson and vermilion. As the slow group, scuffing on the rough cobbles, came abreast of them Laura saw, at the end, a very old woman draped in black inching weakly after the others. She was bent almost to the point of being hunch-backed and walked with her feet apart to achieve a measure of steadiness. Her shoes were men's and she wore no stockings; her bony ankles showed white, dirty and tiny above the black leather. As she drew abreast of John and Laura she stumbled and fell on her hands and knees; apparently too weak to rise and unnoticed by the others she remained there emitting monosyllables in a foreign language.

Laura was horrified. She started toward the old woman. When she reached her she tried to help her up but the old woman would not or could not budge. She was weeping.

"John!" Laura called to him. "Come here!" John came over to them. "You'll have to lift her up," Laura said. John put his hands under the old woman's arms and tried to lift her. She remained slumped on the dirty street, crying.

"You'll have to carry her," Laura said urgently.

"What?" John said incredulously.

"Carry her," Laura repeated. "Look, she's crying—she's got to go with them—*carry* her!"

"She doesn't want to be carried," John said, horrified. "They'll come back and get her. Come on." He started to leave, with an embarrassed final glance at the old woman.

Laura started to cry. "John, you come back here and carry her," she pleaded. John walked back to the old woman and, stooping awkwardly, pulled at her narrow shoulders. Clumsily he tried to raise her but she was so bound up in her grief that she was oblivious to his efforts. At last John lifted her by the waist to her feet and tried to set her down but she would not walk. It was at this moment that they both had a close look at her face—it was hideously ugly. The eyes were gummy and her nose was running. Hairs bristled on her scraggy, jutting chin and she was toothless. She smelled very bad.

"Carry her," Laura said in an agony of urgency. The spell of the church was still with her; she felt they must help.

John, stiff with revulsion, put his arms under the shoulders and knees of the woman, lifted her and started off up the street after the dark group of mourners. As they walked along Laura thought how wonderful John looked carrying his frightful burden and shuddered at her appearance. She kept anxiously beside them and stared into the old woman's open, milky, stunned eyes.

For two blocks they walked and then a fat, oily-faced man from among the mourners looked back and came to them. With hostility he said "I take," and pulled the old woman from John's arms. "Walk, Mumma," he rasped to her, and said something to her in a language John and Laura did not understand. He dropped the old woman's feet to the pavement and she managed to stand totteringly, her clothes askew. Then as he pulled on her wrist she followed weakly, without a word or sign to Laura and John that she had taken in their presence. The mourning pair went raggedly up the street after the coffin and Laura stared anxiously after them. She did not notice John had gone. When at last she turned she saw he was sitting on his bicycle, looking at the ground. She hurried back to him. He did not look at her.

"Any other chores you want done?" he snarled at her. "Are you *mad?*"

Laura was stunned. "But we had to help," she protested. "And I couldn't carry her."

"We didn't have to help. You just went all hysterical." John was furious and his face was white. "Look," he said, finally turning to face her. "Don't ever ask me to do things like that. Don't ever." He paused, gave up and shoved his bicycle angrily away from the curb. "Filthy old woman!"

Shocked, Laura went to her bicycle and wheeled it blindly to the curb. As John bicycled up the street she looked after him. Brave leader, she thought with contempt. The brave, brave leader.

Slowly she mounted her bicycle and followed him.

# THE LEGEND
# OF GRAY MOUNTAIN

TWO MEN stood by a fence in the pasture. It was hot but a breeze blew up from the valley below them and the leaves on the birch groves glittered in the sun.

The old man grasped the rail fence and shook it to see if it was firm; it proved loose and unsteady. But his attention wandered and his eye took in the rough pasture below; he appeared very worried. The young man with him, holding an axe, also watched the valley below and turned and scanned the slopes above where the beech and spruce woods met the pasture. Sweat stood out on his forehead.

"How do you know it's today?" he asked the old man.

"Kate told me," the old man said. He was stooped but his shoulders were solid and powerful; his white hair was plentiful and grew close to his handsome head. He wore steel-rimmed glasses and his muscular face bore the look of one who had endured much. He wore a blue shirt and shapeless brown trousers over a big frame; his shoes were heavy and dusty, planted on the singed coarse pasture grass. "Why'd you bring that axe?" he asked the young man.

Elihu did not answer but dropped the head of the axe to his feet and looked down at it, embarrassed.

"You think the old women'd get you?" the old man asked him with a bit of a smile. He stopped smiling. "They're not concerned with you." He waved away a swarm of gnats absently.

Around the two men was a New England scene of beauty, rugged and lonely in the sun. They stood on the side of a large mountain whose rock top was just visible above the woods. Beside them and below stretched a long upland valley in the soft varied colors of ripening late August; dark blue cloud shadows spotted the yellow and rose fields, the blue-green woods rising and dipping down to where the streams ran, the swelling mountain range across the valley from them where Burn Mountain, Hartshorn, Tappan and Old Snow rose at first gently, then steeply to flattened rock summits where the light played in ochre, pinks and flashing white. Long and intense blue, Ash Pond lay like a fish along the center of the valley. Beside it could be seen glimpses of the dirt road that led to Whippen, whose sparse houses were just visible below the rocky, steep pastures and black spruces beside them; all of the houses were gray with sharp square lines made clear by the morning sun.

It was nine o'clock.

"Say, Dana," Elihu said, turning to look suddenly at the other man. "Will your wife be here?"

"Yes, she will." Dana briefly examined the back of his hand and looked across at Old Snow. "They'll all come; it can't be stopped."

"Do they like—to be—watched?" Elihu asked. He was only nineteen and looked uneasy. He licked his lips and ran his hand under his nose swiftly.

"I brought you up here to see this because I had to come and I durst not to come alone, if you want to know," Dana said. "No, no one's been up to watch before, don't know why. It's going to be the end of Kate, and that's the end of me. No one ever lived through one of these things." He looked every bit of his seventy-five years and, in the bright morning light, pale and ill. Two brilliant drops of water stood briefly in his small, bright blue eyes; he cleared his throat and leaned on the gray fence; his big hand plucked at the lichens growing there. "It won't take long, as I remember," he added. "An hour, maybe." His voice was faint and husky.

"Why don't you stop it? Why don't we all stop it?" Elihu demanded. His uncut brown hair hung into his anxious eyes. "I don't like this. I hate it."

"Look," Dana said. "It's always been this way. Every time there's a new crop of old ones, they do this. It's in them, I don't know why." A crow flew across the pasture below them, blue-black and deliberate. He lit on the top of a small spruce. "Tand and Whippen, they never mixed. See, Tand, being over Gray Mountain here, is our nearest neighbour. But folks never get along in the two towns, and, funny thing, I don't know and you don't know and nobody knows what started the women doing this but they have gone at it since the first settling here, a long, long time ago. Something starts it—it's always in the summer, though—and from what I hear this time the thing that set them off was a woman over from Tand spat on Bettsey Loveless. Spat on her. Men don't do that." Dana looked at Elihu and gave out with a mirthless laugh. "Might's well set down," he said, looking blankly around him. He lowered himself to the ground.

Elihu stood, however, tensely, and again scanned the valley and the pasture above where dense clumps of spruce in various sizes grew strongly, quivering in the breeze. His hollow chest and thin cheeks contrasted with Dana's solid build; he looked as if he were at bay.

"I sure don't want to be here," he said, looking off. Then he said, "I see someone."

Dana got to his feet and looked down the hill. Climbing steadily though slowly came a thin figure in black. She was carrying a sickle and every so often swung at the hardhack or bullbriars as she passed them. She did it with sureness although she was brittle and must have been eighty. Occasionally she disappeared from sight behind the big puddingstone boulders scattered through the field. She could not see the men hidden behind the fallen, huge trunk of a blasted maple.

"Tirzah Williams," Dana said, squinting down at her progress. "Alone."

The old woman, her long white hair done high in a blown·bun, had the rounded narrow back of the very old; tiny wrists stuck out from the shrunken black sleeves of her shapeless dress. When she came to the biggest boulder she stopped and looked up the pasture towards the woods.

"Looking for them," Dana commented, his lips dry.

"Where's all the men?" Elihu asked. Again he said, "Why don't they stop them? Why don't we stop them?" he repeated desperately, looking at Dana with huge reproach.

"You don't understand, boy," Dana said tiredly. "Around here it's what they do. They're brought up knowing about it and they, well, they like it. How can you talk some woman out of doing what she likes?" They looked over at the old woman. She was sitting awkwardly at the foot of the boulder, looking alertly down the mountain.

"There's someone else," Elihu whispered. Past a birch grove there appeared two figures laboring up the slope; one was a vastly fat old woman in lavender who was trying to help an aged hunchback a foot and a half shorter than herself. The fat one carried a hoe and the cripple a kitchen knife.

"My God, even Dora Swope," Dana said, peering. "With Millie. Millie Grinnell. They aren't friends; at least they never was." The large woman in lavender was pointing up the mountain. "Guess Dora can't see over the bushes," he added.

"Mrs. Letts has been in bed for twelve years," Elihu said. "Do you think she'll come?"

"They'll all be here," Dana said wearily. "They all always make it, somehow; they help each other; they get excited about it and rise right up and get up to this pasture—seems like they build right up to hating so's they can't hardly wait to come up here like this. Funny thing, they never come here except for this. Peacock's Pasture. Best pasture this side of the valley." A late thrush sounded near by and another answered him farther off. It was a perfect day.

More figures were appearing at the bottom of the pasture. Five old women climbed into view.

"Good thing you haven't got no grandma," Dana said. "She'd be coming up here too." He stared down at the approaching group. "Serena Watts. Margaret Pew, Lily Gates, Amanda Buck." He was looking for his wife. "And Coritha Lewis; she's been down sick, like to die this week," he added. "Look at her climb. Made the best rhubarb pie."

The three who were already at the boulder watched the others come but no sign was exchanged. The old women did not talk. Lily Gates had a shawl wrapped around her shoulders but she carried a chunk of firewood thicker than a big man's arm. A tall, bent old woman with black hair had two kitchen knives. The others carried a scythe, a cross-cut saw blade, a hammer.

"Where are the other men?" Elihu asked desperately.

"I don't know," Dana shook his head. "Down there, watching 'em leave, I guess. Watching 'em go." He stiffened. "There's Kate," he said tensely. "By the great Lord, there's Kate." He leaned heavily on the hard, solid old bole of the fallen maple. "She used to tell me she'd never do this."

Alone, wearing white, a slim old woman stood below them looking up at the group around the boulder.

"She's got my axe," Dana said. "Well, at least she picked something better than a chunk of wood." He watched his wife's slow progress up the hill. At last she was near.

"Go out and talk to her," Elihu urged Dana.

"I have talked to her," Dana said, his huge hands gripping a dead branch of the tree. "Just this morning she made my breakfast and said she wouldn't come. She's older than me," he added irrelevantly.

Behind Kate came a crowd, short, medium, tall, wearing pink, blue, brown, purple, armed with assorted weapons to be found in the farmyards. On all the old faces was a common look of determined hatred.

"Who told them when to come?" Elihu asked. "How do they all get up here at the same time?"

"I don't know. One of them tells another, I guess. There is no leader. Except I think Bettsey Loveless stirred them up, finally," Dana said. "Yes, I think it was Bettsey. But I don't see her." He looked at the gathering of, now, about twenty-five old women. "Yes, there she comes. White as a sheet, that one," he said, watching a squat woman climb. "Guess they're all there except Mrs. Letts—and Joanna Whipple I don't see."

"How do the Tand women know about coming over the mountain?" Elihu asked. His shirt was soaked with perspiration.

"That I don't know either," Dana said. His eyes were fixed in agony on his wife. "Fried fish we had, and muffins," he recollected softly. "Who would have thought it." He watched the white figure of his wife sitting alone in the shade of the big boulder. She was looking up the pasture towards the woods. He saw her get up. Looking himself up the mountain he saw a group of old women jerkily emerging from the black woods and descending the pasture. "Look," he said.

"Now they'll fight, won't they," Elihu said, his hand closing around the axe handle. "What'll we do?"

"Nothing." Dana answered. He was looking at the women coming down. They would not be as tired perhaps as the women who had had to climb up. Climbing was usually impossible for these old ones; they never went beyond their front yards and sometimes never even outdoors, even in summer. And not interested in anything much except one or two remembered facets of life; if they talked at all it was about times far past; not interested in those around them; not eating more than bread and tea or a little sweet pie, love all gone in all of them. In these wild parts of the world a sort of stark hate grew in its place.

Another pair of souls came in sight at the bottom of the pasture. "There's more," Elihu said, pointing down the hill. "Look at Joanna, almost running up. This'll be her day, she hates everyone. Like as not she'll chop up her own. Hasn't been herself since her father threw her out for not reading the Bible verse right to him."

"Mrs. Letts," Dana said, pointing. Past the two men, not seeing them, came another old, old woman, bent and white but wearing pink. Upon her cheeks and hands were liver spots. She had short, thin white hair blown in the wind; she was a nice sight in the sun. Her old, sunken face was tranquil and squinted but slightly. Pausing near the men and by a spruce of the right size she gathered up her skirt and squatted to make water; the men, seeing, were repelled by the sight of the ivory haunch and looked over at the group of old women, now bright with something to be done.

"They're coming close," Dana said, straining to see past a branch to where the Tand women descended, not stopping, not slowing down. The Whippen women stood up in awkward poses, their weapons poised for the first blow. Steadily the Tand women, all old, all possessed with fury and committed to the next half hour, closed in on the Whippen group by the boulder. Suddenly the two groups had partially mingled; the old women stood looking at each other, and the two men thought this might be the moment when they would change things, not fight, and dodder on home where they belonged. But a big, determined shape reached out her hand and pushed down an old Tand woman so that she fell and hit her head on a rock. The fight started with that; warily the women approached and the first inept blows were exchanged, but, mounting in anger, they became harder. Treacherous and full of intent joy the women were, grim and newly strong.

Scuffling in the hardhack a fighting pair backed and hewed each other towards the place where the two watchers were hidden; Joanna Whipple, breathing hard and bearing down was going to kill first; the men could see as Joanna's sickle tore the flesh of her bony opponent. She had a wooden mallet and smashed at Joanna's hand to break her hold on the sickle. But with a final stroke Joanna caught the woman in the eyes; the mallet dropped and the woman gasped and sank to her knees, holding her face; Joanna hacked again and the woman lay still, her neatly laced shoe projecting from under her navy blue skirts. Elihu held his hands clasped tightly over his mouth while he watched in horror.

The battle spread out and in the tumult some of the women disappeared behind the thickets and boulders. The men saw Margaret Pew, bosom swinging, cleave the head of a tanned old thing in blue; others of the feeble started up and with mad strength and singleness of thought bent to it, slaughtering in blind hate, glorious in their moment to themselves but to the men terrifying as the dark blood fell and spread and lay unrecoverable, old and now spent amid the grave beauty of New England. They watched as Joyce Peabody tripped a short hunched woman from off the rock, ineptly beating her with a stone; she spat and turned to meet her end when a fat woman from Tand jerked her down by her apron strings and killed her with a rake.

What thoughts stirred in those old heads as the birds flew overhead and the grasshoppers hummed steadily the men did not know. The women died for the most part unaware, clinging not to life nor to anyone, memories all gone, old beyond caring, big at this time in their primal gust of death beyond which came they knew not what, nor had thought of, if at all, for some fifteen years or so. Church had not seen them for as long; song had left their lips; speech became only aimed to the past; the present touched them not even as they died except that, oh, they hated. Hate for what? Had life used them so? Did this remote mountain neighborhood start in them such bitter frenzy, imprisoned in dim hearts, bringing them up to this pasture at last?

Elihu was faint; before him Kitty Best had rammed a kitchen knife through and through a Tand opponent who died with faintest murmur, mouth askew, and here at last a pair of eyes that questioned in their last agony. Too late these aged bodies knew the truth, that death at the hand of another human being is the worst, in hate.

Dana wiped his hand across his forehead. "It takes a long time," he said hoarsely to Elihu.

Changing shadows crossed the grunting remains of the crowd that started in to fight. Of them all two sets of old women fought, and then two fell, one against a rock, her white face blank. Two only were left, fighting on the boulder, one in black, from Tand, the other, in white, was Kate. Against the green-black background of the spruce forest beyond they stood out.

At the sight of this Dana cried out, a mighty, hollow voice, rending the pasture's silence: "Stop! Stop, you," and broke from behind the tree to run towards them. But the women did not pause; and as they strove the white struck down the black, who fell off the rock upon the ground and did not move.

Kate stood on the rock, still in the position of her last blow. Saliva hung from her jaws and her empty old eyes gazed unseeingly across the pasture.

"Come down, Kate," Dana said urgently. "Come down to me." He held up his hand to her.

Kate shifted her focus to take in this new disturbance, her bloody axe clasped hard in her two worn hands; blood splattered her white dress and the big rock.

"Here, I'll come up," Dana said, and began to heave himself onto the rock. Elihu, a few yards away, saw what Dana did not: Kate lifted the axe, maddened by the battle, and brought it down on Dana's white head. Dana did not know what had struck him; he was dead immediately, slumped by the puddingstone.

Kate turned her back in total coldness and began to climb down, not forgetting the axe which, from habit of frugality, she would not leave behind. Elihu watched, paralyzed, for a long moment in the morning sun. Then the hate from the old women caught him and he felt it rise in him at the winner of the hideous battle.

"Kate! You, Kate—get on with it. You got to kill me too, you damn old woman," he yelled, sobbing. Kate, who had killed his friend, Kate, who had killed her husband, who should be dead of old age herself, was stepping down the hillside, free. He began to run down the mountain and almost fell against her.

"You're a-coming back to Whippen, and then you'll see, you old rat," he screamed, grabbing her by the skirt. He dragged her, stumbling and falling, at a dead run down the pasture, the hardhack and hay whipping at them. Gone the sweet view, the scent of summer, the bird flights and the cool breeze. The hating pair reached the pasture bars and the road in the village torn, sweating and heaving, more dead than alive. Elihu yanked Kate along to stand in front of the quiet grey houses where the men and younger people were gathered in silent groups.

"Here's an old bitch—old bitch—OLD BITCH," Elihu screamed, tearing the axe from Kate's fingers and giving her a vicious shove. Hate caught from the sights in Peacock's Pasture drove him earnestly as he threw back the axe against his thin shoulder and brought it down again and again on Kate until she lay broken and unrecognizable.

Two men caught Elihu's upraised weapon at last and pulled it from his hands. They stared at him in silence. Then one said, "Boy, don't you know she'd a gone off into the woods? They don't never come back."

"Let be, son," the other man said. "Let it all be." He drew Elihu away from the dead woman, down the road. By a black cherry tree he said finally, "Up here, you got to let them be."

Elihu straightened and looked at him. The hate was in him now; it felt good. He felt like a man, at last.

# GOODBYE TO
# TWO PEOPLE

TED WEINSTEIN stood in his stocking feet in one of his two show windows putting the finishing touches on a mannequin he was dressing. She had gray-blonde hair, long lashes and was an abstraction of a woman, being made primarily out of chicken wire. She wore an expensive dove gray suit with a diaphanous yellow scarf around her throat. Ted dangled a triple strand of pearls in one hand as he studied the effect created by his window containing three figures, all in rich, subdued colors with only occasional touches of scarlet or black, and fine jewels.

Satisfied, he gathered up a few accessories he had decided not to use and stepped carefully to the opening leading from the window into the store by the boutique counter. There he found his shoes, a pair of well-polished, country-gentleman brogues with thick soles—he did not like the new pointed Italian shoes and since he was the only man working in his store he wanted to create an image of a strong, tweedy personality as a foil or background to the beautiful clothes he sold to women. He wore, today, a Black Watch jacket, spotless white shirt, a Rooster tie and gray trousers. He was a big man with a strong, meaty face and a great deal of pepper-and-salt, curly hair carefully groomed. He liked the black rimmed glasses he wore; his eyes were small and rather close together.

With his shoes on he went out the front door to stand regarding the two windows he had just finished—cruise clothes to tempt the winter trade. Each window was sparingly done with the quiet colors he always chose for his decor. There were the quiet glistening of the hair of the mannequins and of the extra bottles and accessories placed in strategic spots on the expensive carpeting, an embroidered pair of stiletto-heeled shoes, a square bottle of perfume resting on a rich scarf.

All in all he was proud of his windows. He stood in the walkway that formed a shelter from the February winds—it was a good entrance and many a new customer did her first shopping there by taking shelter from the cold between his two windows.

He began to indulge his favorite daydream. Looking at his windows he saw them through the eyes of Honor Canaday, and was pleased. The beige sundress with the narrow pearls would entice her, he thought. She hadn't been in for two weeks, which was unusual. He hoped she was not sick or—his heart leapt with anguish as the thought crossed his mind—perhaps she had gone away. He loved Honor Canaday, his favorite customer, a perfect size ten. His main thoughts, not having anything to do with the store, were of asking Honor Canaday for a date. He hadn't felt the time was right so far, but now he had bought the Pontiac convertible in navy blue and found the quiet, candle-lit restaurant on McGee Street he felt sure she would love. Perhaps today she would come in and he would then suggest dinner. What they would do after dinner had always puzzled him in his daydream. Dancing? His apartment? He was very proud of his apartment, the whole second floor of a house in the better section of town; and he had the candles, the hi-fi, the fireplace, perfect for conversation and dancing. But not for the first date. Perhaps she would like a movie at the nearby art theater. That was it.

A customer passed him and entered the store; he ended his reverie and followed her inside. The woman was standing at the boutique counter and Hannah was waiting on her capably. He busied himself with a small rack of blouses towards the front of the store where he would not miss anything. He noticed a figure standing outside in the shelter of his show windows and hoped for another customer. It was a very cold gusty day; surely she would have to come in to get warm? He went to the door to suggest this and then saw that it was not a woman but a man. From inside the door he stood and observed the loiterer. He saw that he was big and badly dressed; his shoes were bright orange and dirty, worn far over at the heels; he wore a spotted navy blue coat with no buttons, unpressed cotton pants turned up a couple of times at the bottom, a ratty tie that was not pushed up to cover the collar's button; he wore nothing on his head and his hair was stiffly and roughly combed back to hang over the specked coat collar, turned up. His face, as he occasionally turned it to where Ted could see it, was terrible; the furrowed brow sloped back to a high hairline, the nose turned up like that of a clown; he had a short upper lip and a lower lip that hung down, showing the bottom of a few stained teeth. He had no eyes; they were gone. On one jaw was a great scar where no hair grew; the man was otherwise unshaven. He carried a white cane and stepped miserably from one foot to the other, trying to keep warm. He was almost standing in the neat, smart drinking fountain for dogs that Ted had proudly set out recently.

Ted decided not to ask the man inside; he reasoned that the man would be embarrassed and anyway no doubt had a home somewhere. He tried then not to imagine what that home would be, but as the morning wore on pictures of what it was like came to his horrified mind: a flophouse; a room in the dirty tenements down by the tracks, with broken glass on the sidewalk and small, dirty, ravenous dogs sniffing their way through a troubled, untidy, empty world. The man stood shifting from one foot to the other for an hour in the morning and came back that afternoon just as Honor Canaday breezed into the shop.

Ted was waiting on Mrs. C. George Wilkinson who was being persuaded that Junoesque women could indeed wear sheer night wear and was happily flopping nighties open so that she could picture herself in them. Ted allowed himself to smile warmly at Honor but continued solicitously to wait on Mrs. Wilkinson. Honor shopped decisively but bought so much that she would certainly be there for some time.

At last Mrs. Wilkinson made up her mind to a black and a white and left. Ted was free to give his attention to Honor, who welcomed him with a frank, happy smile. She was looking at the ski clothes.

"Planning a trip?" Ted asked her as he muscularly shoved the unwanted sizes on their hangers out of the way.

"Oh, the usual," Honor answered vaguely, reaching for a burnt orange jacket with a hood. "How've you been, Ted?" She took the jacket off the hanger.

"Missing you, as usual," he ventured. His tongue clove to the roof of his mouth as he thought of the imminence of the refusal of his invitation. He could not speak out; not today. He turned his attention to his rack of sophisticated clothing and held out a white ski jacket with fur. "How about this? White is daring, you know—means you don't spend a lot of time falling on the slope," he added, wanting to sound knowledgeable about skiing. He had never done any.

"I like the orange—and just to please you I'll take the white, too," Honor said, glancing at him mischievously. "Now I want about one each of everything else in your store." She moved from one counter to another, from rack to rack. As Ted waited on her, enthralled with her quick decisions and good taste, he noticed for the thousandth time how her natural look topped all the bouffant hair stylings, the Brigitte Bardot mops he saw, the poorly applied makeup on so many of his ladies. She was scrubbed and rather pale, dressed simply in a plain green wool and a casually worn mink coat. He had never seen her house but imagined it as large, spotless and fresh-smelling.

"Ted," she said in the middle of it all. "What would you think of a man who is—very nice—but hangs around bars all the time?" She was turning over a thick pink sweater.

"Not right. Not right at all," he said promptly, glad it was not he who hung around bars. An occasional beer was his only drink. He was delighted at this small confidence. Let her think of him as a father figure; that was something, anyway. "You can't tie yourself to an alcoholic," he said seriously.

"That's just it," she said, frowning into space. "But he's so damn handsome." She smiled at Ted. "Oh well, I always have you, don't I?"

"You certainly do," Ted said heartily. He could not, still, bring himself to ask for a date. He had been a little shaken with the reference to the handsomeness of her current beau. He never thought of himself as handsome, though people told him he was attractive. Wasn't it better, more long-wearing, to be attractive?

"Well, I've bought really enough, don't you think?" Honor said with a fulfilled sigh. "Send these things, would you?" She started to go, glanced out the door, and turned back to Ted. "Who is that terrible-looking man out front?" she added softly, in horror.

"Oh," Ted said, looking. The man was still there. "I don't know. Poor devil."

"Well. Off I go," Honor said, turning toward the door. "Goodbye, and thank you." She smiled and was gone.

Ted sighed and turned to the counter to straighten the stock. But Cora, one of his salespeople, had everything neatly back in place. With nothing to do Ted went to the door to look at the weather. It was, he saw, sleeting, and the blind man stood, again shifting from one foot to the other. He was still there when Ted left at six, and the sleet swirled so that the street could hardly be seen. Uncomfortable, Ted ploughed through the weather to the parking lot to climb into his luxurious, cold car.

That winter had made money for the store—more money than it ever had before, and it had always been prosperous. People— women—had flocked in. Ted was troubled now, however, because the blind man had evidently decided to make Ted's store his shelter for the whole winter and for two hours in the morning and perhaps two more in the afternoon he stood, monumentally unattractive, in the walkway in front of the store. More and more of his customers commented, in varying degrees of dismay, some angry that they had to look at him, some compassionate. Ted thought about him daily, his attitude vacillating between anger, revulsion, resentment and pity.

His business now began to fall off unaccountably. At first he thought of this only as a normal mid-winter slump. Then it began to worry him. He could not account for the fate his store seemed to be having. What made things worse was that Honor had not come in at all. Ted decided the blind man in front of his store must have something to do, in fact everything, with the poor business he was doing.

He made up his mind to do something about the man. He pondered at night in bed what he could do. Speak to the police? This seemed harsh. Speak to him, himself? He hadn't the brass to do it.

Suddenly he thought of Honor. He could ask her, with her taste and kindness, what to do. If he could see her, if only she would come in. No. He would telephone her. This actually was the opening he had needed for a more personal relationship.

He thought about this gambit for two weeks and then, one night when he got home, still wearing his coat and hat, he picked up the phone and called her. She was in and answered the phone herself.

"This is Ted Weinstein, Miss Canaday," Ted said into the instrument, using his lowest, clearest tones.

"Ted—Weinstein?" Honor was puzzled. He realized she had never known his last name.

"Yes, of the Smart Set Shoppe," Ted elaborated.

"Oh, Ted! Yes, Ted, what can I do for you?" She was sophisticated and poised, as always.

"Miss Canaday, I thought—well, I have a problem, and I wanted to discuss it with you," he went on. "I thought perhaps you would have dinner with me, perhaps this week, and I could discuss it with you."

"A problem? What is it, Ted? Nothing about my charge account?" She was obviously surprised at these developments.

"No, no," Ted said smoothly, hiding his agitation. "Well, it's about—it's about the blind man who is continually outside my shop—perhaps you've noticed him?"

"Oh—yes," Honor said. "What is the problem?"

"Well. I have felt that, frankly, he's hurting business being there all the time—a dreadful looking fellow, actually—." Ted groped for the right words. "I've wanted to think of some way to—well—get him to go somewhere else to pass his time, and I don't know quite how to do it. I thought—two heads are better than one—perhaps you could suggest a kind way to get him to leave—." Ted bogged down. He was sweating. His hands made damp marks on the phone and his neck suddenly had a crick in it.

"Why, Ted, I don't really think there's anything I can suggest—he's a poor soul all right—but suppose I ask Daddy about it? and have him drop by to see you—." Her voice trailed off, remote, cool. Ted realized his dinner invitation should not be repeated.

"Well, yes, let me know your suggestions," Ted said. "I've missed your coming to the shop, by the way—was it because of that man, by any chance? I hope not," he said desperately.

"Oh, no. I've been away, and—one thing and another," she said casually. "Well, I'll speak to Daddy," she said with finality.

"Thank you *very* much," Ted said. After saying goodbye he hung up miserably.

He got very little sleep that night. The blind man's fate haunted him.

The next day he was standing by his shop door looking out. He saw a green Cadillac draw up by the curb and a firmly-fleshed, well-dressed man got out gracefully. He wore a well-fitting topcoat and a hat and looked the soul of poise and product of good living. The blind man was standing in his usual place. The man who had gotten out of the car approached him and began to speak to him. Ted could just hear the conversation.

"Excuse me. My name is Harold Canaday," the new man said. The blind man said nothing but stopped moving.

"Now, I have fifty dollars in my hand for you," Harold Canaday said. "The management of this store doesn't want loitering outside—a fire hazard, you understand."

The blind man said nothing. Harold Canaday moved to him and pushed the money into his hand. "Okay?" he said with brisk finality.

"Nga," the blind man said, and after a long pause during which Harold Canaday seemed to be regarding him with amusement, and Ted sweated with horror at the scene, he moved clumsily away from the store and down the cold street. Harold Canaday got back into his car which was driven, Ted could see, by a chauffeur, and drove smoothly away.

Ted turned to the nearest rack of clothes and began mechanically to look them over. He did not want to think. A woman came in just then, perfumed and chic. Mechanically Ted greeted her and fell to the job of serving her. His hands shook a little, though. He stopped looking out of the front of his store and became busier than ever.

# THE PINCH

Lou was up there again and Lorene couldn't stand it: "Git down goddamit," she yelled. The rest of the ladies sat sodden in their colorful plastic chairs watching what they could see of *The Brighter Day*, not enjoying the sight of Jane making out with Roger, but they would have missed the sight and sound of the television if they had been deprived of it; sometimes they were.

Lou continued to stand on the chipped varnished chair where she could reach up and hold her hand flat against the television set; on the palm of that hand were two dimes and four pennies. No one knew why she showed her money, earned by doing errands for the attendants now and then, to the television:; but every day at one time or another she did this, her loud cotton skirt, too long, hanging down from underneath a linty black blazer, two sizes too large, her feet in runover black oxfords with Cuban heels placed any old way on the chair, her socks a violent pink with holes. Her dry white hair was chopped off at her ears and stuck out in back. To herself she chirped cheerful comments that did not make sense, even to Sally who sometimes went on the errands with her. Lou was too old to get raped, or to have it matter if she did, so she did not often need anyone to go with her; Sally was sent because sometimes Sally got on the attendants' nerves so much she had to be gotten rid of; she was glad enough to go to the Community Store of the hospital and stuff on glazed doughnuts and sodas the attendants gladly paid for.

"Git down," Lorene yelled, getting up; she was hugely fat and tall and this had happened before; she had pulled Lou off the chair and looked down on her hurt body on the floor with flat small eyes, not glad she had won, just content that she could daydream further at the sparkling set where pretty things showed.

Lou got down, talking to herself and smiling around vacantly at the room; leaving the chair where it was she rambled out into the high-ceilinged dim hall waggling her pockets. The ladies left behind stared on, their fat bosoms uncorseted jutting unloved, untended in front of their blank faces.

In the back row of bright chairs Violet sat dreaming next to Ruth Etta Stadelmaier. They often sat together because then no one interrupted their dreaming, unless Mrs. Potter or Mrs. Etkind came storming in and made them do something: make tea for the attendants or get out and see the men play baseball. Neither of them liked to have their dreaming butted into and their bond was that they hated this and particularly Mrs. Etkind who was huge and strong and starchy and made all her ladies do dirty jobs when she didn't want to do them: clean the toilets or peel the vegetables. Violet was afraid to death of knives and feared doing vegetables; she thought she might kill someone; secretly it was Mrs. Etkind she was most afraid of killing; but anyone, anyone, she might kill; even Ruth Etta. Mrs. Etkind drove them all to the washing area where they sat on splintered benches in the raging sunlight that lit the buff institution walls and dimly scraped and cut huge stacks of ice cold vegetables; they were not clean and they did not do it well at all but Mrs. Etkind had won; later at dinner they ate the things they had worked on, many helpings sometimes, unaware of the connection between fixing and eating food.

"O god," Violet said, out of the blue. She was not saying it to Ruth Etta; she said it frequently, more to her family in Albany who rejected everything to do with her than to anyone present. Ruth Etta turned large empty eyes upon Violet and then looked back at the show. "Looa that," she said as the man in the scene slapped the girl very hard. The rest of the ladies rocked slightly or sat still, some not even looking, as the hard light came in through the harsh starched white curtains to turn their pasty cheeks and fat or emaciated arms green. Two rioting potted plants stood by the center window; Mary was systematically stripping the leaves from the stems. Corinne saw her. "Mrs. Etkind," she screamed. "Mrs. Etkind, she's doing it, she's pulling them leaves . . ."

"CUT THAT OUT, hear me?" came a squalling voice from the door. Mrs. Etkind did not come over to Mary or Corinne; her voice was her weapon. "AND DON'T NONE OF YOU OTHER LADIES LOUSE ME UP THIS AFTERNOON—Om weak tudday. No smokin for youse ladies if I catch you Mary doon that again."

Mrs. Etkind turned and walked swiftly, muscularly away, her bright white cap twitching on her stiff gray hair.

"Think he's coming," Violet hazarded to Ruth Etta.

"Who? Oh. Oh yuh, him." Ruth Etta mused, her beautiful empty eyes roaming the moulded tin white ceiling with the painted sprinkler system.

46 □

"He's an hour late aready," Violet said. She picked a thread from her neat scarlet sweater that almost matched her plaid skirt; on her thick short legs she wore darned crimson knee socks that did not match anything; on her feet she had the wholesome black Cuban heeled laced shoes.

She looked around the room. She sort of wanted him to come this afternoon; she kind of liked him. Cute, like. Somethin different.

"Say," she said. "Wanna go see where he is; don't need to say nothin to Etkind; just say we're going to the store. Wanna go to the store?"

"Yeh," Ruth Etta said, getting up immediately.

This was the afternoon when Jack Whipple, disc jockey from the station downtown, came to the ward and entertained them. He would talk for an hour on anything and the ladies listened and dreamed, and he went away, the waters of their minds unmuddied in the least by anything about him; except for Violet and Ruth Etta, who smiled at him and to whom he therefore directed his many cheery jokes.

It was easy enough to get by Etkind; she was knitting a complicated stole for her mother and glad to have some of her charges get the hell out, as she told them, counting again.

Ruth Etta and Violet put on their ten-year-old coats, nearly down to their ankles; they took their purses from where they had hidden them under their mattresses along with the fig newtons and scapulars and were let out with a great key-clanking by Etkind.

There was a strange peace and silence in the stairwell, dirty, chipped, slippery with spilled food.

"Let's light up," Violet said, stopping and groping in her pocket. Ruth Etta stopped dutifully and waited while Violet took out her squashed package of Luckies. At the foot of the stairs Corky, the half-wit, was mopping with filthy water and smoking; "Got a light, Corky," Violet said with coyness. Corky was said to be in love with her; she liked being kidded about it; she had never had a boyfriend and now she was fifty-four she thought maybe she ought to really settle for Corky. Corky pressed his wet cigarette to theirs and, lighted up, they went out the door into the sunlight.

"Where do you think he'd drive in," Violet asked, stopping.

"Oh now we ain't goin to go lookin for that fellow," Ruth Etta said, her pretty long black hair falling over the dandruff on her shoulders. She looked around uncertainly.

"The parking lot," Violet said, starting down the hill. Ruth Etta followed; they both felt better doing an errand. They knew he wasn't coming but they could pretend he would be there; Violet speculated on what sort of car he'd be driving but could not think of the names of any. Ruth Etta dreamed as she walked daintily beside Violet; asked what she was thinking she could not have said; it was never much, but it was never about the hospital. One thought she did have; she wanted a pretty orchid bedspread with a cute bed doll on it. Other than that she just flittered from one slight observation to another and almost never spoke or wanted anything. She drove the attendants crazy; they could do nothing with her.

The two women came to the rough gravel of the hospital's west parking lot and stepped cautiously among the big strong cars, glancing at the personal belongings in them—a tiger toy, a baby's seat, two full suitcases—without any longing, without wanting to have them or to go anywhere.

Violet stopped by a yellow Studebaker; "LOOK," she whispered, pointing. Inside they saw Jack Whipple asleep on the front seat, his boyish face relaxed as his head rested on the seat. A lock of black hair sprang up from his high forehead; they saw he had grown a small moustache since last week.

They stood looking.

"Wake um up," Violet nudged Ruth Etta.

"Ohhh," Ruth Etta demurred. They stared hungrily. Jack went on sleeping. The windows of the car were locked and shut; the sun rested on Jack's legs and body. He wore sport clothes and a bow tie; one hand rested on a newspaper on the seat beside him. The women saw his signet ring, his boyishness, his nice clothes, his differentness from all they usually saw. They did not want to wake him up; neither wanted to spoil the dream they were having at the moment.

The gravel crackled under their feet as they turned and walked slowly away, up the hill towards their old dumb building.

"Know what," Violet said, staring smiling into a bare elm. "I'd like to a seen his cock. I'd like to a just taken down his pants there. I bet it's cute." She gave a coarse guffaw. "I seen a lot of um in my time; moren seen, too, kid, you better believe it. I even seen Corky's. Yes mam I see that the other day when you wasn't looking er Etkind or any of them goddam gals."

She turned to Ruth Etta. She was not capable of surprise; she felt nothing except that Ruth Etta looked different. She was crying silently.

"Smatter?" she asked her, poking her with the back of her wrist.

Tears flowed silently down Ruth Etta's face. She did not wipe her eyes when Violet handed her a used brown and orange flowered handkerchief; she went on crying. They walked in silence back to the building. As they came closer Ruth Etta's crying became audible, more and more so; Etkind was at the door waiting to let them in because she had heard it.

"NOW WHAT THE HELL," she squalled, locking the door behind them. "Smatter, Ruth Etta? Hahn?" She poked her in the ribs.

"SMILE NOW OR I AINT GONNA GIVE YOU NO SECONDS ON HOT DOGS TONIGHT," she said loudly, turning away.

"Say, Violet, whatsa matter with her," she stage-whispered to Violet. Violet was looking smug as she took off her coat.

"Absolutely nuthin; some fella at the store wouldn lend us no money, is all," Violet said, her face shut. She went off down the hall to the day room, back to her chair at the back. She could hear Ruth Etta's uncontrollable crying, mounting to screams, and was unmoved. "Goddam women," she thought.

*The Edge of Night* was on now; she relaxed and began to think about Corky and what it would be like. She would have the hot dogs for supper, then after that she could sit for maybe two hours before bed, thinking about Corky. She was content.

# THE DRUM CONCERTO

THE PICTURE by Pugnoni stood framed in gold on the parquet against the carved bookcase. On a great velvet pillow Georgia Vroom sat gracefully, looking at the picture.

"Not his best. A certain satisfaction, though... light from heaven coming in; nice, isn't she," she added, speaking of the Virgin who held the holy baby as an executioner exhibits the head of a vicious criminal.

Georgia was speaking to Leonard, who stood stiffly on the perfect floor, his long narrow feet tentative, his dark gray double breasted suit keeping his tall narrow body safe from speculation as to what man kept his counsel underneath. He had been described by a classmate at Ruela as "lean and quiet and dirty and mean"; a certain tension held his pale face, his glasses were rimless and glowed in the late sun, his gray hair was perfectly groomed. Dirty certainly now he had ceased to be; wary, a man to miss nothing, a man with a withheld vocabulary but words packed neatly inside for instant precise use whenever a moment came for them; a man in control. His position at the head of Italy's best, although not largest, publishing house showed in the look he had of having involved himself constantly with people against whom he figuratively rubbed so that he had no angles, but no plumpness.

He was not a man for a small woman. He was, too, a man for whom the woman must be exquisite at all times, who must never let down as he never let down; even sleep was controlled and illness never cast him down. His chosen companion must not ail, quaver, or weep unless in laughter. As he was spare with language, she must run hers out along the conversational line with ease but above all with a civilized guard up, no mistake in judgment must be heard from her, no looseness of fibre or pride be visible. All the great virtues of the mistress must be hers, but above all she must make each thing seem something other than what it was. Thus, love was humor, or even trivial; a party was not an important diversion or method of controlling one's friends; it was a small game played by her and him with certain rules that could be changed each time, but they two would know these rules and would not descend to any of the small attitudes of anxiety— above all Georgia should not, must never, show anxiety—and he would know if she contained the slightest trace; her smell, her motions, her speech would betray her. They must neither of them complain, make platitudes or generalities unless they were ambiguous enough to force some thought; must not seem to value anything while at the same time valuing life so intensely that the playing of the game of life, the routing of their days toward participation in,—they did not admit of infinity—a chic flashing out and away from the old things so as not to be tiresome. Death for them would be some sort of triumph alone, done neatly—and was the life blood they lived on, which was a great bond.

"Not too fine a fellow, that Pugnoni," Leonard said, turning away to choose a small cigar from his case. "He became a monk in some order and then went from this town to that stealing other men's women. Someone cut his throat and I believe also other parts of him . . ." He smoked, staring down at Georgia, then away. "I'll be in Rome tomorrow," he said after a silence. His cigar gave the room a smell like nostalgia for rain in a once-seen Greek island.

"Gottwald's book is an utterly pure outpouring of bilge, of course," Leonard said, sitting down on an eighteenth century chair that gave off its best gold light in the now setting sun. "Where is Maria? No drinks?"

"Gone, couldn't stand the smell of her hair any longer so I asked her to buy some mussels at the shore," Georgia said, smiling at his queer gaze as she mentioned the bad hair. She knew he loved to be shocked with her American frankness and knew too that later on he would decide she was quite beyond the pale, but at least better than the women his friends got in now and then or for longer. But none of them had lasted for eight years as had Georgia; both of them sat quietly and thought of this fact; Leonard looking brilliantly at a corner of the divan, Georgia looking at him, assessing, remembering his subtle courting of her when she was with Hamish after they came to Italy, to Siena; they had been standing in front of Hida's murals in the Moorish tower eating jelly beans pointing out to each other the characters that best represented their parents and what they had done; all were black and this gave Leonard a piquant curiosity tinged with distaste for the odd candy; the magenta edges of their conversation drew him, how- ever, and he came over . . . After that she had been drawn by an intense desire to belong to someone who needed no one; he had been drawn by her beauty and her ability to enter into conversations that ordinarily only men were able to take part in. Much later they found that love making was for them a vast adventure that neither of them could find words for or let alone; each held a mystery for the other that, though both had the insight born of a terrible past much considered, much damaging, with grand despair at the back of the whole, they could not draw even in their minds the outside limits of the other or totally possess. The civilization of each was intensely loved by the other; each fed on that of both, growing towards the state of complete sophistication that is a sort of immolation not of the common world; it is of the geniuses of living, of angels walking between the places where things happen, driving out the plain day and making it wild, rich and suddenly revealing.

Leonard went to the table by the window and chose a bottle. He poured with dignity and also with generosity. He gave one large glass to Georgia and held the other as he stood in the middle of the cream rug, his head cocked toward a spot on the ceiling.

He said "I wonder; I wonder about these people I'm seeing tomorrow. Cantessa is a saint, that we know, after his dealings with Christian. But Santelini cannot be said to be anything but second rate and I wonder at their friendship. Also at what they want from me. Ah well." He drank, his long hands holding the glass well.

Georgia always looked for his commentary on the people he saw; she compared it with her own thoughts and derived extra vitality from mention of men who wrote the things she read. Beautiful at forty-six, with a mind retentive, hating those men and women who constantly leaked nonsense in the presence of others, sickening with the waste they exhibited, she thought of cedars, cedar trees, the contrast with the wasters, the toughness and fragrance of the trees and the scanty lives of the talkers.

The telephone rang down the hall. Leonard stood quietly as she rose and walked away to answer it. They never took each other's calls or admitted to others that they were together; people still thought they were rigidly intellectual friends; where the whole town sought and found sex daily, all the time, and discussed it with tedium, she and Leonard were regarded with interest, speculation and always the conclusion that both were not in need of anyone.

Leonard heard Georgia speaking, the conversation was not long. She returned with the look of someone who has had a great change suggested for her life in some way.

"Well. That was Mrs. Abbey," Georgia said, sitting down again on the cushion and placing her hands in abstracted patterns on it. Looking down. "Mrs. Abbey."

"Where is she?" Leonard asked, watching her face.

"She's here. She, and Fern," Georgia said. "And, Leonard, I of course told her to bring her here; it was—necessary, of course..."

"Of course," Leonard said. "And—when?"

"Right away. They're driving around here in half an hour. I imagine I won't see you for a little while, darling. I'll be a homemaker in a slightly different way..." She continued to make patterns with her hands; then she looked up confidently. "It will be fine. We'll just find a lot to do; Mrs. Abbey is a very good person, really. Fern's just the same... Mrs. Abbey got her hair done... it's rather charming, she says..." She rose; Leonard watched her grace and felt a bitter thrust of passion, not to be fulfilled for many days. Fern, the simple daughter, the terror of their life, another man's doing, not his... had it been his, he would have handled it differently because he saw her as a hopeless constant; he would free Georgia from her dread motherhood, her conscience that he both lauded and hated; this hopelessly endowed daughter now in her late twenties was the constant threat that hung over his relationship with Georgia; fastidious he was but it was not this that made him want the relationship ended; it was something Georgia would not treat with; she had been adamant.

"I'll go now; you'll want to see to arrangements and I am to have dinner with that degenerate, Konrad," he said, putting down his glass. He went to her and laid his hand on her hair. "You can reach me at any time. Let me know when—they leave," he said gently.

"Goodbye," she said, watching him go through the door into the hall. She could not accompany him, see the front door shut and locked behind him.

Leonard drove in his small dove gray car to the restaurant where he was to meet Konrad Moses. He parked easily on the wide street where blue shadows stretched restfully; large old poplars lined the avenue and there were several elegant shops, now open in the cool evening air. He paused to look again at the emeralds in Morandi's window; he would go there soon to buy something for Georgia.

Passing under the awning of Brut's, he entered and bowed to John and Kathleen Morris, just leaving. He did not like them, so correct, so constipated in their worship of all things Italian and so negligent of their own country. He did not slow his steps in passing them; he knew he would be regaled by Kathleen with her discovery of Henry James.

Konrad was already seated dramatically against a crimson and gold wall panel and was drinking.

"Ah. Konrad."

"Leonard. This is fine. I'm happy."

Leonard sat as a waiter held his chair deftly for him. He looked at Konrad approvingly, a slender elegant man in a dark Cardin suit, a tiny pink in his buttonhole, his tie a beautiful electric blue. His grooming set off his handsome introversion. His eyes were black and surprisingly small but the heavy brows and hooked nose gave him character.. Deep, Leonard thought; deeply complex, rather foul; fascinating...

He ordered a strong drink and then said "So. You've finished it." "Ah, yes. And I don't believe it—that I've finished it or that it happened to me..." Konrad began to narrate a synopsis of his book as the restaurant filled slowly and they ordered more liquor.

He had traveled widely always; his last trip was to Iran, a wild mountain area where the people lived on as they always had, relying on horses, tents and the sword to sustain life. Konrad, alone, had ridden into a high rocky valley and had spent a week with one Nessim, his goats, his two women, one middleaged and used up, thin and silent, one young and sly with a small baby, eating cheeses from goats' milk, rabbit and lamb. It was terribly cold at night and they sat on a rug in the tent drinking kumiss which did not make them drunk because there was always danger of fire, of murder, of storms...

One night the wind, always roaring there, pitched screaming against the tent which billowed but was held firm by huge rocks. Out of the storm a priest, smelling of fat and with huge bare calloused feet, came to visit Nessim. He lost no time in running his hand up under the young woman's layers of clothes and he was silent, concentrating, his lips wet.

Nessim said this hospitality was usual. The priest, seamy, dirty, bearded, began to laugh and, guzzling more kumiss, hinted that the baby lying swaddled beside the old woman, was his. He had come for him, in fact. Nessim was elaborately polite at first, thinking he was joking. But as the night wore on the priest had drunk vast quantities and had staggered to his feet, moving to pick up the baby.

Nessim, now infuriated, was there first and picked the child up; he cast it then on the roaring fire in the middle of the tent and, holding his dagger over it, prevented Konrad or the others from saving the child. The priest went, eventually, out into the raging night, making a rude gesture at Nessim before the tent flap fell behind him.

Later, as dawn straggled up and the wind lessened, Nessim explained in a dull fatigued voice the customs of child-rearing there: a father could do as he wished with his children and death was dealt out quite often to prove paternity.

Konrad, sickened, sat on the rug and listened to Nessim going on about his life; he seemed unable to stop and unable to sleep. The women lay motionless under more coverings.

Nessim spoke of the comforts of goats, most like a human woman of all animals. He spoke grimly of the lack of flowers; he had seen some once at a desert market he had loved.

He spoke of warring with other mountain men and of the fact that when he returned from these affairs he was somehow left without himself; at such times he could not sleep.

But one forgot, slowly . . .

"You find us romantic, do you?"—he asked Konrad, after a long pause. "You know, I'd like to see the sea. I believe it would—make a difference. Then I could contract my suicide. I want—the end . . ."

He said, too, that he had never owned a picture.

Silently he seemed then to ruminate and said no more as a watery sun rose and the women crawled out to prepare the rabbit for a meal.

"Ah, Konrad, you see you have charmed me out of eating my dinner; yes. We shall publish your Nessim book. It has a new dimension, does it not?" Leonard had no appetite for food now; he ordered brandy. He sat abstracted; once he drew in a deep breath, mouthed silently and looked sharply at Konrad. "Well, and did all this change you?"

"No, it made me more—more myself, do you see. A box, to be filled. A package, I am, I'd say." Konrad saw a friend passing and waved. His lack of emotion for the terrible story he had just told irritated Leonard, who finished his brandy and signaled for the check.

"I'll be in touch," he said, rising. Konrad beckoned to his friend who was wearing a yellow suit and dark glasses and who sat down in Leonard's chair. Leonard left the restaurant, going relieved into the fresh night breeze.

As he drove to his apartment he felt weighted with the knowledge of the mountain child's death. He had not known much horror; now it bore him down. It was, he thought, the loneliness of it all . . .

Loneliness, he saw, was a being apart in a silence, somewhat soiled, no doors to pass through, no speech with anyone however inadequate; it was to have no future or past; there was no going or arrival; being was boundless torment surrounded with self-doubt. Leonard, observing himself, saw he was about to change, had changed in some major way.

Considering what to wear, what the bedrooms needed, flowers, she busied herself as the terrible half hour passed. She was wearing a full blue silk and was just setting out a generous plate of Di Laschia's bon bons when she heard them at the door. With desperation and determination, she walked into the hall and let them in, looking with resigned fatigue at the face of her daughter, Fern, who wore a fine tweed suit with complete lack of grace, her overweight body sagging, her white round face unaware; she had been crying again and was angry, Georgia could see; how well she knew those times; how exhausing, impossible, they were; she looked with compassion at Mrs. Abbey.

"Your apartment is so restful," Mrs. Abbey was saying, standing near but not too near Fern, alert, in navy blue, tidy, fresh and strong, giving off a bitter smell of moth flakes. "Fern, would you like to take off your jacket, dear—" She moved to help Fern who walked further into the room towards the candy and stood by it picking out several pieces that she stuffed into her pockets, also eating. She turned, chewing, to Mrs. Abbey.

"Now what shall we do," she said, confusion blending with impatient boredom in her flat eyes. The new hair arrangement already had the matted unbelonging look Georgia remembered from other attempts to make her aware of herself. "You don't like me," she added, looking with hostility at Georgia. She began to hum tunelessly to herself, looking doggedly at her mother. She went on humming as Mrs. Abbey led her out of the room towards the bedrooms.

Georgia followed them, her mind flying from the horror of this whole, this complete failure, this ungodded time, the continuum of nothingness, this epitome of the hopeless, to Greece, to Leonard having dinner with at least a man with a mind where life had muscle and disaster could be let alone, borne, arranged; she knew when the flowers came they would take on the qualities of her daughter; even flowers were forced to failure in the presence of this creature of certain limbo.

She stood in the doorway watching Mrs. Abbey seat Fern, comb her hair efficiently and begin to unpack, making cheerful statements to the discolored empty woman stuffing candy into her gray mouth.

Georgia forced herself to speak energetically and forced herself to address Fern who removed an orthopedically designed shoe and was looking absorbedly at it.

"We're going to have picnics, since it's so lovely outdoors, darling," she said desperately, hoarding in the far reaches of her mind the moments in the future when, in her own bed, she could dream of strength she did not have. "We'll go shopping, too; don't you think that would be fine, Mrs. Abbey? Fern, won't that be fun?"

Fern turned her eyes towards her mother and then back to her foot. She said balefully to Mrs. Abbey "I hate that man on the train. You know. YOU know," she said, and her mouth laughed in an ugly way. "YOU know what he was doing, don't you, Mrs.,"... She stared fixedly at Mrs. Abbey with ugly expectancy. "I know he was against me and he hates my mother too," she added, not looking at Georgia. "The way I hate her." She began to hum again, rocking herself rhythmically in the pretty boudoir chair. She picked her nose suddenly and stared off at nothing.

56 □

"Why don't you give Fern a bath, Mrs. Abbey," Georgia said. "I have some bath oil in your john." She gave up at that moment trying to reach her daughter; the bath oil, the high beauty of the cathedral in the lavender twilight that she saw from the window, the individual opening a casement gently across the way, the sound of traffic below, all called her to live; the murderous pale scuttled thoughts, the scatological and grimy trend of Fern's ways would unseat her completely if she gave way further; she felt the sudden weight of age upon herself as she dropped her motherhood in the blue evening moment, accepting the burden of the divorce of herself from that state to make life and the living the large present of herself. The strong fear and hatred, weariness and groping she had felt in Fern's childhood left her as she then too gave Fern to Fern to hold or lose, seeing that satisfaction to her daughter, incomprehensible to the well, was in another realm totally from hers.

She left the doorway and drew a perfect bath for her daughter, watching the pearls of bath oil slide into the clean water with a sudden joy, an unlatching of a new door, she a bride of living wholly now, loving as before but loving more; released; the rehearsal for life she had experienced had made for her the groundwork of a vast and now unshakable serenity. All things were possible, she felt, almost reeling with relief and the marvel of it all. She called to Mrs. Abbey with strong tones and decisiveness. "Would you come here, please?" The woman came, eyebrows raised in readiness.

"It is best, I find, that you and Fern not stay here after tonight," Georgia said. "Now is the time for the stay in Switzerland we discussed in our letters and I'll make arrangements tonight; you'll go there tomorrow. I know you love Switzerland," she added with a smile, the smile caused by knowing she would give no explanation to Mrs. Abbey. "So. The bath is ready; and then we'll go to dinner downstairs in the dining room." She went to the door. "I do thank you, you know, for everything," she said gently. "You are good." She left the room and walked down the hall to the great twilit drawing room where her nearly full glass stood on the rug by her pillow. She picked it up and took it to the window, looking out from her high point at the ready and vital city; at her ready and vital life.

Without examining her feelings, her decision, she felt strong, complete, of a cruelty that was a magnificence; she had now the decisiveness that must have motivated a Patton; a bold cleverness, a fine thwarting of fate that promised some clear depression to grasp her in the future, though not now, exhilarated her; exhilaration rose about her in flickering strongly colored pillars, supporting her new sky of a well borne present, a self-designed and self-ordained future where she could walk open-eyed past the other savages to the altars she had helped build: of tolerance, of mystery, of compassion only for those who could feel it, and of another sort for those who could not; altars to wit, decision, the incompleteness of life where even so there was the infinite possibility of supplying any lack...

The severance of the moment past withdrew sustenance from the beast of conscience and poured ingots of untold nameless marvelous shapes for a future always to ripen in the sun of her strength. The stone of the past had melted; she knew it would be found a burning stairway for another; for herself it forged a summit of forgiveness.

The dinner hour with Mrs. Abbey and Fern passed in a haze; they retired afterward, Mrs. Abbey firm and cheerful as always and Fern tearful, hostile; as soon as they closed their doors Georgia went to the telephone. She must speak to Leonard and tell him her decision; she felt he would understand; she must see him, she must see him immediately; she wanted to put out her hand and touch him; she wanted him.

"Leonard," she said when he answered. "Listen, please..." and she described her afternoon after he had left and all her subsequent thought. She described them well, articulately; she concluded to him "I've parted with motherhood, today, Leonard..."

There was a silence. She pictured him fingering the small topaz beetle or the Limoges shepherdess on his telephone stand as he thought out his answer and ensuing invitation.

He said finally "That, I think—I find now I think—is an ultimate cruelty of a monumental sort—in spite of opinions I have given voice to in the past. I think, considering the actuality of something we have discussed a great deal, that this is a degradation for you... I am depressed. But... you must do what you think you must do. As I told you earlier I must be in Rome tomorrow; then New York... when I return I shall ring you up and see if you can't work out a readjustment of this decision. I have new reasons for thinking as I do and I must talk to you about them... Goodbye, my dear." He hung up.

Loud the traffic outside, the rushing hectic mindless night spawned from the tricky, soft, formless and vacant twilight whose morality she had trusted, whose poetry had lured her to a new morality of self that had been a moment's glory, a certain freedom, the beginning of a new time; the silence, too, was loud in the perfect drawing room as she stood staring down into the street.

# FRIEDA'S STORM

"HUM, HUM, hummmmmmmmm," he sang and spoke rather humorously as he poured a lot of sherry into a cut glass tumbler. "*Like* what I did today. I *like* it," he went on.

His wife on the porch outside, one step down, was standing bent at a wicker table that supported a rococo green ceramic vase full of goldenrod; it was that sad time, for most, the end of summer; she was reading the headlines.

"Mh," she said. Outside a clean cool wind blew across the baseball field of the camp and across the big screened porch.

Hudson Narcoonis stood in the doorway with his drink looking at his wife's heavy tall form with the heavy graying hair in an old-fashioned arrangement over her chalk-white jowly face that trembled whatever she did. He saw with flinty despair her solid buttocks, thick waist, heavy straight calm legs, the broad feet in woven summer shoes with thick heels; he recalled she bought them in Panama on her trip with her sister. His bearded brown face was dead as he contemplated her. As he looked, though, he composed her for his next painting—something abstract. Devil Reading. She-Devil. Naked Bourgeoise. Titles flowed through him with the sherry. Various titles in his own language—Finnish—occurred to him.

She straightened and turned her back, pulling her yellow boucle sweater down taut over her figure. He did not see this; his gaze had gone off across the long lake, very blue (a shade he disliked) and comfortless. He did not like lakes and he was foreign to summer camps where everything was so two-dimensional. He did not like children. He wore a smooth-cloth city suit, a colored vest and a black tie with a small white fleck in it. He was narrow-built, tall, a little stooped; he gave a black impression with sharp prune-colored eyes, rather small, his coal-black head of hair and the neat full beard. On the little finger of his right hand—a well-shaped, strong hand—was an obsidian ring, plain with a gold setting. His feet were long and narrow; he wore black shoes with a good polish. One wondered how he would look without the beard; he was certainly presentable with it.

"Well. What is for dinner?" he asked Frieda with his heavy accent. He knew he would not like it; it would be too little, and dull. He longed for a plate of calves' brains with whiskey, cream, potatoes, swordfish, roasts with gravy.

"Mh." She waited and thought. How narrow her shoulders were, he noticed, and looked away. "I think we'll have cereal and some, um, peaches," she said, moving slowly toward the door. She did not look at him with her exophthalmic, veined eyes, but stood in front of him till he stepped out of her way. She smelled of—skin, he thought, gulping a large swallow of his drink.

Frieda walked the cool length of the huge living room that was tanklike and dark, rising to the roof two storeys up; a balcony was set around the second floor as a way to reach the vast bedrooms. The borrowed house was just like Helen Goss—she would build big enough to hold the whole Radcliffe class.

Frieda tried not to look at the gaping nostrils of the stuffed moose head attached to the balcony on one side. She secretly liked it, all but the nostrils, and the stuffed wildcats and deer, though all thought of going out in the woods was against her nature and a gun was something for very different people. Her eye flicked over the peeled wood furniture in the big room, the big stone fireplace, the Indian rugs, the magazines she subscribed to but rarely read, the big bookcase full of detective stories that Hud liked; at three in the morning she would hear him come downstairs from his room to pick out one he hadn't read. She herself liked books about anthropology, or botany, and yet she could never discuss them.

Hudson Narcoonis moved out on the large porch now that the unpleasant presence of his wife was gone, and gave himself over to contemplating his life through the perspective of a whole day of painting on an abstraction. The sherry did not affect his view on anything; he could drink quantities of alcohol, smell strongly of it, and maintain an astounding grip on the conversation. He was a valued guest at parties and he always went when invited and almost never took Frieda. Having her in the house with him most of the day was terrible enough—although he was aware when he at last turned towards whatever studio apartment he called home at the time that he counted on the pillar-like presence of Frieda to dispel his mind's weird and amorphous devils. For instance he was troubled by dark shapes, of anything, directly seen or indirectly, and always turned on all lights in his vicinity, leaving them on all night. He would tolerate no animals in the house for this reason. At times his overcharged artist-mind fancied, or day-dreamed, of odd, even mad, situations, which he knew were unreal but whose presence for a moment became prolonged, because of a sort of richness-value they in their originality had, a jewel-tone, a consistency, a juxtaposition, an intricacy, perhaps; and he could not jettison so valuable an experience no matter how unsettling. Frieda was distant and unreachable, foreign to him yet with familiar outlines. They formed, the two of them, a silent orbit, each rotating on an axis around their possessions. They were as in touch, too, as two planets. They were more alone together than they would have been physically solitary.

Frieda sought the broad shallow stairs, where too a big bunch of goldenrod stood, and went up with firm steps, her cheeks shaking, her big dry hand on the bannister. She was intending to change her dress and wear a floor length India print she had chosen as the proper thing for the wife of an artist—in one of her clearer moments of thinking—mostly she thought in patches—"That linen is too long . . . shall I go . . . will he be in . . . the dress I'm going to put on is . . . golden-rod . . . hate it . . . hate . . . hell . . . oh god . . . god, *damn.*" Often her thinking went like this. Her own large shape in mirrors kept her from analyzing her thoughts as neurotic or even odd; she was heavy and big and her large face looking at her exuded calm with the fact that she had jelled into a satisfactory middleaged woman who sustained a brilliant artist as husband. The fact that they did not ever share a bed, and had not for fifteen years, made no difference to her, she decided as she absentmindedly tossed his pillow onto his bed and drew the spread none too neatly over it, one day.

She arrived at the balcony and turned to go into her big bedroom. Going to the closet she looked for the India print, found it hanging with a sachet of lavender on the hanger, and brought it out. Slowly she divested herself of her sweater, her suitable size twenty light plaid cotton and her damp but clean underclothes. They never swam and it did not occur to her to buy a bathing suit and try it; besides she would be sure to run into Mollie Hawkins, the camp director's wife and a close friend of Helen Goss who had lent her the house on the basis of a rather amorphous friendship at Radcliffe where they had been officers together of a classics club. She did not really like Helen Goss, who talked a great deal about Zen and wore flowing saris at the most unsuitable times and gave her Siamese cats names like "Sandor." If she did stroll to the beach she would be sure also to be cut off by a gathering of brown little boys in camp uniforms yelling BEEPETY-BEEP-BEEP, or bellowing cheers while their young athletic counselors stood up as she approached. She had nothing to say to youth, never having been young herself.

She put on clean white under-bloomers, a generous brassiere and her long slip, then the print. She brushed out her hair with a brush whose bristles were made of whalebone.

And all this time, working in her, was an unusually strong feeling of discomfort; usually she was mildly uncomfortable—the reason for which she ascribed to small matters like tight shoes, pressure of world events, the necessity to get brown sugar for the oatmeal she always fixed for breakfast, deciding (or not) to give away her raccoon coat, so warm always.

But tonight she whispered to herself "god damn" more than once, and realized it was quite conscious. She became aware that she smelled something—and it was Hud's shaving lotion, pervading the upstairs. She thought of closing off his room but knew he would wonder why she had done this. She went to his door, her hair hanging bushily over her shoulders, and stood looking around. She rarely looked at Hud's work but tonight she took stock.

His room was enormous, suitable for a studio. Ranked along the walls and on the floor were large canvases, finished or only partially executed. Slowly she made a circuit, the lowering sun casting warm rays to light the collection.

First, a breasty abstraction in green and taupe, standing on his bureau; obviously liked.

"Oh," she whispered, ashamed. She was ashamed that she had not inspired the breasts, the torso. "Tit-bladded," she said aloud, vindictively. She did not hear Hud come up the solid stairs to stand quietly in the doorway. "Pretty tittyish," she stage-whispered scornfully. She moved on to a red leaf against a blue plate, huge and vibrant. "Sssssssssss," she whispered. "I can't. I *can't.* Piss," she remarked vaguely. Turning, she confronted a large multicolored abstraction, a purple stratum bordered by red and white. "Tut. Phooey. NOT," she added. "God, damn these, god, damn them all." She continued on her circuit of the room and the attached sleeping porch, saying "MURDER; TWADDLE. Thumbs down. Piss..." the worst words she was capable of.

Hudson listened, stunned. Never had he thought his big wife could turn against him. That he should be against her was eminently correct; she was a Philistine, a penny-scrimper, a bore, a big ugly shape; she owed him everything she had... "Nuts to them" she went on, squatting to see one better. "Lord have mercy," she said. "Hell. Urine. URINE! Dirty bath... sink... sweaty... old *smell... big* smell ... bathroom!"

Hudson's shocked feelings as he listened made him break out in perspiration. He began to understand certain things about Frieda. For one thing, she had no feeling at all for his work, or him. For another thing, she had been so sheltered—or deprived—that the only vocabulary she had for expressing what was obviously a murderous loathing, was derived from naughty little-girl words or from that most private and desperately personal place, the bathroom; that he totally misunderstood and failed this big, homely, lonely, empty woman; and, last of all, he could not change any part of the situation because he needed her there, and he saw that little though she had, she would have nothing if he broke up their relationship. He left her, her last words that he heard being "unspeakable *urine* ... old *smell* ... god, damn this..!" as he went down the stairs.

He was about to go to the kitchen and get out the china and cereal, something he previously had never done, when a piercing shout from just outside came to him:

ELIGANOO GANICK GANACK
ELIGANOO GANICK GANACK
WO-UP WO-UP HULLIBALOO!
THE NARCOONISES!!!

It was a group of twenty small boys smiling earnestly up at the windows as they overflowed in good feeling towards everybody.

Silently Hudson stood back in the shadow against the cupboards while the children yelled "Come out! Yay! Come on *out!*" And then, running and shouting at random, undismayed at having no response, they galloped off.

# THE VON

FREDERIC VON Voss lay deep in the grip of a terrible dream in his tent in the pasture halfway up Cold Stream Mountain. Dark buildings and sky lowered over a scene of murder blended horribly with sneering smiles and one long tortured mad laugh. It seemed he was both sought for and also involved with the torture.

He woke on his cot; for a moment he could not shake off the horror of the dream. Then he turned his head and looked through the tent's flaps at a gray foggy morning; the usual view of the rest of the range was hidden. A high wind threw the branches of the big trees around; the sky, as in the dream, was leaden.

He lifted his arm from the blankets to see the time on his watch; it was half-past six. He lay for a few minutes more in the comfort of the bed and then got up and put on his wool shirt over his pajamas. Going outside to relieve himself behind the huge maple that sheltered his tent he felt the cool morning air on his naked skin, a curious sensation comprised of pleasure and helplessness. He felt a certain pride of possession for this stream of pure quite beautiful urine flowing from him, a pride he felt in everything he was and did and owned.

A goldfinch flew past him in swoops, silent in the fog. Frederic went back to the tent, feeling cold and fit, and set about making a fire outside. He did this methodically and the wood caught quickly, beautifully. He soon had a hot blaze going and heated a pot of water to shave with in front of the steel mirror he had attached to the tent pole. He shaved firmly and evenly, pleased as usual with his tan and his ice blue eyes and his straight rather long blond hair; when he had finished he stepped outside and swept his hands through the dripping hay; with the water he wet his face refreshingly and was content to be thus primitive.

Breakfast was large and healthful: wheat toast, fried eggs and a handful of dates. As he got it all ready he hummed his favorite sections of Rossini's *Stabat Mater;* under these circumstances the dream's presence faded to an almost pleasant exciting experience; he might even make use of it in the book.

He was anxious to get on with his first chapter which he had started only the day before; the two previous days had been spent getting set up and walking the terrain nearby; he had made several trips down to his Buick parked on Mygatt Road to carry all his supplies to the pasture; he had stopped courteously at the Totten farm there to let them know he had arrived. He did not suggest to Audrey or Ben Totten that they drop in on him; his was to be a summer of hard work.

He set his dirty dishes in a pail of water and drew up the covers of his cot neatly; then, after pulling on a pair of corduroy trousers and a pair of sneakers, he sat down at his typewriter where his notes and earlier typing were tidily laid out with stones on them to keep them from blowing away. He reread what he had set down the day before and, occasionally referring to his notes, went on with chapter one.

He felt good; he liked what he had written; he knew all the people he had known in Germany and England at the universities would enjoy reading THE BOOK OF THE BLESSED, to be a big novel about life on a campus. It would include references to situations he had known in all the many positions he had held in the past eleven years and would concentrate particularly on the stories and situations to be found at Cameron College, the progressive school for men at which he had been employed for the past two years. He believed that in a novel you not only could enjoy writing down the true facts about real people, you were morally obligated to derive from life, of course changing the names—and for this he felt he had a special gift. He himself had been given the nickname "The Von" at Cameron by Paul Savage, a tennis colleague; the rest of the faculty who liked him—and this was a rather small but select group—took up the name too.

He felt no compulsion when talking or writing to mean what he said; he found a freshness and free flowing quality in some of his sentences where he had expressed rather outrageous things. He intended to write about his own affair with Naomi and the thing with Mrs. Whiting since he enjoyed including his own personality. He thought anyone who did not like what they found there about themselves had really better look to their own conduct; he took what gave color and flair to his story.

He was deep in a paragraph about Mrs. John Colson, wife of the dean, and searching for a new name for her; he had just thought of Berridge as a good dean-like name when he heard a rustling in the long grass outside the tent. He looked up to find a short stocky old man in terrible clothes standing looking in at him with smoky mad eyes; his purple sweater was darned in several places in the front with huge yarn stitches of bright orange and blue and the sleeves hung down to his gnarled dirty hands with long nails. His uncut white hair blew in the wind; strong smells of his unwashed body mixed with the smell of bacon fat came to von Voss' nose.

"Ahhhhh," the old man said tentatively.

"Yes, sir?" von Voss said, his hands remaining on the keys.

"Say. Want to buy some milk?" the old man asked in a high husky voice. His dark baggy trousers were covered with years of spots; his shoes had no laces and were crusted with mud and seed from the hay.

"Oh. Well. Thank you—you sell it?"

"Yuh. I do; got blueberries later too. Vorlet picks em."

Von Voss had the feeling that this sprite travelled the mountains all night and never slept. "Who are you, sir?"

"Savory," the man said, coming in curiously to look everything over. "Bring up the milk myself in the mornin about eight. Good cream," he added, scratching his neck. His mad eyes stared at von Voss.

"All right, Mr. Savory—bring one quart every morning and I'll pay you each week. Will that be satisfactory?"

"What?"

"I said I shall pay you each Saturday," von Voss said patiently. "Who is Violet?"

"Daughter."

"You have the other farm down at the bottom of the mountain, do you?"

"Ya. Get ya some now," Savory said, leaving and rustling off through the grass. The wind swept again through the tent but it was warmer; von Voss continued his paragraph with satisfaction: "Houghton slammed on the brakes by Fells Hall, seeing Courtney run lightly from the mail room, waving at him . . ."

He paused to think just what it was about Naomi that he should describe trenchantly to make his readers see what he saw in her . . . her warmth, her wit, her fine expensive clothes—no, this wasn't a book for women; men didn't care about fine expensive clothes, even though he did . . .

He sat thinking about possible undesirable readers. Mostly he thought of his readers as a large body of the literate, sensitive upper class—yes, upper class like him and like all his friends; but he had an uncomfortable picture in his mind's eye of kids reading—well, that section in his notes about Mrs. Berridge and their passages in bed or in his car more precisely; she seemed to like that very much; he thought of people he saw in town, careless, tough, cheap, even weird or unbalanced, poring over his carefully polished words, his dear life, his own bright arrangements and successes . . .

He put these thoughts away and went on; passion, everywhere, through everything, he must state, capture; passion and subtlety of thought, wit.

As the wind continued to blow he worked through the morning with only one stop to stand, light a cigarette and eat some of the wheat crackers he found so good for him. He knew the air around his tent too would do him a lot of good; probably get rid of the bad dreams; it occurred to him that he should read Molière or a like type of thing before he tried to sleep; rational living and thinking, and hard work all day . . . he planned a certain time when it was pleasant for sun bathing. He had already walked once the five miles to Broome's store at the crossroads with his rucksack on his back and had enjoyed carrying the ten-gallon can of kerosene back with him. He put out his cigarette and made elaborate preparations to photograph his typewriter with the nearly full sheet in it, then another shot of the lowering weather outside; he hoped this would be fraught with the dour quality of the day and even be a bit tragic.

He went back to his work and stayed with it until he began to be very hungry. The first chapter seemed to him to be entirely promising; he was deep in an atmosphere he had created of that mellow, passion-promising air he had found around centers of learning. Still feeling carried away with this success he made himself two cheese sandwiches and got a bottle of Löwenbräu from under his bed. He stepped outside with the bottle to look at the mountains and saw that the dark sky was breaking towards a blue; it would soon be a beautiful day. It was, he saw, half-past two; he could put in some time in the sun before he had to get into his slacks and jacket to go to Mrs. Paton's party at four. He finished his beer and went into the tent to raise the flaps all around and put on his bathing trunks. Waiting for the sun to come out he reread what he had written and swelled with pride at what he found; he wondered why he had waited so long to try this novel when he so obviously had what it took.

The sun began to shine hotly into the tent; he went outside and lay on his blue blanket, mulling with satisfaction certain of his phrases. The sun was good and he knew he would pick up a fine lot of color before the party; the wind still blew the hardhack but lying down he was comfortable. The dream's atmosphere came back in small shreds; he amused himself extracting its mood, finding cogent words to describe it . . . but when the horrifying laugh recurred to him he turned over uncomfortably and reminded himself of the Molière. He dozed.

He slept lightly for a while, turning once to regulate his tan; then he became aware of being very thirsty and realized that Savory had not come up with the milk. He thought he would walk down to the farm and get it. He went into the tent, put on the sneakers and a shirt and went down the pasture to the broken fence that marked the boundary of the farm. He saw ahead of him a violently sunny space; as he drew nearer he saw the house again, no trees around it, a splintery gray cube with endless sagging porches. On the nearest the old man sat on the railing darning his loud sweater while he still wore it. One chicken stood in the bare yard; there was no sound from the house. Then he heard a pan crash and a thud; the screen door slammed and a girl came to where the old man sat.

"Vorlet, I'm hongry."

Violet leaned on the railing. She was colorless and flat chested; she wore a man's black cardigan and a spotted orchid skirt. She had no shoes on; her hair was dark and short, frizzy and held flat to her forehead with a fancy rhinestone bobby pin. She caught sight of von Voss walking toward them and stared; he lifted a hand in greeting as a loudly racketing wreck of a truck raced into the yard. A young man in dungarees and nothing else, about twenty-five years old, climbed out and also stared at him. "Want somethin?" he asked belligerently.

"I have come about the milk—your father said I could buy some here?"

"Oh. Ya." The young man went across the yard to an old barn where many boards were missing and hay stuck out the holes. He disappeared; then, when von Voss did not come, he put his head out of the door and jerked his arm to indicate he should join him. Von Voss went across the dry grassless yard and into the cool barn where the young man was pouring some milk, well sprinkled with small pieces of hayseed, from a pail into a glass jar. "That enough?"

"That is excellent. I have told your father I will pay each Saturday. I will myself come for the milk each day."

"Okay. Name's Bruce." He went out, leaving von Voss to screw a top on the jar and follow into the sunlight.

As he was returning through the yard to go back to the pasture he heard Violet from the porch say "Ey." He walked towards her; the old man was no longer there. "Who're you," she asked him.

"I? I am Frederic von Voss."

She looked at him with no expression on her face, her arms folded across her chest. "I got a swell pa." She turned to swing a thigh up along the rail. "What do ya think of some ole pa who likes his own daughter," she asked him, running her finger under her nose.

"Oh. I think it is a very fine thing for families to like one another."

"I mean he thinks I'm his wife," she said with an ugly laugh that showed her bad teeth. "Gah."

Von Voss turned to go, waved and said, "It was very nice to have met you, Violet." He walked away; the grass smelled sweet when he got to the pasture and the spruce smelled strongly in the sun. He thought with distaste of Violet sleeping with the old man, and who knew who Bruce got together with. When he reached the point in the pasture where a hillock would hide the farm from him he turned briefly to look down; Violet had gone in and the farm looked peaceful like an etching. He walked further up the pasture and passed a light brown cow with a sweet face staring at him as she chewed.

It was now time for him to change his clothes; after putting on a white shirt that would set off his tan nicely and his gray slacks and a sport jacket he got out a scarlet and blue silk scarf and tied it around his neck inside the shirt's opening. He dropped the flaps of his tent and left to walk to the road where he had parked the Buick. This took him steeply down a path through some woods, beautiful with the sun and wind through them; it occurred to him that some of this should go into the book; he pondered a scene with a yet-to-be-chosen woman, with himself, there in the woods, that ended with her running away from him, dismissed, down and out of sight.

He passed the Totten farm without seeing anyone, went to his car and unlocked it, and got in, enjoying the fine upholstery and the deep roar of the engine. After five minutes on the dirt road he arrived at the macadam which he followed for twenty minutes, reaching Centerville and, a few minutes later, the Paton gates, covered with woodbine. Deep shadowed stands of ferns grew at their base; the long road to the house was gravel, lined with locust trees.

The party was beginning. Near the house von Voss stepped from his car just as the two occupants of a handsome station wagon were getting out. The man, strong and heavy with white hair neatly brushed, his meaty face empty of expression, held out his hand. "Henry Quinn, and this is my wife, Jewel."

Frederic shook hands with Henry and bowed slightly to Jewel, who wore a lime linen dress and had extremely blond hair. They walked toward the large white house across a closely trimmed big lawn shaded with many elms and horse chestnut trees. Other guests, already with drinks in their hands, stood talking; von Voss, estimating the importance of the gathering since he had only been here once before, saw that already about twenty people had arrived; if the Quinns were to be typical he anticipated a good couple of hours. The sea lay at the far end of the lawn, sending a blinding path of sunlight back from its whitecapped surface where several sails leaned with the wind.

Approaching a table where bottles and canapés stood von Voss saw Paul Savage seated in a wicker chair, his elbows on his knees, staring down at his shoes that he had turned sideways. His shoulders jutted and his gray hair was blown; he was as always graceful but looked as if he was there because he had nothing better to do.

"Ah! The Von!" he bellowed, not getting up. Beside him in a chair made from the horns of wild game Sherman Hyde, whom von Voss had met at the other party he had been to here, sat examining a child's toy with concentration; he was slumped almost on his shoulders spinning the propeller of a bright yellow and red tin airplane. A four year old boy in a lavender knit suit and newly cleaned white sneakers stood watching him. Sherman's graying hair and lined, horselike face contrasted with his spotless white shirt, his bleached seersucker trousers and his long narrow black shoes. His socks as well were black.

Without looking up Sherman said, "Von Voss, see what we have here, young Knight and I." Von Voss walked to the table and looked down at the plane. Savage looked fixedly at him but said nothing.

"Hello, Hyde," von Voss said.

"Sherman is making it go," Knight explained tensely to von Voss, who poured himself a drink at the table.

"Lovely stuff, this Japanese junk," Sherman said, spinning the propeller again. "Takes me back to the time I had a broken leg when I was seven. My world was made up of this sort of thing."

Savage snapped a loose piece of wicker on the arm of his chair. "Moretti and Evelyn took off," he said.

"Ah? Now what does the discarded Nick do?" von Voss asked, smiling gently.

"I think he's after your Naomi, frankly, so sorry."

"Frederic," a silvery quaver came from the veranda. An old woman in black voile stood in a classic posture, one slender hand raised bone color against the shadow of the porch, her watery old face under an old Panama hat eagerly pointed at von Voss. Carrying his drink and also picking up a small roll containing creamed chicken, he went to stand by the wild rose bushes below her. The flowers sent forth a heavy smell; the old woman looked parched above them. "How is the writing coming—I'm so interested," she said in her light voice.

"Just getting started, actually."

"Well. I'll just see if Olive is ready to come down." The old lady, turning first one way and then the other, waved vaguely and went through the dark doorway.

"Oh, god, Olive," von Voss heard Savage say.

Von Voss looked towards the spot near a carefully planted canna where Henry Quinn, drink in hand, was watching Jewel, far across the lawn, talking with a tanned dark haired young man in tennis clothes. Henry in lieu of a smile pursed his lips slightly at von Voss and said "I am observing nature." His eyes, slightly squinted and very cold, returned to his wife who began to laugh with her companion and laid a hand on his shoulder. Von Voss walked over to Henry, who said, "You read all these articles on how we behave when we're not so young any more; what am I supposed to do? I don't particularly love her but all these years together must mean something."

"But you have had marriage; for that I envy you."

"I've been around. I've seen life. I ought to know this is just run of the mill living. Everybody does it." Henry put his hand in his pocket and took it out again. "Well, what's your problem, if any." His cold eyes looked into von Voss'. Frederic looked at Jewel and the man she was with. "I think like most women she's busy collecting for a rainy day. Which may not, after all, come along," he said lightly. He continued to observe Jewel who now was walking with her companion beside a bed of delphinium. Von Voss looked forward to having some innings with this lady and knew from experience that he could succeed in doing this. To cover his intentions to her husband he said, "The lad seems a bit young for her, perhaps?"

"Ah well." Henry drank long from his glass and turned his back on his wife. He now confronted a man who, seated on a white bench, was talking to a big woman in rose boucle who stood beside him. He was small boned; his skeleton showed disconcertingly at many points. His face was small and yellow and his teeth were also yellow and folded over one another. His clothes were starched and his neck rose from his collar like a bunch of celery in a jar.

"It is a form of hysteria," he was saying to the woman, though he looked up briefly at Henry and Frederic. His lips were wet and saliva shot from his mouth as he talked. "You do not have to be democratic. Just keep yourself civil and you will be thought of as democratic, anyway." He laughed and gouged a bite from the piece of cake he held in his hand.

"But Sandy," the woman said, sitting down beside him persuasively. "You would not allow then for militant democracy—say, in the black condition. You really have no imagination or you could picture yourself as one of them." She drank, dribbling a little. Her dark waved hair formed a neat topping for her groomed self.

Sandy looked sharply at her and her glass and said wryly that he thought that what she held in her hand was a very big reason for her courageous talk; he did not feel that most people were courageous any more. He certainly was not. He looked suddenly at Henry and von Voss. "Don't worry about it, Henry," he said, his gaze on the far edge of the lawn. He was not talking about democracy. "She's just feeling the summer windsweptness." He added nasally, "Don't you feel that summer windsweptness?" speaking to the large woman who threw her head back and laughed soundlessly.

There was a rustle in the grass and Mrs. Paton approached supporting a thin middleaged acutely pale woman who had a pink crocheted shawl around her shoulders; she wore a cheap white cotton dress two sizes too big for her and carried a bunch of roses.

"Roses for festivities, I think are always nice," the old lady said vivaciously, talking to the unresponsive face of her daughter. "Sandy, get Olive's chair from the porch, you and Henry."

Olive had the look of a housekeeper, ailing, who spent her days sitting on the porch of a nursing home. Her large knuckles went ill with the creamy full-blown roses and her nose was red with a drop on the end of it. The large woman went to hold one elbow of the invalid and tried to think of something to say to her. But she looked at Olive's face and the forbidding insularity of the woman took all thought of conversation with her from her mind. Sandy and Henry came from the porch with the chair with its chintz cushions and Olive was settled in it near a table. Her mother said, "Isn't this nice, now, Olive, all of us here together on this lovely day." Sandy pretended to be looking for something to pass around from the table to be able to absent himself from Olive's presence.

Von Voss was again watching Jewel and saw that Henry's drinks were not doing him any good; von Voss thought contentedly that he could use all this. Savage strolled up to him and said in a low voice "Taking notes?"

"Ach, always. And what of your Brünnhilde, there—our Anna?"

"Gone off to Puerto Rico so you can't stick her in your catalog of the seven deadly," Savage punched his arm lightly and strolled away to pour himself another drink. Von Voss felt good; something good to drink endlessly available through the rest of the afternoon and all these involvements to see into. He glanced over at Olive who was being offered cake and was saying no to it; she did not look at him or at anyone. Her mother was saying to Henry, who had lowered himself into a chair beside her and offered her his whiskey, "Oh, I never can drink that, isn't it terrible," her moist eyes darting around the faces of the people near her. "Olive, have a cooky"; she motioned to Savage to pass them to her. "Where is Jewel, Henry?"

Henry got up and crossed the lawn to the intent couple now standing near the sundial; he took his wife by the arm. "Mrs. Paton wants a word with you," he said reasonably, nodding to the young man. Jewel, distracted and sulky, walked back across the lawn to stand in front of the old lady and Olive; she managed by choosing to discuss the flowers in the garden to chat animatedly for the prescribed seven minutes.

Von Voss had been aware of her approach and waited for a chance to talk at length with her. When at last she moved away from Mrs. Paton he went to her and offered to get her a whiskey. She looked up at him with happy appraisal and accepted. "Make it a healthy one," she remarked in gutteral tones for his ears alone. When he brought the dark drink to her, also holding a fresh and strong one for himself, she said "Rah! Cheers—are you German? What do you say for a toast?" He simply lifted his glass to her with an accomplished deep look into her eyes; he saw before him a completely happy woman. He knew he was considerably taller than the man on the lawn.

They talked for the length of their quickly drunk liquor; he said then "I have a wish to walk a little somewhere; would you care to walk with me?" She smiled, lifting her eyebrows, however, and nodded firmly. She glanced over at her husband, then put her hand lightly on von Voss' shoulder. "I'd love to," she said, setting her glass on the ground.

"Let us walk down the drive," he suggested, turning towards the gravel. She walked beside him in the breeze and sunlight; for a little while neither of them spoke.

"Do you walk, as a rule?" he asked her as they approached the curve that would reveal the gate.

"Not usually, for some reason; Henry doesn't either; he's always thinking too much," she added, quite kindly.

"I find my thought flows better on a walk," he said, looking up at a few fluffy white clouds overhead. "I'm just now starting a book," he decided to say then. She was enthralled and as they turned off onto the macadam they became deeply involved in discussing his novel; it seemed to be exactly her type of book and she was delighted he was writing about people he knew, frankly and no holds barred. She told him she could give him some really ripe material and as they walked on and on, turning off into a narrow cart track into a huge heath-like area, she talked about friends and their personal difficulties—and she had had many friends and their difficulties had been colorful and really ripe. She obviously came to life best when on these topics.

They talked with such absorption they did not see the sky cloud up and did not notice where the track had taken them. He was telling her about his new quarters on the mountain and allowing her to feel invited there to share a little time with him in his tent when he saw that they were now in a surpassingly strange place and the sky was again like lead.

Here the earth was hard, black, trampled, without grass, and everywhere grew thick black alder bushes with shiny trunks. The grove of alders stretched far ahead and they had penetrated so far that he could not tell how to return to the common. He stopped, looking around him; she was saying, "Pansy Perkins, the one with the fixation I told you about, started wetting her bed in her thirties—"; then she realized they had stopped walking and also looked around her. "My God," she said, looking at him, sobered. "We should have dropped a trail of white pebbles or something."

Von Voss saw a movement far into the avenue of alders ahead of them. It proved to be made by an enormous black hog; it was leading a whole herd of others, also black; silently they came near and then surrounded von Voss and Jewel. It began to rain large cold drops; there was no sound except the impact of the drops on the leaves and an occasional blowing from one of the animals. They were as big as bears, he thought.

" Come," he said to Jewel, snapping his fingers ahead of them over the backs of the nearer swine. "Move ahead gently, so . . ."

Slowly they made their way in the dim light; the pigs continued to surround and push them and it now rained in torrents; immediately they were soaked. Von Voss found himself waiting for a mad tortured laugh to break out somewhere; he began to sweat with dread. The swine jostled them, blowing and snorting; they did not grunt.

He thought if the laugh started here it would go on and on. He wanted to run but they could only take slow small steps.

Jewel took his hand; for a moment he held hers but dropped it quickly. She could not know this was a battle to him; that he had real demons in his head that he would not tell anyone about; he wished even that he was alone with the herd, the deluge, the horror to come. Then he could scream.

For an endless half hour they moved slowly through the huge grove, the black animals and tree trunks gleaming wetly, a solid evil smell rising from the beasts; the water poured on them, diminishing them.

At last they were pressed against a rusted barbed wire fence hidden in the wet weeds; with difficulty he held the strands apart for her to crawl through, and somehow got himself outside the sty. Stolidly the swine saw them leave; von Voss looked back, feeling a presence in the grove he had somehow become horribly at one with; where was the laugh, when would it tear through the heavy air?

Beyond a soaked stretch of sloping hay the roof of a building showed. Now they could walk more easily and again she took his hand; again he let it drop. She could not guess his exhaustion, his defeat. Her dress stuck to her figure and he did not care. Her hair was dripping and she had lost her shoes; he could not care.

"Jesus," she said as they came to the edge of a deep sand pit. The roof belonged to a bright green diner on the floor of the pit; the road passed just beyond it.

Somehow they slid down the coarse orange-red wet sand and made their way to the door of the diner. It was locked as was the back door when they tried it. He pointed towards the road and they walked to it and stood beside it in a patch of rough grass. They looked both ways for some sign of life, of help; the road was empty; there were no houses. They silently turned to the right and began to walk. The wind had risen and battered the cold water at them. After they had gone about a mile, still in silence, they heard a car's motor roaring behind them; von Voss desperately stepped to the middle of the road and stood with his arms spread out.

The car, a dirty pickup truck driven by a fat young man, came to a stop; he leaned over and opened the door. They dragged themselves onto the seat beside him; von Voss slammed the door and they went on.

"Just ben to the hospital buhcuz my wife's havin a baby," the man said, driving wildly. The visibility through the windshield was almost nothing but he kept the car at sixty. "God, bleedin all the way—you must be settin in it. . . ."

"Where ya goin?" he asked them finally. Jewel said "Mrs Paton's." "Oh-kay," he said, swinging the car into the turn near her place. The rain was stopping; huge puddles were everywhere and the trees dripped. At last he drove them down the gravel lane to the house where they climbed out. They did not thank him and he did not say goodbye.

Only von Voss' car and the station wagon remained parked near the house. At the sound of their arrival Henry appeared at the door; he came out and walked towards them. Jewel started to walk to him but stopped; he joined her and they stood looking dully at von Voss.

He shook his head slightly, wearily, and climbed into his car. Then he started it, backed it onto the neat wet lawn, leaving deep tire marks, and drove away.

# PRATHER SCULLY

PRATHER SCULLY took aim well, swung his thin arm far back and threw the horseshoe lovingly. It revolved in a dignified way going through the warm still air towards the stake and dropped on it perfectly with a combination clang and thud, making a small puff of white dust. Prather stood as he had when he pitched it, legs apart, the toe of one clean basketball sneaker pointing down, his right arm dangling out, pink, empty, rested, content; he was content all through. His scalp under the gray clean curling hair, neatly parted, tingled a little; fourteen straight ringers. He let his arm fall and stood straight, squinting across his sunken clipped lawn to the flat light concrete beyond. He was happy seeing the cars flash and sparkle past, some going seventy he knew, but those were good drivers, all watching the road well, all well coordinated; his people were those things, and also quite a nice looking group.

He turned slowly, restfully, and looked at his house, covered with morning glories, the well-placed cinder blocks hardly showing but he knew they sat true. The house was one and a half storeys high with an off-center gambrel roof and tin smokestack. The weedy grass was clipped short and he had some flowers for the first time, this summer. He walked over, his hands on his flat buttocks, to stand and look down at the marigolds. Cute, he thought; cute of you to come up when I don't know anything about planting you. He thought about his boss at the garage, Joe Kendall, who planted pink petunias with the marigolds; he himself planted nicotiana, fond of their star faces and the smell at night. Lanky and a little stooped he went around the corner of the house to look at this bed. Looking down at them he thought about ice cream and determined to have some. It was supper time. He was always content with whatever the hour brought during the day but time for supper made him the most content.

Before he went in he looked to the right at the house where the

Solomons lived; smoke rose straight up and he could hear the gurgle of television from a dark open window at the side. He pictured Larry heaped on a velours chair drinking a highball while Reba got their fat, huge dinner. Their green bungalow was pretty in the late sun, Prather thought. He glanced the other way to look at Meehans'; he thought of Mary inside because he had no one to say a living thing to. He knew he wasn't much on talking but there were times when it would have been nice to eat a sandwich and drink a bottle of orange soda with some one of his own.

He opened the screen door and stepped into the neat cool kitchen. The cars were thicker on the road, it being the weekend and the dating hour; this gave him a good feeling of companionship.

For supper he thought he would make a meat loaf with some late corn and tomatoes and a dish or two of the peppermint stick ice cream from the El-Ba Restaurant down the road. Relaxed, tidy, he set about making the loaf, using veal, pork and beef, spices, eggs and some new cereal. He set out the new package of cinnamon buns and put the pan of meat loaf into the oven. He set the corn pot over a cold burner to heat later, drank a long glass of cold water and went out into the yard to wait for the meat loaf to cook. He had a wooden chair he had painted a dark green; he carried it over to the shade of the big sumach by the road and sat down, watching with care to see if there were any wobbling wheels or partly open doors on the cars.

As he sat there he thought about Ireland which he had left twenty years ago. He thought about his dead parents, gone ahead without him; and his brother, Diman, seven years younger; he had not wanted to come along to New York. No word since but he knew that was Ireland for you; the world was a pest, to Ireland.

*Diman, look at these fat fast cars and them in them with their talk; and these with their four, no, six children under seven; and the great truckload of hot dogs; ah, Diman . . .* Prather pulled himself free again of the longing for company that was especially strong when he thought of Diman, and got up to go inside.

He looked down the highway from which heat rose in waves and saw a man in a white shirt and black trousers, carrying a large suitcase, walking in his direction. He turned his eyes back to the traffic passing him and admired the size and speed of Hannay's Potato Chip tractor trailer as it drummed by. The beauty of the day and the sweet smell of his lawn pleased him, made him happy; he chose once again from the passing cars the one he would have when he had saved enough.

A gray-blue station wagon shot by; he liked the panels of imitation wood; that would be a good one to have, a lot of room back there. A Volkswagen slowed to stop in front of him. A very dirty man about his own age asked the way to the Speedrome and Prather stepped over to explain clearly where it was, just up the road. The car got up speed very fast and turned back into the right lane, just missing another car. Prather went back to his chair and sat again, breathing quietly. He tipped back a little and looked south again.

The man on foot was very close now and Prather could see his face clearly. A man in his thirties, black haired, big mouth, a bit too big; big nose and a brown skin. But the main thing Prather noticed was that he seemed at close range to be exhausted.

The stranger at last came abreast of Prather who saw that several yards behind him a large dog padded also exhaustedly, unable to keep up with him. The young man dropped his suitcase at the edge of the road and looked at Prather. "And hello," he said, his wide mouth spreading in a tired smile. "I'm lookin for one named Scully here in this town."

Prather said, "My name's Scully—Prather Scully . . ."

"Prath!" The young man lifted both arms in amazement. "I'm Diman."

Prather stared into Diman's face that he had not seen for so long. "Diman, boy—come and sit down and rest you—God and you're tired."

Diman dropped onto the lawn and lay back and shut his eyes. The dog at last caught up with him and lay down too nearby, panting.

"Why didn't you send a card saying you were coming," Prather asked. He seemed unable to stop the happy grin that pulled at his face.

Diman was smiling too though his eyes were shut. "Have you then got a bed for me?" Prather could see that his shoes were torn and dirty and his hands badly blistered on the palms.

"Did no one give you a ride? And where are you from, now?"

"The old sod, on one stinkin ship."

Prather started toward the house. "I'll get you something to wet your whistle," he said. He went into the kitchen and took a bottle of the orange soda from the ice box and opened it; he also filled a saucepan with water for the dog.

When he got back to his brother he found him sound asleep. He sat watchfully, excited and happy, while the traffic continued to flash past. Finally he thought of the meal he was cooking and, carrying the suitcase, he returned to the house and sliced a big plateful of tomatoes and dropped the corn in to cook in boiling water. When it was done he put the food on the table. In the center he put four bottles of the pop, two grape and two orange; cold drops of water slid down the glass.

He went out to get Diman who was just sitting up in a dazed way. When he saw Prather he climbed to his feet and held out his hand; Prather grasped his wrist because of the blisters and they embraced for a moment silently.

Diman laughed. "Walked from New York, me and Sandy there.

You got one big country." He went to the dog. "Poor old feller, he had to come." He turned to Prather and then to look closely at the house. "Ah and it's nice." He walked towards the door. Prather followed; the dog roused himself enough to lap some water and then flopped over again.

Diman sat immediately at the table and rested his arms on it, examining his hands. Then, laughing, he held them out to Prather. "Hamburger it is," he said and then fanned them in front of him. He saw the good meal laid out and began to eat as if he had never eaten. Prather sat too and they ate steadily in silence; once Prather reached over to refill Diman's plate.

At last Diman leaned back in his chair. "I stink, is what," he remarked and laughed. He looked at his brother appraisingly. "Old brother," he said softly. He shook his head once in incredulity.

Prather left the room to look for bandages in the bathroom. In a box on the back of the toilet he found gauze and a tube of ointment and brought them back and bandaged Diman's hands. Diman sat watching and smiling. "Boo," he said then to his brother, making like a monster at him. Prather smiled and smiled. They looked at each other.

"Oh," Prather said, and opened two bottles of pop. They swigged silently. The dog whined once outside the screen door and Diman got up and let him in. Prather put the bit of meat that was left in the pan on the floor and Sandy wolfed it down, continuing to nose and chase it after it was empty. "Give him a bit of bread soaked in water, why not," Diman said. Hungrily, wary lest it be removed, the dog ate that too. Then, not looking for a better place to lie, he slept again.

"I got chased out, brother," Diman said from his comfort on the brown couch where he lay. "The old sod couldn't digest me. Ah."

"I wish Ma could see you today," Prather said, still sitting by the dishes on the table. "You're big; the biggest of the lot."

"They liked that," Diman said. "That's the I.R.A., you know. They used us with the size, they did. And oh I loved the men and what we did." He cocked one leg on the other and wagged a bad shoe. He stared through the screen door into the soft evening. "Dublin's a grand place, Prath; was you ever there then?"

"No. Was only in this country and I've only seen this state. But it's the size of the whole of England, this state. You'll see. When I get my auto. We'll go around."

"Auto, is it? Ah," Diman said, turning to look at Prather. "Autos, houses—you've got good work, then?"

Prather described his job at the garage where pretty music was played all day on the radio there.

"And you like that?" Diman said. "Tell me about old Mother passing."

"She was poorly always, never strong. She just sank, bit by bit. One morning in the winter I went in to her and she was gone. Just poorly right along. I remember it was a blizzard so I had old Mother for a few days like that—ah, well . . ."

Diman dropped his jaw down once understandingly and nodded; they were silent for a moment.

"And do you know what happened when the ship—the Hispaniola, it was—sailed from our harbor?" Diman asked, laughing once more. "There was a wonderful girl I had, Fiona; she said, drinking one night, she'd set fire to the shore if I left and I, oh, laughed and forgot it. But out in the water I saw everyone go to the rail and she'd done it—she did set fire to the shore. Oh what a great blaze."

Prather tipped back in his chair, not minding that no one had ever set fire to a shoreline for him; he fiddled briefly with a spoon and put it down. "I hope you're going to be willing to live here with me," he said. "There's room, you know—nice."

"Ah now thank you, Prath. And I will. Thank you." Diman held up a hand and saluted.

Prather got up and cleared the dishes from the table. Quietly he washed up and left the dishes in a pile to dry on a towel. As he worked, Diman described the reason for his having to leave home and when he talked about the fighting Prather turned to listen carefully. This brother of his was nothing short of a hero and had been fighting since he was fifteen. That and a cooper's job with the brewery in Dublin. All his spare time and all his money went to help Ireland.

"Now, this Fiona," Prather said, sitting down again. "She's your girl?"

"Ah, one of 'em," Diman said, examining his bandage. "She's lovely though. I love her. But then there was Mary Feeney, too, I loved, and Barbara. Oh, and Barbara's got my son." He looked up smiling. "I got a son, I have." He folded his arms and lay thinking. Sandy groaned and stretched in his sleep. "Left 'em all—had to. But they'll be fine. All pretty . . ." He paused. "Prather. Something. I've got to readin." Diman drank from his bottle with enjoyment. "Everythin, I read. I know so much I'll be a joy to you." He looked soberly then at his brother. "And Prath, I have to tell you a bad thing. I drink and I drink. Lord and I love the stuff. And I have to have it, it seems."

"I never took to it," Prather said. "But at the Five Acres along the road you can get what you want if they know you. They all know me, anyways. We could walk there if you think you're fit, now? Not far."

"I'm all right. I'd love to celebrate, you know—and that's how it goes; if I've something to celebrate I drink and if I'm low I drink and then if it's just everyday, I drink. That covers it all, does it not," Diman said, stretching. Prather thought what a handsome fellow his brother was; they had only the blue eyes in common. Diman took after his uncle, Francis. Uncle Francis fished off Dingle, he recalled.

"So it's to the Five Acres now?" Diman said, getting up. "And I've just got the price and that's about all I've got."

Prather stood and they went outside into the twilight. It was eight-thirty and the traffic had thinned out. They walked by the side of the highway past the few other small houses of the town and under a few huge elms. After ten minutes they came to the Five Acres, a squat cinder block building, small and set in a pitted gravelly parking lot. About twenty cars were nosed against the bar's scrawny hedge. Beer signs glowed invitingly in the small windows.

They went through the battered screen door. It was dark inside and full of men at the bar and in the booths. The air was heavy with smoke and the good smell of liquor.

At the bar a healthy looking fat man in a cheap wig greeted Prather, shot the drink he had just mixed across to a man in a bibbed overall and said "Yup?"

"My brother Diman," Prather said. "This is Bobby." They nodded. "Diman and me want a bottle, Bobby. What do you have?"

"Just Fleischmann's and one Seagram," Bobby said, looking beneath the counter. He straightened and waited for them to choose.

"How much, man—I'd like two, any two." Diman said.

"Ten."

Diman tried to reach in his pocket and then had to get Prather to take his money out. Bobby slid the bottles with care into a used paper bag saying "Drop in again."

They went out through the crowd, some of the men saying "Ey, Prath." It was darker outside now and the warm evening was still. Crickets sounded and the edge of the road smelled good. As they walked Diman took out one of the bottles, managed to get the top off and drank deeply.

"Hoo. Have some?" He held out the bottle.

"No, no thanks," Prather said, smiling. They continued along this way; back in the house Prather could see the bottle was a third down. They sat up to the table again and Diman seriously drank; they spoke little.

Prather went into his mother's old bedroom and looked it over. He should make up the bed. The room had always had a bare look the way his mother had wanted it but the plain cardboard-framed photograph taken of his father when young still leaned on the poor mirror. Prather dragged the peach colored rayon spread from the bed and took sheets and the two blankets from the bureau which smelled sweetly of old wood and old women.

When he was finished he went back to the kitchen, filled a tumbler with water and went out to pick a bouquet for his brother's room. In the dark he found a few sprays of marigolds and several of the white nicotiana and took them inside. Diman smiled; his glass was again full of the straight whiskey. He lifted it to salute Prather and drank. Then he roared out, "To the boys at it back home—I think of you, Brendan—Joe—Little Will—Diman's with you . . ." Prather clapped him on the back and told him his room was all set.

"Ah. I thank you. Now, sit a minute—I've one more bad thing to tell you." Diman swallowed more of his drink. "Now, Prath, this drink—I'm told it's gettin to me and I've been told to quit the stuff—oh, forever ago they told me that. But—I canNOT quit—it's so lovely, you know. I was just to see O'Neill—remember him? lives by Wad's Bog—he says I'll be gone in three months, now. Up there with the boys and old Mother, I mean . . ." Diman took another swallow steadily. "So—it's Hello Prather Scully—and, pretty soon, goodbye Diman Scully." He looked at Prather with his wide smile. "Well. To bed with me. I'll finish my tea in bed." He got up and walked with the nearly empty bottle towards the bedroom. He stood in the doorway looking in, then sighed and, going to the sagging bed pushed the pillow in position so he could lie down and still drink. From the bed he said "Thanks, Prath."

Prather stood a moment longer in the doorway looking at Diman. Then he went out through the kitchen and the door to the garden.

He was full of thought. It was all about his brother and then spread out into consideration of the world as it was. He knew Diman would not be with him for long, now, and this made him sad. But Diman had lived a lifetime, he could see; he had a son, he had been a soldier, he had filled his mind with his reading. Prather had read very little but he knew life could be described and explained in books in ways he liked. What if Diman drank—and would die of it? Why shouldn't he burn through a short life if it was so good . . .

Prather walked to the back of the house where the stars of the nicotiana scented the soft air and paced comfortably back and forth. The night was high, big and quiet; no sound but the crickets could be heard.

Prather thought about his own death to come and that only briefly; it really was of no concern to him now. Diman did not care about going and had been busy and happy, both brilliantly; so, he was cut a bit short; he was sure it had been good.

For a long time he walked and stood in the quiet night, turning over his thoughts of Diman's coming death, his mother's death, death and night. The night merged generously with death; the flowers smelled good; the air was gentle. At last he turned back to the warmly lit house, at peace and thinking how it would be for them tomorrow.

# THE COUNTRY DOCTOR

THE EVENING of the picnic was soaking wet. It was the time of June when there was too much green and the sky between rains was brassy. In the station wagon Sam, Peggy and Ann turned off the highway into the Wiese's overgrown yard and stopped by a cluttered barbecue. A wet robin hurtled by and the traffic roared on the road. Beyond a ragged meadow a new taupe motel stood with one bright blue car in the drive. Beyond the road and an acre of fields and woods was the long gray lake with its opposite shore dotted with summer houses; above these the land was broken into farms; a train with orange and red freight cars made its way across blowing its whistle.

The house was a nondescript shape, previously a farmhouse, painted white. It looked unoccupied except for the kitchen light and the door standing open. A carton had fallen apart in the rain by the snowball bush and on the porch the screen door lay on its side against the clapboards.

Suddenly a little girl shot out of the kitchen door and ran over to the station wagon. She was about ten and wore cheap red shorts with rickrack and a novelty sailor jersey. Her long brown hair was tied back in an untidy pony tail with a rayon scarf and her ears stuck out.

"Hi," she cried shrilly as she leaped at them. They climbed out and Sam and Peggy greeted her and Peggy said "Ann, this is Beatrice." They all picked their way through the long grass and bushing peonies and up the splintered kitchen steps. Noise burst from the kitchen door; Hedl stood, arms out, a long cigarette in one hand, to greet them. She was short and solid though not fat; her mouth grinned widely over tobacco-stained teeth but there was a permanent frown between her black eyes. She wore jaunty faded blue denim and looked more like Long Island than the sticks.

She broke her theatrical stance and embraced Sam and Peggy and was introduced to Ann. They wound their way among the crowded furnishings in the kitchen. There they stood and Hedl flung her arms around Sam's waist and laid her head, eyes closed, briefly on his shoulder. He kissed her scalp and patted her. Then she stood upright, snapping her eyes at the others. The smile spread readily and she said "So, what do you hear from Marcia? Oof, have this ashtray—I NEVER never have enough—*do* I, Sam?" She darted one onto the drainboard between Sam's and Ann's elbows. Arms out, cigarette in mouth, she twirled between the refrigerator and sink. "Now what must I get for my guests—Tell me, how's Marcia?" She was on her knees rummaging in a dark cupboard.

"*Mama.*" Beatrice had come in and whined in a spoiled voice. "When's Daddy coming?" She hunched her shoulders and knocked her knuckles together, arms out in front of her. She ogled up at Sam, who smiled back. Hedl got up from the floor in a swoop, holding a set of colored aluminum highball glasses. Abstractedly she placed them on a carton and looked around as she said "Oh, Papa'll come—tonight we have EIGHT POUNDS of steak for five and one-half of us to eat!" She seized her daughter and hugged her. "Now. Sam. What to drink. I think I have left some gin—gin and 7-Up, no?" She looked around the group. All smiled and she dove away again for the gin. Peggy picked up a jar and read the label. "Oh. Marcia's barbecue sauce. You know she left Harcourt Brace and isn't doing anything. Can't get over Walt."

Hedl shook her head violently, scattering her cigarette ashes in sympathy as she wrenched the tops off bottles. "Never will I forget Marcia that night he got killed. She was marvelous. Marvelous. It was I who screamed and wept and she was perfect—" She paused to pour the drinks untidily.

"The night who died, the night Walt died you mean," Beatrice begged, to be in the spotlight. "Can we eat the nuts?" She began to pass them, helping herself.

Ann went out onto the dining porch off the kitchen. A cheap oak table, several unmatched straight chairs and a low rattling studio couch with a damp maroon and chartreuse cotton chintz cover filled the space overly full. She sat down with the gin and 7-Up. Sam came to the door, looked at her and said "I hope you like people."

"Oh, I do," she answered vivaciously as a truck passed, shaking the house. "Good stuff," she added, holding up her glass and then drinking. It was terrible stuff.

Sam and Hedl came out on the tiny porch and a gust of big raindrops blew off the trees onto the roof.

"You are not from around here?" Hedl said to Ann.

"No—from Massachusetts," Ann said.

"Ann's an artist," Peggy said.

"Ahhhhhh!" Hedl yelled. "An artist!" She turned back suddenly into the kitchen, forgetting the group on the porch, and said something in rapid German to Beatrice who ran off through the house.

"Ach, Hansie is late always. I hate to love that man, honestly I do. But a doctor—" She shrugged vigorously as she came back onto the porch. "Oh. Yes. An artist, and what do you paint, or do you sculpt, or draw or what do you do?" She sat suddenly, her smile drawn up, crossed her knees and jiggled her foot.

"I do everything, really," Ann said. "Any old job that comes up, I do." She smiled but thought how vapid it sounded. The ugliness of the place was total, she thought. Small doodads were nailed up on the clapboards of the porch without rhyme or reason and the cold light shone in on a collection of tense suburban garden furniture mingled with maroon-painted Victorian pieces in the sitting room inside.

A car drove into the yard and then the porch door slammed. Beatrice galloped onto the porch squalling that her daddy had arrived. In a minute a fiftyish bald Jew walked into the kitchen, his black eyes sparkling, his smile showing good teeth. His mouth was generous and sensitive and more youthful than the rest of his face. He was youthful too in the way he moved. He was about five ten and must have weighed a hundred and ninety but he was quick and sometimes playful the way he moved; his bare forearms were very muscular and his hands were not the hands of a fat man. It was easy to picture him on his rounds at the hospital; even more he belonged in the operating room.

He clamped an arm around Peggy and around Ann too right after they had been introduced, and hugging her comfortably as if he had known her for years looked twinkle-eyed into hers, his hand comfortably swatting her hip. Suddenly the playfulness fell from his face, he let the girls go, and he boomed into the kitchen, "Where the hell's *my* drink. Did no one fix Hans a drink? Boo hoo." He fiddled around with the bottles and came back to the porch beaming, his wet mouth full. He and Sam looked each other up and down gauging how much weight each had put on.

"Lookin fit," Sam said to him.

"Ahh, all I do except my work is eat, eat, eat," Hans said, slapping his stomach. "I don't sleep; I never sleep. Ask Hedl. Hey, Hedl, do I ever sleep?"

Hedl was upstairs and hollered something unintelligible in reply.

"Well, all sit why not. We do not have to eat this minute." Hans sank down on one end of the poor cot, ignoring everything about it. His quick, handsome, pouched eyes went from one guest to the next. "We were at New York last month again," he said. "A medical meeting, thank God, came up. I took Hedl and we did a lot of things."

Hedl came out on the porch and stood dramatically holding a toasting fork.

"The UN building we saw—oh, it was magnificent, simply magnificent—Beatrice, darling, pass around the nuts again, huhn," Hans went on. Hedl picked a tooth with a red fingernail. "Also we saw three plays and that show by Goldman and Olaskwicz. We ate half the food in that town, too'" he said with enjoyment, draining the last of his drink. He got up energetically. "Now let us take that darling steak down and cook it by the lake and if it rains, to hell with the rain, we shall have steak." He reached out and hugged Ann again, enjoying her embarrassment. "Mmmm?" he said to her, and let her go.

"If it is going to rain perhaps we stay here?" Hedl said, looking at her husband.

"Nah, nah," he said, restlessly tossing things into a carton. "We go. If it rains we go in the shack."

Ann thought of the story Peggy had told about Hans and Hedl losing their seventeen-year-old son down by the point where they were evidently going to sit and eat. "Why don't we eat here?" she said, looking at Sam for support, but no one was listening. Hans snatched a piece of chicken from the ice box and was eating it quickly. He reached out for his wife's shoulder. "Go, GO," he yelled, tossing the chicken bone into the sink. He took up a box and basket and without looking back charged out to his car, a huge brand-new dirty Buick. Beatrice followed, capering. The rest got together the other things and just as a brief but hard shower started they were rocking along the ruts through the meadows and second growth to the lake shore.

A wooded point protruded gently into the lake and the .barbecue, rustic table and a sagging lean-to were almost lost in the big glade. Soon a clutter of bread wrappers and cartons littered everything. The rain stopped but the sky, though pearly here and there in the distance, was metallic and unfriendly still.

Hedl was ordering everyone about. She had put on a baseball type cap and scarlet jacket and new lipstick, somewhat crooked, and was still smoking. "Darling, you have matches—Sammy, get the barbecue going. *Thank* you," she squealed at Peggy who started to set the table. Hedl set clumps of knives and forks with bone handles out and pointlessly moved napkins, mustard and salt and peppers where they were not needed. Her mind seemed on something else, but she talked ceaselessly. "Beatrice darling you should have brought blue jeans— you must bring here a pair to leave and wear when it is cold like tonight—do you like barbecue sauce, Sammy, here I knew you did," she said, stretching the smile over her teeth in a travesty of coyness; her eyes were strained and seemed to avoid everything. As soon as she could she sat down, uncomfortably, at one end of the table and started to eat like a cannibal. She did not seem to see what she was eating but she crammed it in as if she were hungry. In one hand was always a lighted cigarette. Before the steak was ready she was humped over a paper plate loaded with pale macaroni salad, wolfing it down, slobbering and champing and talking gaily, battening on the remarks of the others and laughing too much at the slightest joke. Hans stood concentrating over the fire turning the gobbets of steak. Everyone was quickly provided with beer and Sam demonstrated his ability to belch rippingly; Hans and Hedl were delighted. Peggy bent over her plate trying not to protest; at last she said "Dear, please," trying to smile. Beatrice skipped stones ineffectually and Ann gathered wet pieces of driftwood, each greeted effusively by Hans when she delivered them by the barbecue. It was too cold, damp and a place heavy with memories and they should not have come, Ann thought.

Then with screams from the table and great exclamations from Hans the steak was brought and the noisy feed began. On everyone's plate was a huge rare slab.

"Mmmmh, darling's GOOD," Hedl said, stabbing another piece. Ann agreed although the maroon uncooked part of the meat was already showing. Hedl passed everything continually. Beatrice bent close to her plate but her bright eyes darted from face to face as the others talked.

"Are you pregnant yet?" Hans said to Peggy. "Time you should be." Peggy laughed and said no, she wasn't; Sam stared at her unsympathetically and took a long drink of his beer.

"You'll manage it," Hans added with tact and not any of the usual leers. "You are good kids and you should have a lot of babies. Look at these farm people; new kid every year, all right, like a slot machine," he said and burst into a roar of laughter. He suddenly looked at his daughter. "That's not for your lit'l ears, my doll," he said sternly.

"Why?" she asked pertly with a smile of precocious knowledge.

"Just not," he said, going back to his meal. He used his knife with his right hand, stacking and packing the food on the fork; with his gusto it looked good to Ann who was watching. He would cut a fatty, unattractive piece of meat in two, whatever it was, then pile on macaroni and a piece of roll sopped in barbecue sauce, and clamp his mouth shut over it all. In no time it was gone; he ate very fast. Ann noticed that his hands were impressive and sensitive; on his left wrist was a Swiss watch that had seen much use.

The rain held off but the sky remained heavy and lowering. There was no wind and the lake lay glassily beside the picnickers. Ann thought the set-up was lugubrious and wondered how Hans and Hedl could come down here for picnics; she thought they might have moved away or at least chosen a bright afternoon to come down. She could not think of anything to say.

Hedl was now busy pouring coffee into plastic cups for everyone. Ann saw her gaze lift briefly to the gray water and then return to her work. Sam and Peggy walked down to the water and stood at its edge. "I want to go in the water," Beatrice said, pawing her mother's shoulder.

"Ach, too cold," Hedl said, darting a sharp glance in the direction of the lake and then looking back at Beatrice. "Tomorrow you can."

"No, NOW," Beatrice insisted.

"Too soon after eating, anyhow, dolly," Hans said. Beatrice pouted, pushed her mother and sat down and wolfed some potato chips.

There was a rustling in the bushes by the shore and Ann saw an old woman come around an alder and stand looking at them. She wore an old rain coat over a print dress and dirty sneakers. She had a ravaged once-lovely face and wispy white hair falling in her eyes. They were a cold blue and her teeth protruded from the upper jaw.

"Mrs. Wood," Hedl whispered, seeing her. Hedl was white and the cigarette in her hand was shaking. "HANS, Mrs. Wood." Hans turned and saw her.

"God save us," he said quietly. Mrs. Wood continued to stand there in silence, her bony hands hanging by her sides.

"She was the one that found Bobby," Hans said to Ann. "What in hell is she doing here? She'll tell us, that is one sure thing."

Mrs. Wood began to pick her way through the wet grass towards them. She was upset, it was plain. Ann waited for the words the old woman would come out with.

"I come here to pray. You come here to eat. With beer," she added, looking piercingly at what was on the table. "You have to come here and carouse." She left her mouth open, staring at them. "I should have the sheriff throw you out," she added. "Callous. Just have no feelings, have you?"

"Now, now," Hans said quietly. "We can't always be thinking about it."

"Well, I think of nothing but," the old woman said. "Our beautiful shore is haunted, now, thanks to your family. Once I came down here to look at my chickadees and in season the thrushes. Now when I come here all I see is that boy, washed up on the shore, just lying there. You Jews, always surrounding yourselves with parties and noise. You've scared away the birds today, I want to tell you." Her eyes sparkled brilliantly and a smile played around her lips threateningly. "I'm telling the sheriff about this and I'm going to write the paper." She turned to go, her bent back under the stained raincoat infinitely ugly. As she passed Sam and Peggy she gave them a long hostile look and then vanished around the alders.

"You MEAN woman," suddenly Hedl shrilled, standing. She lit another cigarette, shaking. Beatrice began to cry.

"Forget it," Hans said with a sigh. "We got to eat; we ate. Well, we Jews better get on up to the house. Looks like more rain." He began to clear things off the table and put them back in the boxes. Then he stopped working and looked out over the water. "Chickadees," he said, and laughed.

# THE STEPS IN THE DANCE

THE GUESTS were arriving. Alida Withington Chauncy stood under the big white pines that surrounded Abenaki ready to direct people or cars. She wore an elaborately embroidered peasant blouse in lavender with a white linen skirt; on her pleasant feet were well-cleaned old Spectator pumps. Her white hair was swept back into a simple full bun, setting off her brown, fine-featured face. Two Peruvian silver bracelets circled her right wrist; on her left was a tiny diamond-studded watch. She wore no rings.

An old station wagon overflowing with children of various ages pulled up near her and stopped. The children piled out. A wrenlike freckled woman peered out from behind the wheel and called "Miss Chauncy, I'll be back for them when the dancing's over—I must go to the station and pick up Hugh. Bye!" Alida bent from the waist to look into the car as it passed and gracefully swept her arm through the air.

"Hugh," she thought concisely. "Large—balding—sweats too much. Doesn't smoke. I mistrust people who don't smoke."

"Oohoo," she broke into her reflections. "Oohoo!" She ran a few graceful steps forward to prevent a Ghia from going through the sweet fern. "Right over here," she called liltingly, indicating a space in the pine needles.

The car pulled up beside her. She almost jumped when she saw who was inside. A tall old man sat dribbling slightly beside the driver, a beautiful young girl with long hair and no lipstick.

"How are you, Miss Chauncy?" the girl said cordially. Her poise was flawless.

"Fine. Fine," Alida said with taut firmness. Her gaze went back to the old man. "Roger!" she called into his unseeing face. She looked back at the girl. "Bring him over to the slope and he can sit with Letitia," she arranged. She opened Roger's door and stepped back to let the girl help him out. "Dreadful old man, *dreadful*," she thought as she watched him wrestle his way to his feet. He did not acknowledge her presence in any way. "You're looking lovely, Cynthia dear," she said to the girl who supported Roger's stick-like form. "Oh!" She saw a group coming up the lane on foot and recognized Frank Starr and his Experimenters. They were young and laughing, all but Frank who wore glasses, smoked his pipe quietly, and almost never spoke. His gray hair was cut in short patches, by his wife, Alida decided. She stepped along gracefully on the pine needles to greet them. "Hello, hello!" she cried. "Joel, Tijo, Bucky—how are you—hello!" She took Frank's free hand under her arm and walked with them the few yards to the dance platform in the natural woods amphitheater.

"We have Mrs. Palmer to play the violin accompaniment again today," she told them. "She is a charming graduate of Juilliard. She likes jazz, too—singular!" She laughed, a low, pleasing sound. As her eye fell on old Roger standing alone with bent knees under a tall pine she excused herself, giving Frank and Tijo squeezes of the hand as she passed.

"Roger, do sit," she cajoled, not touching him. Quaveringly, in falsetto, he said "I need—I want—uh, where did she go?" There was a drop on the end of his cartilaginous nose. Alida tried not to look and turned in a worried circle looking for Letitia's plump form and the bright color of the afghan she was knitting. She saw her by the puddingstone rock on the opposite slope, and forcing herself to take Roger's arm, guiding his stumping steps over to her through seated groups of brown, attractive young people, past Leonard Beatty and his phthisic wife, Oriel, and their collie, Rasmussen, past Gene Stokes squiring a dumpy, heavy-haired Latin type in an off-the-shoulder blouse that Alida deplored—Gene's inamoratas were scandalous but if they came from another country she always forgave him—past Muzzie Thompson in a coronet braid with her deaf, smiling mother in newly-cleaned sneakers, past Toodie Banks in a black sheath, sitting alone ostentatiously reading Kafka—Bennington is—nice—Alida thought, jumpily diverting her thoughts from the revolting touch of Roger's bone under his thin jacket; she steered his wraithlike form to a sunny spot by Letitia.

"Here, dear; watch over him, Motherbird," she called rather vaguely to her niece with a muscular smile that did not reach her gray eyes. Straightening after she lowered the old man to the ground, much relieved, she stood looking around her at one of the sights—akin to a Boston symphony opening of its season—that pleased her most. Her lovely woods about to be used by her friends and their attractive families for English country dancing made her very happy. Tuesday was a loved day in her week.

She saw Mrs. Palmer stuck with Emma Pease; Emma's swarming

gestures and strident voice carried across the whole amphitheater. Alida walked unobtrusively over to them and said, putting her hand on Mrs. Palmer's shoulder, "Ready?" She smiled warmly at them both and Emma Pease, flustered, said "Oh, I must get a partner!" and lumbered off, her rump bouncing under a scarlet broomstick skirt. Mrs. Palmer, in a white dirndl, took her place near the platform and Alida stepped agilely up on it and clapped her hands twice. Mrs. Palmer, chin clamped tightly to her violin, played the opening bars of *Black Nag*, and there was a general quiet as couples made their way to the floor. "Black Nag, Black Na-ag, children," Alida called. "Hurrah for mankind!" And she stepped off the platform as the groups formed for the dance.

"Tradition. Hm. Love. Poetry and romance." Alida's mind, happily blending with the scene, kept the violin company. She bounced a little on the balls of her feet and her hand inadvertently shot out as Terry Schoonover, aged eight, started in the wrong direction in the dance. A light knock on the head by her older brother brought her back in line and Alida returned to her musical reverie.

"Paris—London, tea, love, romance, gentlemen and ladies— wine—violins—" Her gaze wandered unfortunately to old Roger across the way; he was gazing blankly into the woods, his large mouth an open, black cavern, his stiff knees drawn up, his white Panama hat on the ground beside him.

"Dreadful," Alida thought. Her mind became flustered. Unbidden a mental image of the old man sitting there wearing no clothes crossed her thoughts. Revolting! her mind screamed—but the image crept through it, taut and engraved. As the music of *Black Nag* continued Alida Withington Chauncy lost herself in that unwelcome reverie that came so often, even now.

She was in Paris and twenty-four years old, unmarried, free, exploring a new country, a new world. It was in her flat on the Rue des Saints-Pères, eleven o'clock in the morning, and she had just gotten up after a late night of reading Rilke with Roger. She recalled his tall figure, well-built and vigorous. He was fifteen years older than she, a brave, witty, strong, talkative man who seemed to have no roots in his native New England, here in Paris, or in India, Turkey, Cairo—not in any place where he had travelled and he had travelled much.

On this particular morning in Paris Alida was filled with a feeling of well-being. Time stretched ahead of her invitingly although she often felt, deep within, great questions: what am I? where am I going? what can I do? She sometimes awoke late in the night and wondered about the people she had seen during the day, preparing subtly for a night of love-making. Thoughts of them upset her because in them she felt a reproach to herself; marriage would come in due course, some day;

but the sloppy arrangements, she felt, of a liaison, were repugnant to her. Once Roger had said "You love ideas, not people." She had felt this most unjust; she had regarded herself as closely attached to her family, her friends—but, she had to admit, her friends were all of one kind, either English or American, well-dressed, mannerly, contained in the same bubble of security all around, never making rude demands, never asking a commitment to each other—it just was not done. She had watched with a certain avidity, the night before at the cafe, a fattish dark man sit the whole evening, not speaking a word, with his arm around a woman who was large, also plump, wearing black with dandruff on her shoulders. She had been envious of their warm contact and repelled by their look. Other people she watched—and now, this morning, she realized she was always watching—the white, abstracted concierge of her building, fifty, graying, wearing mustard dresses and spotted sweaters, who lived with a thirtyish short bald man who was a watchmaker. The seventeen-year-olds in the apartment adjoining, also unmarried, who fought, burned their food, had nothing, were committed, at least for now. It was the impermanence that made her wonder; if it didn't last, what good was it?

She had a glass of wine for breakfast, this particular morning, as a concession to something vague—perhaps today a new thing would enter her life, she would be someone's focal point. She stood in her negligee, a soft gray, with the tumbler of Riesling, in front of her mirror, in which was neatly placed a notice of the poetry reading, coming up, of Georges Imboges, and saw that she was willowy and classic of feature, a guarded expression on her face; she did not often assess herself in any mirror; her long hair gave her a poetic look and with her back to the light she looked rather mysterious. She watched herself take a sip of the wine, inwardly rebuking herself that it was only a sip; she took a large swallow, finished the glass, and turned away to pour herself more. She went to the window, that overlooked a closed cement warehouse and a row of narrow, cluttered houses, and stood, warm in the sun, drinking.

There was a knock on the door. Usually she would have called out to find out who it was; now she walked smoothly to the door and opened it. Roger stood outside. His face did not have its usual bland, mischievous familiar look. He pushed past her and closed the door. He looked as if he had not slept.

"Take your clothes off," he ordered, starting to wrench off his tie.

All right, her morning mood counseled. Take them off. She slipped off her negligee and stood in her nightgown several feet away from him as he yanked at his clothes, removing them, so that he stood, almost immediately, naked before her. She had never seen a naked man in her life, and gazed seriously at his changed, flushed face.

"Well, take it off," he ordered hoarsely, and moving to her, wrested the nightgown over her head. She stood, also naked, before him, feeling ruffled, her hair tangled, herself unwashed, uncertain.

"Come on," he said roughly, and drew her towards her narrow bed. She saw he had not shaved.

A sudden hilarity overtook her for some reason and she drew back. "Let's talk, Roger," she suggested, sitting down in a sudden flood of poise at the foot of the bed. Coupling with this urgent, uncouth stranger, in the morning, seemed suddenly unthinkable. Naked together, she suddenly felt unfettered and able to say anything, no matter how frank or obscene—but to go into his—yes, bestial—arms was laughable. She felt a warm wind from the casement around her and looked interestedly at Roger's nakedness. He lay as if flung on the bed, a hairy, heavy rebuttal of all he had been to her before, the urbane, uncaring, proper, clothed man who had fitted so nicely into her scheme of things.

"Alida, you're driving me crazy," he grated. "Get into the bed."

Aware of herself as desirable, cooled by the breeze, fortified by the wine, Alida said what she felt was marvelously apt for the occasion: "Satyr and nymph," she observed, laughing. She was not afraid because she felt free and in control. She had no knowledge of desire and in spite of the wine, the bed and the nakedness she knew this was a folly she would not commit.

"Roger," she said, leaning to put a hand on his icy, bony foot, "This isn't for us. Go to sleep, my dear." He lay, hot-eyed, looking into her face.

Suddenly he leapt to his feet and crossed the room to where his clothes lay scattered.

"You laugh, do you," he muttered. "Jesus Christ. You laughed." Dressed he stood at the door. He looked at her, his eyes dull. "Alida, no more of you for me," he said. He stood a moment longer, then opened the door and went out, leaving it swinging a little.

◁ ▷

"Miss Chauncy!" A hand was on her arm and she roused herself to see that Betsy Traver was bending her well-groomed head towards her as if she were deaf.

"*Yes*, my dear! I was dreaming," Alida called, not yet quite returned to Abenaki.

"Roger is unwell—Roger Bayliss. Can we take him into your house?"

Betsy was perspiring.

"Oh! Do! Yes! I'll go to him." Alida looked across the pine needles to where a small group hovered around Roger, lying flat. "Boys!" she called to Tijo, a muscular boy of about seventeen, and his companion, Joel Witherill. "Come! Carry Mr. Bayliss into my living room." She glided gracefully to Roger's side and coolly, all who watched felt, handled his pulse and loosened his scarlet tie. He was covered with perspiration. "Just heat, I should think," she said calmly. "All right, you young men," she stood back so that Tijo and Joel could lift the tall, frail form. She preceded them to the house.

Don't let him die here, she found herself praying as she tossed the embroidered pillows on the couch aside. Not here. No death here.

The boys brought the old man in and laid him on the couch. Alida was presence of mind itself. As she talked to the gathered concerned group who came in she noted that Roger had come to and was vaguely looking around and breathily mouthing words to himself. He seemed in no pain.

"All right, Roger?" she called into his face.

"Yah," he mouthed, his breath sour, his eyes off in the vague distance.

"Then I think Cynthia can get you home to your own bed," Alida said crisply, fighting nausea. She felt perspiration on her forehead, she, who never perspired.

"I'm right here, Miss Chauncy," Cynthia said.

"Good-oh!" Alida said. She saw a used Band-Aid stuck to the sole of Roger's shoe. Oh God don't let him die here, she breathed as she helped to hoist him out to the car. Strains of *Gathering Peascods* floated to her from the amphitheater.

Let not death enter this lovely scene, her mind prayed, revulsion tensing all her muscles until she got the old man settled in the little car.

"Goodbye, Cynthia dear—let me know how he is," she cried as the car bumped away.

*Gathering Peascods* went on under the sun-dappled pines, the sweet fern smelled fresh and heady.

But Alida felt age upon herself; and, yes, something else too; there were to be no more chances for her.

# THE PUPPET KING

THE SHADOW lying on the ground beginning at his feet looked like a gnome's; Dudley Forbush felt uncomfortable that it did and changed his position to see if the shadow would look more dignified. He felt comforted as he reasoned about shadows: toward sunset they lengthened and he should look at his then. Perhaps he would look more like Prince Philip with his long tailored lanky relaxed dignity. Standing in the dirt by the barbed wire behind the army kitchen building he wondered tensely what chance there was of his queen and her consort coming across the sea to review the troops he was part of; how he would honor them in his earnest loyal Scottish heart; he thought of how he would instruct the dolts in his platoon on protocol and the backgrounds of the royal pair; he could; British history was his hobby, no, his passion; all of it he had at his fingertips and he never knew that his buddies spent long complicated hours thinking up different questions, reaching far back to the Celts and so forth, to stump him with. He always knew the answer to some extent and spared no trouble looking up further data so that they too could become enriched. It warmed him to have them ask the questions; his pale fat face with its dreadful straggling black moustache looking like a patch of poor sumach took on some light that even Toby Sutherland, the dishwasher, thought made him look better.

He was standing by the fence because the other men on the kitchen detail were taking a smoke; he was against smoking or breathing in anyone's smoke or even breath and so he always came outside where he knew the tropical sun would do him a great deal of good. He also took those times to do memorizing if he had something he was learning; the language he employed in his mind was carefully worded as if he were speaking to a bishop or even Her Majesty herself; he held himself in readiness for the time when he could address her just once in his lifetime. His unattractive body and face, flat head, his eyes like black dead snails, his uncut nails, his bad legs and pot were invisible to him; the only realities were Britain and things belonging to her; and he, he belonged to her. If he died in her service it was only right; he tried to tell his companions this, and why this was so, when they cursed army life, each other, the food and the local women they could not have. Then they would curse him; but he knew about saints, he knew about messages; they could curse him but he was right, he knew.

It was four o'clock. Supper would be served in an hour; before that he had a lot to do getting the trays set up; he had not swept the floor after dinner and Olfield had chewed him out wildly; he never swept it well because he was without any muscle tone and was also uncoordinated. He busied his mind too all the time with his facts and could not possibly be practical about anything; no one ever tried to explain the army or life or women, how things really are, how he stood in relation to anything or that kind of thing; in fact only one person ever thought of doing it, the Jesuit camp priest; but just when he was going to approach Dudley in a friendly manner Dudley had turned to him, eyes on the dirty floor, loose lips poked out as preliminary to a vast statement, then said coldly, "Father Cassidy, how can you stand Catholicism in the face of the fact that our Queen is Anglican; I consider you a traitor." Never looking at him.

Father Cassidy looked once again at the cold face before him, poked out his own lips wryly, raised his eyebrows and moved away.

Dudley now noticed the usual commotion at the entrance to the camp; A singular dirty black delivery truck was stopped by the guard station there. He could just make out the words KIRK'S MARIONETTES and some more lettering below he could not read. The truck was passed through and drove bumping over the dirt track to the administration building. Dudley thought about it as he climbed the unpainted steps to the kitchen and went about his work; he barely saw the surrounding brown boards and the placarded walls, the sweating windows or the other tired men as he pondered marionettes in this place. Shows of all kinds came and went, usually pretty terrible; but this one he thought would do something, or, could. As he sat sideways, alone at the end of one of the long tables chewing his early supper he ignored the tough gristly meat, the huge, hot dark-spotted potatoes and the dumpy sweet, thinking about the coming performance. He was not in any way artistic but liked to think Britain was a cradle for all fine things and could always argue this into existence if any one would listen. He forgot to go out and see if his shadow looked any more like Prince Philip's, cleaning up after the hot stinking meal; when it was done he went to the administration building to look on the bulletin board for facts about the show for tonight. His tight accurate biased little mind noted the time and place and that the whole thing was put on by one man alone. A Scot, too, he thought pompously, roaming around the sere grounds alone, waiting for show time.

This was eight o'clock at a spot in the area known to the men because it was where they were made to walk with double packs for punishment in the sun for hours; it was slightly sloping so a crowd could sit looking downhill and see over each other's heads. It had begun to rain as it always did at this time of evening and the mosquitoes were out; nevertheless Kirk had set up his staging; his truck, open at the back, stood by exhibiting bright materials and electric cords vaguely inside. While Dudley stood tensely taking it all in, two men he did not know strolled up and discussed the coming performance. After walking down to the staging and taking a look behind they came back up, moving faster on and away from the place; Dudley heard one say, "Buncha goddam dolls. Bet the chap's a queer, right as right."

The other man said something Dudley could not hear and the two men broke into hoarse gasping laughter, hitting out at each other and giving shoves. No one else came along; at eight o'clock Kirk, a small handsomely youthful man with an alert face, good teeth and clipped gray hair, mounted his staging and stood looking at Dudley. Kirk's face was tired and the black work suit he wore accentuated his small wiry frame.

"Well, soldier," he started in. "Are you my whole audience?"

"I'd like to say something to you, Mr. Kirk, "Dudley said eagerly, stumbling and slipping down the slope to stand in front of the stage. "May I ask, sir, if you too are a Scot?"

"Yessir," Kirk answered, slapping at a mosquito.

"Well, then, can you tell me why more Scots are not signing up to come over here and fight for their Queen?" Dudley demanded.

"Oh. Well. Well, you know Scotland really didn't get such a fair shake from, uh, her great great grand-daddy, and so forth, soldier," Kirk said carefully.

"Not at all. Not at all, sir," Dudley said, his lips stuck out as he built his words. His buddies knew this to be a sign to get away before his lecture got going. "You see, the divine right of kings has never been truly understood by the common man so that they must be educated to it." He paused, fixing Kirk with his solemn dead eyes.

Kirk said nothing, standing in the rain looking down at the dumpy figure before him. It was getting darker.

"Yes, you see Queen Mary, of the Scots, was one of the troublemakers; I've read a great deal on her and she was a very bad woman, to my mind, very bad, frivolous and ambitious, and we know that she did not revere our Elizabeth the Great, the First. Now," Dudley swung absently at an itch on his back and thoughtfully mashed an insect in his palm as he went on: "The lover Elizabeth had at that time—" He stopped stunned as a row of sparklers and miniature fountains lit the steamy night in front of him; music rose from somewhere; Kirk had vanished. Suddenly marching in front of Dudley came a graduated row of nineteenth-century soldiers of Italy; following came a charming series of animals dancing, tottering, lighted up whimsically or covered with colors of beauty and brilliance; carnival characters and courtesans, children and dancers came alive from behind the black curtain; Kirk could now be seen standing over the stage, his hands working the animation. Stunned, Dudley watched the color and the whimsy, skillfully and briefly exhibited. His heavy mind lingered on his loyalties, his duty; still for a moment here and there he looked and saw something briefly to divert him.

Kirk put on his whole show. Indians danced, horses performed, minuets and polkas and Israeli dances were shown, gay, colorful, imaginative; the time passed and Kirk's face above the stage was tense and serious. Dudley's, as he sat in the still falling drizzle, was empty and serious; he questioned the whole thing. How could something so trivial be good; how could humor honor the British empire. Frequently his mind wandered to his favorite daydream in which the queen arrived and he alone ministered, he alone understood, gave, supported, and of course, in the daydream, died.

Offenbach and Smetana, segments of operas, Scheherazade, all poured their fantasy before Dudley's eyes. He was unaware of the lateness of the time; the show continued until eleven. Whitely his face stood out in the soft tropical night. He thought of Kirk as a triviality, out of step.

He decided to make him toe the line, see the light, change his ways, when the show was over; in fact, he decided he would stop this worldly exhibition right away and speak to the man about his aims, his service to the Empire.

He was tensing his muscles to get up when the last of the show ended. The lights went out; there was intense silence. No sound came from anywhere.

Then, music; *Scots Wha Hae* rose in the night; the stage was suddenly blindingly floodlit; Kirk himself stood there, with two British flags in either hand; he began to dance a sort of variation on a Scottish sword dance. He was graceful and inventive.

Then, at a break in the music, he leapt gracefully down from the stage, still holding the flags; he danced up to Dudley and held a flag out to him. Dudley was thrilled suddenly; the music fired him up; the flag was the last straw; how he honored the flag.

Kirk took his wrist and to the music they began to march around the area in the mud, in the dark. Kirk waved his flag in time to the music; Dudley held his as if it were the Grail and marched with all the perfection his uncoordinated muscles could summon. He did not see the desperation in the face of his fellow as Kirk measured their march around the dirt, empty of audience; he did not detect the artist's fatigue at the end when the music stopped and only the bright lights from the stage held the mood he had created for this one man who for some reason bothered to watch his magic.

With a magnificent clipped salute Kirk silently said good night to Dudley. Dudley, aware of who was the significant miracle worker of the two, stuck out his lips, saluted also, about-faced and marched out of sight into the murk.

# OZENFANT

IN THE doorway of Elise Pote-Harris' apartment Jacob Ozenfant saw a tall woman in brown silk welcoming him in a cool voice. He entered the hallway and stood with her, finding her a quiet presence at the end of his turbid day.

"You are Jacob," she said with a smile. She placed a long hand on her graying hair that was arranged in a loose bun. "Ghattie's said many fine things about you. And you've brought the poem she wished?" She laid a hand on his arm and drew him down the hall towards a murmur of voices. "Some here may not understand what you read but I assure you some will. I will," she said warmly.

Ozenfant glanced at the walls as they went towards the living room and saw many pictures that he liked very much. He noticed a large steel engraving and stopped to read the description on its scroll at the bottom. Elise stopped too and looked from behind him; she took the opportunity to admire his height and his smooth silver hair. His suit, good although nondescript, pleased her; his dark shoes were polished and had seen much use; she noticed his big hand absently holding the edge of the frame.

"They all have what was described as *full* eyes, in these, don't they," he commented and turned to follow her.

Entering the living room his glance fell first on Ghattie, sitting on the floor in a long blue mumu, her torrent of clean red hair surrounding her Beethoven-like face. She was talking to a small man in a greenish suit but she looked up when Ozenfant and Elise came into the room. Then Ozenfant was introduced to the five other guests: "Jacob Ozenfant... Hamish Cessholm"—this the young man in the greenish suit, a large nest of wavy blond hair jutting off to one side of his high forehead, his cheeks a healthy red, very full red lips—; "Mary Peabody"—sitting tensely against one corner of a large dark plush armchair, very thin, in pink, two dark braids coiled around her head, her features neat and almost pretty if it were not for two lines from nostrils to the corners of her mouth; "you of course know Ghattie, and this is Palmer Ormiston under the lamp"—a long thin young man with chiseled features and thin dark hair over a large skull; "this charming vignette with Hyacinthe on her lap is Corinna Maliga"—a plump blonde woman in black with casual hair cut probably by herself; "and now, my august husband"; Ozenfant saw a big man who stood as they came in; he wore a dark suit of smooth cloth with a fussy design in it, something Ozenfant had noticed was very popular with the Viennese.

Ozenfant nodded to each with a sober assessing face; they too looked quietly at him, some with a smile.

He looked around the large room, low ceilinged like all those in the old big buff dwelling places in the city; the walls were light and covered with more pictures, big and small. A huge bouquet of lilacs stood on a grand piano to one side; the rug was Persian; he did not intend to sit down on it. He looked for a chair and saw a straight mahogany one near the lilacs. He was near Corinna and could hear the loud purring of the cat and could smell Corinna's potent perfume.

"Sax is my name," Elise's husband said, appearing at his elbow to offer him a large glass of wine. Ozenfant thanked him and was pleased that he drew up another chair beside him and sat too. "Now, Elise is the poet of the family," he said. "I listen and object."

"To what?"

"Mostly when she makes out she's bored with anything; she's never bored."

"Horace wrote about boredom and mentioned sweating, I believe, in the grip of it," Ozenfant said, looking into Sax's heavy face. "Actually, there are no boring things; only boring people."

"So true." Having established comfort between them the two men drank slowly. Ozenfant saw Ghattie looking up at him with the same expression she wore in class when he was discussing poetry or more especially when he was reading his own; it was powerfully gratifying. He wished again for a daughter, such a daughter.

"Have you a wife back in America?" Sax asked him.

"No, no wife. I always seem to prefer thinking," Ozenfant said. The smell of lilacs was delightfully strong. He thought of Cambridge in the spring when the bushes on Brattle Street were blooming. There was in the room too a pleasing smell of butter.

An elderly stocky woman in a lavender plastic apron entered with two plates of small sandwiches. She had a hurt indrawn mouth and wore smeared crooked horn-rimmed glasses. She glanced around and nodded gravely to Ozenfant.

"This is my cousin, Suzanne Pryor," Elise said to him. Suzanne,

102 □

wearing a pair of neat pumps of a plum color, went among them with her plates. As she passed Ghattie she rested a friendly hand on her shoulder briefly. Ozenfant noticed a smell of baking meat and some odd spice as she came to him. She completed her circuit and left the room.

Elise walked to the piano where she played the first part of *Pavane for a Dead Princess*, standing up. "Dr. Ozenfant will open for us," she said as some of the talk died away. "This will be most informal," she added. She sat down in a scarlet upholstered chair and leaned gracefully to one side. Hamish placed his glass on the rug beside him and rested his chin on his hands. Ghattie, Ozenfant saw, became even more intense, feeling for him. He had told her with what torment he read aloud, one time after class when they were having wine at a cafe.

"Well. This I call *Miserere*," Ozenfant said, taking a folded sheet of paper from inside his jacket. He looked down at it seriously and read it well; it took a very short time and when it was done he put it back in his pocket as if deprecating it.

"I like your phrase 'the sound man slept unexcitedly,'" Elise said, leaning forward. "And are you religious?"

"In a certain sense only," Ozenfant said. "I don't go to church but I do go into churches, often; particularly here. There seems, definitely, a presence..." He thought about the Stefansdom the previous day with Ghattie, the great twilit nave, the baroque altars with the half-dead simple flowers in the cheap glass vases that did not match, Ghattie afterwards as they ate together in the Michaelplatz offering her usual unusual interest in everything he said, holding her breath almost as he spoke about the new poem which, he told her, was about a young girl.

"Someone I don't know," she had guessed correctly; it was also someone he did not know; a phantom, complex good-bad individual, he had told her, although a little reluctantly, not wanting to grind the girl out of existence with heavy verbal handling until he got her on paper. Certainly it was not Ghattie, but yet, the daughter he thought about so much these days—even at the opera where he went almost nightly, to rub out the pressures of the young Americans he was instructing in his small class. They all looked so underfed and their watchful eyes questioned so; never had he encountered this much doubt. He was including the doubt in the poem, he had told Ghattie.

Hamish spoke. "Why do you say 'your lips are loose with patience,'" he asked, rather irritated. "I think people tense their lips when they're being patient."

"Some do, some don't," Ozenfant said thoughtfully. "You look around and think about it," he offered with a little smile. He returned for a minute to his thoughts about the students in his class; particularly he thought about Lindsley with his mad thudding voice and the poems he wrote that matched it, and his great shock of hair that seemed so full of electricity. Then Ozenfant's mind returned to the warm big room and Elise again commenting, "Where did the image come from about the sand? Have you been in a desert?"

"I confess I learned about that from a movie I saw." Ozenfant felt rising in him the old near-nausea that came from particularizing about a poem; his anguish made him gentle lest he jab at the mood of the gathering. He saw Sax and Corinna looking pensive; she stroked the cat and stared across the room; she had nothing to say then and would not, through the evening, he guessed. To rest his mind and diminish his tension he looked at her hair, her restfully plump body. Again he thought with contentment that he was tied to no woman who became large or went everywhere in his thoughts like a balloon tied to his finger.

Ghattie was making patterns on the rug with her hands, thinking. "I thought you said the other day that dead trees were a cliché to be avoided," she said then.

"Yes, I did; but there needed to be one at the point in the poem where it occurs," he explained. He reached for his wine and drank deeply. It helped to be somewhat, just a little, tight, when he had to anatomize like this.

Elise seemed to realize that he had had enough for that time and proceeded to ask Hamish to read; he offered a violent series of lines that contained a great deal about death and some explicitness on sex. When he had finished Sax said "Why so much semen on the sheets? I mean, what does that have to do with the murder you describe—I think it's a murder."

Hamish was leaning back, daring them to fail to love what he wrote. "Oh, it all ties in, I think," he said. "The love scene was violent, too."

"Ah," Sax said, as if enlightened, drinking. He was not yet offended.

"Anything goes, now, you know," Hamish said. Ozenfant looked at Ghattie who was looking up at him. He realized she wanted him to make definitive guidelines for the crude Hamish; he was not going to take on that hopeless burden this evening. A thought passed through his mind so vividly he wondered if he could be going mad: *All tracks lead to the grave.* But this sentence came to mind at other times— during the operas, while he taught, as he had sat quietly at the foot of the Brahms statue beside the awkward muse playing her lyre there; with Ghattie during some of their times together. No, he rejoiced with the usual clarity that came to him when he wondered about his madness: no, he was simply of that part of life, seeing into madness and all the other dark interstices of it; his neuroticism wrapped him like a damp but warm clock and he rejoiced in it, if it could produce the poems; and it could.

Ghattie read now, a long poem about life as a play; the idea had been done over and over in various ways before but as usual she made it fresh and included ideas even he had never heard from her. She was indeed gifted and of course had nerves like his own. Again he wished for her as daughter and suddenly looked forward to their next private conversation somewhere, somewhere beautiful of course, in this lovely city. He would be refreshed.

Her title was *The Big Laugh: A Word Opera*. Actually she had very little laughter in her and this was one of the things he enjoyed about her. He had always avoided the big laughers; he suddenly realized she had taken this theme from a conversation they had had and he felt again acutely their rapport.

She finished the poem and drained her glass. "I must *must* have some more, Elise," she said, holding out the glass. Elise took it and filled it; "Thank you," Ghattie said. She drank again. How alike we are, Ozenfant thought, lifting his glass to empty it; how sadly alike and how wonderfully. Something was making him marvelously alive. The wine, the room, Elise, something about the great cat Hyacinthe—it all contributed. The friction and even horror of teaching his class receded.

Hamish had the bit in his teeth and was attacking the poem. Ghattie sat leaning back on her hands and listened to the end and then said nothing. The poem was good and she knew it; she knew Ozenfant thought it was too.

Poetry readings are just another arena, he thought; but we go; we must speak; for the world's good? No, for its egomania.

All right; egomania; I'm mad, all poets are mad; but what about all the others; he rested, knowing how mad all were, in their way; the mess as usual, he thought, holding his glass for Sax to pour into once more. He drank. *What right have you to say Hello to me, even?* he thought in his strangely friendly and sympathetic mind. He crossed his knees the other way and drank again. *Hello, fools, but I do really like you; just know, we are all fools.*

After Hamish's long diatribe on Ghattie's poem, taken up less brilliantly by Mary, Elise once again orchestrated and Mary took out a tiny notebook which she held up to the light; she read four cold stark poems that crusaded against war, injustice, license and sex. As she read Ozenfant studied her braided hair and thin person, took issue with moralizing in poetry and knew he would be too kind and, now, too mellow to comment so on what she had produced.

After a small silence Ghattie spoke out and said that she thought such teachings ought to be couched in prose; she did not think moralizing should be done in poetry, except extremely elliptically. To everyone's surprise Mary began to weep.

"I'm sorry, I'm sorry," she kept saying, and finally snapped her mouth shut and put away the huge handkerchief she had used. "Well. I can only write when I'm incensed," she explained. "To hell with the poems, I ought to try to get away from that, as you say, uh, Ghattie..." She picked up her glass in sudden confusion but it was empty. Corinna lazily offered her full one. Mary took it and fell silent, sipping and looking at the floor.

Ideas poured into Ozenfant's head:... before the music starts I hear... the death of plot... isolated tissue I am... and so is Ghattie... the tomato is, botanically, a berry... sing in chorus with me about... oh, daughter, Ghattie, be my daughter without all the bother of... frenzy... Suddenly he felt trapped, almost ill. All of us straining at whatever the evening is about; he himself was surrounded, defeated. He was exhausted simmering in all this. This was a constant reaction he was familiar with; his classes affected him this way and writing his poems for any length of time did the same thing; not writing them affected him even more so.

He fought for calm and now Elise was reading; it helped. He watched Ghattie as Elise spoke; Ghattie turned to look at him and he suddenly realized that what he saw on her face was pure adoration. Adoration; all the times they had been together in the city's beauty she had adored him, he old enough to be her father; but she was not seeing a father in him; slowly as he looked at her she blushed. Choked, frustrated, he drank again and looked away, seeing a large painting of great beauty across the room from him, a Bonnard, glowing with healthy color and subject, some of the color slightly jarring....

Elise's poems—there were two—were in prose and she had a gift with this style. She read quietly as Suzanne came in again and passed a plate of smoked salmon and cream cheese sandwiches. She was heavy and the apron rustled as she moved. Ozenfant lit a small cigar and watched her as she approached Hamish who shook his head with impatience and did not look at her. This seemed to diminish her to herself. Mary glanced at her tensely as she held the plate towards her and quickly took two sandwiches; with them in her hand she looked again down at her feet which she had placed precisely beside each other. She flexed her thin shoulders, ate quickly and again became hunched and watchful.

Elise concluded, saying, "The ocean is enough." Then she said, "I usually like to play music that I think fits what I've written, afterwards...." She rose, dropped her papers in her chair and went to the piano; again, standing, she played a strange composition that Ozenfant had never heard and to which he took a vague dislike. He knew the dislike came from his uncomfortable discovery of Ghattie's feeling for him and the sense of loss he was trying to absorb and press beneath his consciousness.

Then Elise's music became both strange and harmonious; it ended on slowly spaced resolving chords. She stood briefly looking down at her hands as the vibrations died away. Then she smiled and went again to sit on the red chair.

The old woman, Ozenfant saw, had to wipe her eyes and left the room clumsily. Elise saw this too and got up to follow her. Ghattie too left the room. No one seemed to have a remark to make on this reading; Mary hunched herself further into herself; Ozenfant felt interest and felt warmly towards Elise and in fact towards everyone, but he could not put it into words at the moment. The traffic in Molker Bastei made a little sound; a church chime rang.

Ozenfant, now that Ghattie had gone briefly, knew he would see her home and knew he could not at that time define what he felt towards her in the proper words, thus blasting what he realized her hopes now were. Sax got up and took a decanter from the top of the piano; passing gracefully among the group he refilled glasses and had a warm squeeze of the shoulder for Mary who glanced up at him with gratitude. Palmer rose and went to the piano, sat down and proceeded to play. His tastes were modern and fitted well in the big room. Ozenfant thought of a long green field waiting elegantly with wheat; Palmer's delicate long nose led the eye pleasingly to his grim mouth and taut chin. Ozenfant wondered what the three women were doing down the hall and emboldened by his wine which he carried with him, got up and sought them out.

He found them in the kitchen sitting having tea together; the old woman was talking rapidly and laughing breathlessly. Whatever had weighed on her after Elise's playing was gone. He stood in the doorway sipping his wine. The three women at the table were calm and together made a fine picture. Ozenfant felt full and warm, effulgently relaxed, until he remembered. He wanted the night to go on for a long time and did not want to be alone with Ghattie until he was cool and could summon the right words to rearrange her thought towards him.

Elise drank the last of her tea and suggested they return to the others; the music came down the hall compellingly. Suzanne remained seated, her gray dim eyes gazing unseeing across the room as she sipped. A partially crumbled hard roll lay on a blue plate before her; one of her apron straps had slipped down her shoulder. She seemed content. Ghattie looked at Ozenfant, rose, and the three of them went down the hall that was quietly lit so that several oil paintings glowed beside them. Ozenfant told Ghattie that he found her poem very fine; she smiled and tilted her head with a little shyness. Then she said, not looking at him, and quietly, "What was the matter just now?"

"The matter? Why, nothing," he said as they came to the doorway of the living room. Sax was just lifting Hyacinthe from Corinna's lap to Mary's. Mary immediately sat back stiffly against the chair and held herself away from the cat in horror.

"Oh?" Sax said, looking down at her, concerned but wanting to do something kind for her.

"*Please!*" Mary said, staring into the cat's eyes as if trying to will her off her lap. Sax said "Well, now," and took the animal back into his arms; he stood smoothing her fur and then went back to his chair and continued stroking. Ghattie sat on the floor beside him and looked up at Hyacinthe. "Pussy cat," she murmured. Then she subsided, her mouth turning down at the corners. Ozenfant settled himself in an armchair where he could watch Palmer play. He looked over at Mary assessingly and saw her look around sharply. Her glance fell on Ghattie and she perceived she was pensive; she said "Ghattie, when are you and Jacob going to have some news for us all?"

Ozenfant was appalled, trapped; he looked back to the piano waiting for Ghattie's response.

"Oh. Well," Ghattie groped, smiling weakly.

Ozenfant realized he must say something conclusive and perhaps this was the best way, among all these people. "Ghattie and I are best friends, didn't you know, Mary? True? Ghattie, my dear?"

"Thank you," she said with a half laugh. "Well, so, best friend, would you like to walk me home? It's getting late, Elise," she said as her hostess sat forward in her chair to remonstrate.

"All right," Ozenfant said, setting his glass on a bookcase and rising. He went over to Ghattie and helped her stand. "Let's walk by the Palace, shall we?" He smiled at her.

"Fine," Ghattie said, not looking at him but reaching to the floor for her papers.

"I'd like to go with you, I think," Mary said, rising suddenly.

"Ah, but you know, I think Elise has more in store for you than we," Ozenfant said kindly and yet firmly.

Mary said "Oh," and sat down again, looking at Elise expectantly.

"Do stay," Elise said to her. "I believe we can get Sax to sing with me." She looked at her husband who bowed low sitting down.

Palmer was now playing Chopin quietly; the lilacs quivered in the light atmosphere; Hamish, still on the floor, had let himself lie all the way down to listen; Corinna was watching Ozenfant and Ghattie closely as they waved and left the room. Elise rose and went to the door with them; with thanks to her and Sax they went out into the hall and down the curving stairway.

As they walked slowly along the street in the cool air Ghattie went on talking energetically but her face was averted towards the big city night where, perhaps, there was peace.

Or, perhaps, immolation.

# SCHNAUZER

WILLIAM PENN Lucas was happy. He was working on an appraisal of costs for the ventilation system of the Arrow Cleaning Company. He had just started; it was eight-thirty in the morning, a Saturday. No one else was in.

Ordinarily William's desk was bare and neat because all figuring and planning was done by him out in the shop where he discussed costs with his customers. His efficiency was his pride and solace. Nothing excited him more than setting up the solution to his sheet metal problems; if he himself could cut the metal on one of the huge and dangerous cutters he was all the more pleased. Today he could get most of the figuring and groundwork done. It would be an expensive job; his conscience told him a dry cleaning establishment needed extra ventilating and he had Stuart Place's architectural plans on his desk representing the already built Arrow Company.

Many sheets of paper were used for William's neat sums minutely working out the shafts and excavations needed. He allowed for a trim edging to show of the metal and for generous and handsome openings outside, well above parking spaces and sidewalks. He had passed or stood pensively in front of many such outlets analyzing their patent faults which at times if they were egregious enough he attempted with the owner of the place to correct at a fair price. Usually the owner was perfectly content to be inconveniencing the public.

In the present ecological crisis William gave infinite thought and study to ways of dispersing or getting entirely rid of the bad air flushed out by his solid systems. He read far into the night how coal mines, ships, skyscrapers, ordinary cellars of homes, industry, all handled this challenge.

William created order wherever he went and the world he dealt with held him in great esteem although he was only thirty-seven. He was not a big man; he was slight and trim. He always ate a small cheap lunch that he brought in a paper bag and he saved small bags where he found them. His hair was black and always cut and groomed. A small bottle of Vitalis could be found with a pair of nail clippers and a shoe cloth in his lower desk drawer.

William had not married and did not seek out women. He was content still to think of a wife as something he would of course have one day but he never dwelt on such an eventuality. He had no close friends, being totally content to occupy himself with his business. He could laugh and joke moderately with his employees but he could also fire them easily and often did, until he found some who were satisfactory. Most of the men caught the spirit of his industry in a short time and liked his solid dignity. The world of handouts and unions was nothing he put his mind to. He rejected these democratic measures totally and thought of work as the only way of life if a man wanted salvation of any sort. On Sundays he could be found early at his business though he would turn on his small Japanese radio to a Baptist program while he accomplished on that day what three of his men would take days to do.

Suddenly he was diverted by a great screeching of brakes and a lot of yelling and commotion just outside his large window. He looked out and, horrified, saw a young child lying beside a hastily stopped new Camaro. He hurried to the door and went out. By then a woman was bending over the child; William looked down and saw that the child was dead and mutilated. A young man of about eighteen hung over the hood of the car vomiting.

The woman straightened and said to William, "Can we telephone from your place?"

"Oh, certainly. Come right inside," he said.

They entered the shop. William shoved his papers aside to free the phone and the woman quickly dialled. "I'd like to report a fatal accident," she snapped. "A child has been killed. What's the name of this place," she asked William.

"United Warming. Maple and Sixth," he said. He could see the Camaro and the gathering crowd. Someone was sobbing beside the child.

The woman hung up and looked out the window. "My God, she's found Cindy," she exclaimed.

"Do you know that child?" William asked.

"I know all these children around here. I'm the crossing policewoman during school hours." She flung open the door and went out, closing it firmly. She went to the woman on the pavement and knelt on the dirty street to put her arms around her. In a few minutes the two women lifted the child to the curb and a police car and ambulance drove up efficiently. The young boy with the Camaro was in tears but the policeman asked him to move his car and then come with him. They put the child's body in the ambulance, spoke briefly to the mother and then drove away.

The episode had taken fifteen minutes. William sat at his desk looking out of the window. He recalled now vaguely seeing a policewoman carefully guiding the children back and forth at the busy crossing; he recalled one summer day when a City work truck came to a stop there and one of the men in it called "Hi, Schnauzer" to the woman. William noticed then that she had a big firm nose and then forgot the incident.

William went back to his figuring and spent the Saturday and the next day busy in the shop.

On Monday, at work at eight o'clock, he noticed Schnauzer at her post, neat in a navy blue suit and police cap, a net around her black hair, gloves and boots also navy, and as children and also adults approached the crossing she energetically piloted them to safety, bowing and bobbing as if in a ritual dance. She was totally committed to what she was doing; she smiled at the small children, called them by name, and struck firmly at one that lurched toward the path of a car. William went to stand by the door the better to see her work. He stood there the three quarters of an hour that the children kept coming and it was with regret that he saw her give a final glance at her crossing and turn into Pat's Place.

He had a new thought. A cup of coffee at Pat's. He turned out his light, put on his jacket and went out.

He found Schnauzer seated at the counter waiting for coffee. He sat down beside her and said, "How's the mother of the little girl doing?"

Schnauzer looked at him with a directness that he liked. "She's in hell," she said. "In fact she took to her bed and won't get up. I'm about to go see her. To think—I wasn't even on duty when Cindy was—just happened by." Schnauzer's coffee came and she began to drink although it was scalding.

"Are you cold?" William asked. He himself never felt heat or cold particularly.

"No." Schnauzer shrugged. "I'm on the move too much. And," she added firmly, "I dress for this. Long underwear." There was no suggestiveness to her remark. She drank a large mouthful. "Say. Do you always work so long and so hard?" She looked at him admiringly. William saw that she was plain and clean; not overweight. Not tall. No smell to her either.

His coffee arrived but he found he did not want it. Schnauzer was finished.

"I'll pay for it," William said, placing a half dollar on the counter.

"Thanks. Got to make my call and do I dread it," Schnauzer said. She got off her seat and went out.

William saw a glass jar containing doughnuts. They looked delicious and he ordered one. He wished he had thought to get one for the woman. He realized he did not know her name. He did not even know the names of many other women. His mother's name had been Etta.

William began to make a habit of buying Schnauzer coffee. She always went to Pat's Place in the morning. At night she hurried home to Mary Street where, she said, she had a room and kitchen privileges. One night William saw her in the A & P and they pushed their carts around the store together. He liked her choice of food and even got an idea or two for himself. She bought tuna pies for twenty-one cents each and he also bought one as a fairly safe experiment. When he ate it he liked it so much he went back the next day and bought four. Cheap and good, he thought. He himself had two rooms on Gussy Place, near his shop so he could easily work at night.

It needed Joe Iggy, one of his workers, to give him the idea of taking Schnauzer out to supper. The workers had observed what the two did in the morning with affectionate concern for the outcome.

It seemed Schnauzer's name was Louise Kochulik and William thought of Louise with calm enjoyment. Romance was not for him but he liked everything about her. She bowled with two other women most Saturdays, did not have a car, parents now dead as were his, a brother in Detroit named Mike.

One Friday at coffee with Louise William said firmly, "I'd like to take you out for supper tomorrow night."

It was promptly settled and William and Louise went to Phil's Chicken House in his neat Plymouth and ordered cole slaw and Harvard beets with the fried chicken. Louise saw nothing strange in being taken home directly after supper; cheerfully she said "Thanks, William," and entered her plain narrow house and closed the door. After that William took Louise to supper every Saturday night, usually to Phil's. One night he thought of asking her where she would like to go and she said she loved pizza. They added The Villa to the places for Saturday night.

William's staff were delighted and were great friends with Louise as she guarded the crossing. They kidded William about his girl, asked him when the wedding would be and gave him advice about Lovers' Lanes in the vicinity. He knew Louise would not like these lanes and he knew he wouldn't. But slowly the thought of marrying Louise grew on him. He learned all he needed to know about her at the dinners Saturday nights. He knew she didn't gab, didn't throw her money about—at Christmas they each sent the other a modest card; and he liked the dress she wore to go out with him in.

It was after a very good week of work at the shop and William was in a great frame of mind; he took Louise to a new place called Rennie's Grille and in the dark liquor-saturated atmosphere asked her if she ever planned to marry. She replied, cutting her veal cutlet, that maybe she would if the right man showed up. William, never devious, said "Louise, I'd like to marry you."

Six months later they were married in a severely frugal ceremony at Louise's Greek Orthodox church on West Clinton Street. Louise's brother could not come so John Mawn of William's shop gave her away. John had a new neat terrible haircut; William wore his other suit; Louise carried mums and the two practical people went home to William's two rooms after a punch was served the small gathering in the church parlors.

At dinner that night at Phil's, William said "I want you to know how much I really like you, Louise," and took from his pocket a treasure, the Masonic ring he had never thought to wear. Louise regarded it on her ring finger with pleasure and nodded cheerfully at him.

They went on eating.

# THE WIDOWS

DAY HAD finally come, high, overcast, windy, warm and smelling of hay and roses. Anna, in a cheap cotton summer dress, stood on the great veranda of the big gray mansard house looking down at the Hudson River, a wide gray presence; the farther shore was still misted.

A rooster down by the tracks along the river crowed heartily; a wren sang in the hydrangeas beside the wide worn steps leading to the gravel walk; an iridescent beetle passed Anna's foot. She did not move; numbly, not thinking, she took in every detail of the morning, the weather; she, so unscientific always, had become briefly a meteorologist. How does a scientist accept a death, she wondered, bruised, horribly shaken, ended.

Up in their great bare room Robert lay dead; alone in his adventure he had gone away and his long thin frame, naked, was stretched on their bed; so peaceful; so very peaceful, she was not needed. Not invited along; not told . . . he lay as if death had come when he first went to bed late in the night. His thick hair was smooth; his shining gray-green eyes, so large and brilliant, were shut; his firm features, exact, controlled, were now withdrawn.

Anna wandered into the cool great depth of the silent house, through the long living rooms, the high dark hallway where the wide stairs climbed upward and the light rectangles on the brocaded walls showed where the many old portraits had hung—a shrewd, contained, solemn withdrawn group of her ancestors, now sold.

Nausea struck her suddenly, then passed; she had not eaten since the cold hot dog and tea with Robert at ten the night before in the shadowed butler's pantry. Robert had had only the tea, she recalled; he had not seemed ill, however. He had been quiet, thinking, thinking; about what she did not know; she usually did not know.

Standing in the hall by one of the long marred mirrors she thought for some reason of violets; her grandfather had had the mid-morning train stop each Wednesday at the crossing at the bottom of his property to deliver a fragrant full bunch of violets to her grandmother; Coughlin, the chauffeur, had picked them up with the foil-wrapped stems and brought them to the kitchen where Vail, the butler, had placed them in a crystal vase and taken them to her grandmother's delicate desk in the anteroom off the hall where she wrote her. many notes to her myriad friends and relatives along the river and to the minister of the small stone church at the end of their mile-long drive, on the River Road.

The violets, the servants, Grace Abbot Stein and Jerome Stein, her grandparents, the frequent trains in the night, all were gone; life had dwindled to her and Robert, alone, poor, both thin, both loving the last of the old place—but there was no money except the small trust she had . . .

The dogs, the full busy carriage house, the fragrant high-ceilinged kitchen where Helen, Maggie, Prudence, John and Peter had worked were gone; were they all dead? Where . . .

Startled, her own movement caught her eye in the mirrors; vaguely she thought how fitting she alone proliferated in that way at this time.

She went aimlessly through the long corridor to the kitchen where she stood by the long zinc table listening to the wind. Robert's being dead did not oppress her; she felt no horror. They had talked about death often and it was in a way familiar country where anything, or nothing, might happen; now, however, she seemed to have lost herself and was not; the world had gone away.

She saw the purple-tarnished heavy silver teapot they had used earlier standing gleaming, malevolent, in the early light; she recalled Cornelia, her cousin, lost in the vast woods and ravine years ago, searched for for days by the Zabriskie men, James Chapman, Laurence Livingston, finally found lying in a shallow pool, dead; she had seen her, white, soaked, young, not beautiful, when they brought her in; the teapot seemed in some way to bring Cornelia back. Laurence, plain, balding, speaking in his beautifully accented way, but briefly, describing the discovery as thoughtfully as he could to spare the feelings of Grace Stein, little, plump appalled Bunny and Happy Cadwalader, Anna, sick with flu, bundled away by Leonore, the poor relative in the beautiful pearls and the lavender plastic apron; the young dark slim visiting prince from somewhere, up from New York and the well-bred group of women friends from the river community took their leave tactfully . . .

Now there was no telephone; there had ceased to be money for any, or money for gasoline for the large black Buick she and Robert had used. Food too was scarce but they could manage that sufficiently. Neither of them cared a lot about eating.

Anna moved to a window and looked out across the uncut lawns to the pavilion, dark green and covered with wisteria now blooming richly; she and Robert had gone there to talk and to be away from people in their courting days—and that was not long ago. She had been married to Robert only four years.

She recalled Evan Moss walking with her to the pavilion—when was that? Evan, dignified, short, thin-lipped, talking endlessly about his college courses and his coin collection . . .

Her mother, not seen for fifteen years, totally involved in Florida in her St. Anthony School of Psychic Reality, fat, brilliant, selfish, and her father, dead these twenty years, a hairy merry young man she barely recalled, her rich busy cousins, so blonde with their Braemar sweaters and cold assessments, their strength, their middle-Atlantic pronunciation; Polly: "peefectly ooful" . . . She herself, thin, dark, with indefinite features except for her Roman nose, a liking for outré ideas and people she had not the daring to discuss or to make her own, outside always but content—all these came to her mind as she stood.

A particularly strong gust of wind slammed a door somewhere. She was too numb to be startled. Her eye fell on a nearly empty sherry bottle standing on the great black range. She would pour some into the handsomest glass she could find in the cupboards and drink it with Robert; she knew surely he was still there, and hers; and she had always loved drinking with him, particularly in bed.

Holding the priceless Italian glass half full she walked the long distance through the house, up the great staircase under the Spanish candelabra, along the hall past the many airy silent rooms, to theirs . . .

She stood by the bed looking at him and sipped briefly; wherever he had gone it was a peaceful experience; his big loose hands lay easily on the sheet, relaxed, ready; she moved to one of the long curtainless windows where the wind shrieked through the screen and set the glass down. She looked now out of the front of the house at the beginning of the long drive lined with huge old white pines; they stood heavy, confident, exclusive of her in the morning light.

She felt drawn to walk among them, to breathe their healthy potent smell, to move, to do something . . .

She went down through the house to the veranda steps, past the full high clumps of delphinium, light blue, dark and white, and stood in the turbulent air. This is real; this was bound to come; this—is real. I'm real. I—AM—REAL . . .

But she was so stunned, so unready.

She began to walk on the soft grass under the pines toward the River Road, her senses working powerfully, her legs moving automatically. Where can I write him while he's gone . . .

Her thoughts reached far away to Vienna where they had visited for several weeks, where history, music and death, brilliant, great, continuing, had filled their lives. And fat ill-tempered women had watched over the homes of the great; . . . the whipped chestnut confection . . . the Goethe statue soaking in a cold rain . . . Brueghel in the palace . . . tombs, operas, marching men, serious hats on all the middleaged women . . . the handsome old man in the park decrying the bandits who had overturned benches . . . the busy efficient banks and hotel people, the tours where everyone had fun with everyone else and digested beautifully.

Her mind flashed busily from Austria to the Alps, to Paris, to Alexandria where they planned to go . . . all, all still there and yet in a way, now, no longer there—so exhaustingly far . . .

Before she reached the road and the chapel she was aware of fatigue; somehow she went on, the spectacle of the high vivacious morning buoying her up. Her long hair blew against her mouth; she choked, gagged, went on; a crow cried out restfully, strongly; she saw him sail on the wind over the trees.

Suddenly, exhilarated, she thought of Japan, China; there, there were mystery, a continuum, a calm . . . still walking in the soft long dewy grass she pictured the great mountain masses, opium, strange crimes, new flowers, strange crimes, crashing sea waves, fragrant crimes . . .

She wondered at the thoughts she had; clung to them strangely . . . bemused, reaching far in her mind, forgetting herself, she at last came to the macadam, the stone pillars where woodbine nearly obscured the name—The Meadows.

The lovely low strong lines of the church merged well·with the stone wall, English ivy, hollyhocks and foxglove; old Dimity was mowing the lawn under the heavy elms. His gray hair blew wildly, but stolidly he continued. He did not look up.

Anna stepped to the road and turned north. It was too early for cars. Far ahead, suddenly coming into view, she saw someone, a woman in black, sturdy, tall. She saw it was Battestine Forrester; how strange, alone, this early . . .

They approached each other and passed without speaking; Anna saw a strong expression of determination on Battestine's fine face; evidently she knew exactly where she was going. Anna recalled that Henry Forrester had died from a fall from a horse ten years ago . . .

As she walked further between woods and stone walls she passed other women, all in gray or black or dark blue, some in silent groups, some alone, all abstracted yet with great purpose; they seemed to say *This place is important, this spot, this in-between locale, because I am in it . . . I'm living here; this is LIFE . . .*

Anna walked indefinitely, still meeting the women who were all plain and strong, all silent. She imagined what an army they would make streaming across some plain in the snow—potent, indomitable, beautiful... there was no pain and there seemed to be no plan, no shaped future.

At last Anna turned to step off the road to rest on a patch of moss in the woods. Small dainty clumps of hepatica trembled in the wind; she could smell sassafras and pine. She felt suspended and unreal. Soon however she was impelled to rise again and walk further on the road.

The sun came out and beat mercilessly down on her. Huge cloud shadows sped across the fields, the road.

And in the distance, tremulously rising from the road, she saw her grandmother's black voile-clad figure and the beautiful large hat with its veil swathing it and her grandmother's face, clinging to the moist nose and mouth. Dimly Anna realized she could not be seeing her grandmother, dead these many years... a vague music came to her ears and a great crowd seemed to be speaking to her about many beautiful things but she would have to ask each person, later, personally, to sort it out.

And Anna realized, with gratitude to whatever gods might be, that she must be going mad.

# SING ANYWAY

GLORIOUSLY HE walked along Mygatt Street. The ploughing, searing, embarrassing interview with Al, manager of the Mohican, was over; Al, standing with him beside celery and Kleenex crates at the back of the store, had said to him "I guess not right now, Mr., uh . . ."

It had been equally bad at Doc Wickes' used car lot; they had sat in Doc's hot Chevrolet outside the big loud parking lot, both of them staring off through the dead bugs at a Sears Roebuck sign down the street; Doc had said "Things are all puttin me in a bind, fella . . ."

At Tomasso's he talked to Ray Noonan who tended bar; Ray had said "Jesus—excuse it, Marion—but you Christers can't tend bar, I mean . . ."

All that was over because Norman Tate who had the framing shop on Beatty Street hired him yesterday, to start right away. Norman was small but a fine religious hard-working guy. Marion would work out in various ways, he thought, folding up a spare piece of paper scrupulously. In the framing work he could learn; being big and strong he could do a lot.

"Nice lookiñ fella like you; how come you couldn't find work?" Norm asked him, looking with a smile, eyes sharp behind glasses.

"Oh, well, I can explain that, I think," Marion had said engagingly. "I talk. I know I do. I just—love to talk. But I positively had the word from my sweet wife about that," he added, carefully keeping his Dentine under his tongue. *Don't run on,* he said to himself, *Don't.*

A million similes, a million apothegms, a million warm friendly remarks rushed to the front of his mind to say to this good little guy. People told him Norm was religious; they could chew the fat on that—oh, he'd help, he'd make them all his friends, he could, he knew. Even the fortyish wizened ex-artist named Vicki. Someone he could charm though she darted at her work silently, unaware her dry back hair was sticking out.

Sweating but keeping his big nice-looking face relaxed though his thighs ached from holding his feet quietly on the floor, he had waited for Norman's big NO.

But instead Norm had spun a little wheel in his thin fingers, regarded it a minute, and then had hired him.

Don't talk, he warned himself—it was agony. He thanked Norm, asked what time he should come to work, and blindly agreed to eight to six. Then he reached out his hand, pumped Norm's, and strode to the door, his big run-over heels tapping pathetically. Dot had not given him a dime extra; he walked an hour to reach his flat in The Windermere to tell her he had a job. Though she served spaghetti with oleo for the fourth night running, her sagging shoulders hanging over her sparse plate, he threw the food strongly into his mouth, mad in a big daydream about the next day.

"Mr. Molice—"

"Call me Marion."

"Marion, I can't get the nail in high enough for this picture," Vicki said. This flattered him, in only just the first hour of work. He jammed his clean, faded blue cotton knit shirt into his belt and looked at the place on the wall.

"I'll fix it, Vick," he said winningly and energetically removed his shoes and climbed on the desk. He hammered in the nail and turned to look down into the large sad eyes of the clerk. He felt well and strong.

"You're wonderful," she said absentmindedly, her lips jerking into her harassed smile.

"*Christ* is wonderful," he chided with a smile. "I just try to help him a bit. Don't you?" He knelt on one knee on a pile of invoices on the desk and ran a comb through his rich, dirty hair. "Well!" he said, and sprang down, sure that poor Vicki found him lithe and good both. He placed a large hand on her thin shoulder in cheap white rayon. "God is with us all the time, recall," he said, looking up. Her eyes followed his and saw only a sprinkler pipe. With a final hearty grip on her shoulder he turned and walked through the gallery's burlap curtains to where Gordon was working on a big frame. He was bawling a tune from *Carmen*, impromptu phrases to the effect that he was going mad. This pleased Marion who felt at this moment needed and completely incapable of insanity in spite of what that doctor in Scranton had said, and—oh, yes, the other two—but that was much earlier.

Leaning on the moulding rack he watched Gordon.

"Know something, Gord?"

"Wot dya know," affable Gordon replied, his wild gray-blond hair circling his high sweating forehead. He continued working; Marion could see he was adept. He knew he would be, too, given time.

"I write quite a lot. Written, oh, say, sixteen hundred pieces, I guess," Marion said with a bright light in his eyes. "You know, I wrote one about God coming down to earth in a school, one time—" He broke off as Norm walked up quietly. "Yes, sir. Now what would you like me to do?" Marion asked energetically. "You know, Norm, I don't want to be aggressive—new and all—but I could make you a real nice stand for all those spare frames around." He cast around for a spot. "Right here, beside this rack." He showed Norm, swiftly wrenching things out of his way.

Norm thought and looked, his thin body in clean white shirt and dark trousers relaxed.

"Okay, you do it, Marion. But don't get in Gordon's way," Norm said with a look around. He left.

"Say, there's a real man of God," Marion whispered to Gordon. Gordon looked up and stared.

"Oh, he's a nice guy," he said, with a shake of his head.

"Huh but I mean, you can *tell*," Marion persisted. "Notice how clean he is, and he don't drive me, my first day. Lets me have an idea. Well!" he said, banging his hands together in a loud report. He began sorting lumber, looking for a hammer.

All morning he was up and down on the floor, reaching, bending, staring anxiously at his piece of rack. When Vicki or Gordon or Norm passed him he would say Excuse me. He felt good. He didn't even daydream like he usually did; about ten-forty-five he realized he hadn't imagined gaining the loving confidence of a great congregation even once; but then he knew he was gaining the love and gratitude of all his fellow workers here. Playfully he went over to Vicki, who was wearing strong horn-rimmed glasses, took them from her face and let his breath cloud each lens before he quickly stuck them back on her. She embarrassedly smiled her half-smile and took them off and wiped them; then she went back to her typing. Marion knew he had won her completely; these spinsters loved attention from virile men. He knew he was virile because he was big; all big men were virile. He was certain Christ was a big man too; and a carpenter, like him, at the moment anyway, at that.

He went to stand beside Gordon, to talk; Gordon liked to talk, he could tell; he told him all about the church in South Carolina he had had when he was nineteen.

"I got 'em with food, boy, right by the belly. Then we'd sing, you know, *In The Garden* and *I Was Lonely Till Thou Camest* . . . and like that," Gordon stopped work and leaned on his work table; Marion knew he had captured him.

". . . so when I left they give me a plaque, no kidding, and they cried—the women did—Geez what a moment!" Marion felt like crying too.

Then he heard someone really crying. It came from behind a closed door at the end of the shop. He knew it was the girls' room; he had seen Vicki combing her wretched hair there earlier. He turned suddenly from Gordon and tiptoed across the shop to listen.

Yes, sounds were coming from the closed door. He would comfort Vicki. He knew how, oh, he knew women.

He wrenched open the door; Vicki sat staring, shocked, from where she sat on the toilet, her thin mottled thighs showing above her dark stockings. "You were crying, weren't you, Vick?" Marion said, hoarse with emotion he felt whenever he was about to save someone.

"I was singing. Please close that door," Vicki said in a loud voice.

"For God's sake get out of there," Gordon yelled from across the shop. "Jesus Christ!"

Marion shut the door and turned to go back and tell Gordon about women. Norman stood blocking his way.

"Okay. Get your things," Norm said quietly. "We don't like this sort of thing."

"But I only—I thought the poor gal was crying," Marion said, his eyes wide, his hands spread. "I'm no sex maniac, Norm!"

Norm had turned away. He spoke over his shoulder. "See me before you go." He moved quietly into the cubbyhole of an office he used.

"Glory be, Gord, it sounded like *crying*," Marion protested. Gord was his friend, he knew that.

"For Christ's sake, women always go off by themselves to cry," Gordon said. He was angry. "I happen to know Vicki always sings in there and she told you she was." He ran his hand through his wild hair and turned back to his frame. "Wooooooo that weeee twoooooo ware Maaaaayeeeeengh!" he bellowed, working again.

Walking past the poor jerrybuilt rack he had begun so well, Marion went to Norm's office. Norm was using the adding machine and went on with it for a moment. "Three dollars cover the work you done?" he asked Marion without looking up.

"Yes, sir, but I—"

"Okay. So long, Marion." The sharp yet innocent eyes fixed him briefly. "See, I got to make a living." Norm turned back to his desk.

Martyred, Marion went to the chipped refrigerator and took out his lunch. Then he went proudly out the front door of the shop. The day was young yet; a day, maybe, for burning, or some great deed—something.

He walked down the street, questing into the eyes of the people he passed.

Some day they would know him.

# DEATH SANS BLAGUE

TAL SCHWAB entered Gerber's Grill at his usual time—half-past five—on a freezing dark day; the plate glass was covered with frost from the steam; since it was Friday he smelled fish along with wet wool and the liquor.

Wearing his usual flashy dark clothes with the new Eisenhower jacket and his rubbers he walked, big, cocky, the liar looking for his audience, down past the chipped green booths not filled yet to the back table near the kitchen where he always sat.

He was surprised to see a girl at the table; she was thin, cheaply dressed, not pretty; very white. She was eating rice pudding; a cup of coffee was beside the dish.

"Ah-HA!" he shouted, sitting down. The girl was startled; she took in his neat longish dark dirty hair and his meaty face grimacing at her.

Helen came up sourly to wait on him, holding her pad at the ready, pink ballpoint poised, her eyes darting off through the grill to the dim movement in the street outside.

"I got a swell cycle," Tal said to the girl. "Ought to see me on it sometime."

Ute Stedman raised her brows faintly and looked back at her pudding, took the last mouthful. She wanted someone, anyone, to talk to; he seemed friendly—maybe he'd pay for her food. She was still hungry; maybe he'd offer her something more to eat...

As the swinging door flew open again she felt the warmer good-smelling air from the kitchen; a man there laughed fatly. Ute picked up the stained beige menu and read it carefully in case this man offered to buy her something. She decided on a club sandwich. Her mouth filled in anticipation with saliva. She thought about the great starchy meals at the institution, their good homemade bread...

"Hell, I'll take ya for a ride on it sometime," Tal said, looking around vaguely.

124 □

"Well?" Helen reminded Tal she was waiting. One hip was stuck out and she sighed and leaned her head to one side, peeved.

"I'll have beans— ah-huhn; bread; lotta butter . . ."

"That all?"

Tal nodded, not looking at her; she went angrily off to the kitchen.

Tal began to clean his long nails meticulously with a small file. Then he combed his hair, his small dark eyes on Ute.

"Stores open tonight, huhn."

"Yes—yes, I think so—"

"Got to buy a stereo. Also a cycle jacket. Gonna have 'Red Rider' in studs onto it. Ah-HA!" He clapped his hands with a painful report; he tipped back in his chair and slid his hands up and down over his chest. "Hahhh," Tal sighed and rubbed his face. "Cold out." He cleaned the corners of his eyes carefully. "I'm a skating champ," he said then.

"Oh?"

"That and skiing. Champeen. I broken every bone in my body also includin my neck."

"Oh dear." Ute didn't believe him but needed to talk. She listened, always, said almost nothing, but she needed to be addressed.

A large dim man in a wrinkled stained overcoat came over to a nearby table and sat down. His rough gray hair was wet with snow, his seamed face lax and gray.

"Ey," Tal said to him, pointing at him. "Hey-hey!"

The old man nodded and nodded to him, not caring; he ordered coffee and loaded it heavily with sugar as Tal went on about his championships. "Betcha never knew a champ, huhn?"

The old man shook his head. He fumbled a dirty rag from inside his coat and wiped his neck and hair.

Helen, cold, efficient, bored and filled with dislike slapped a thick chipped brown platter piled with kidney beans in front of Tal, set down a basket of cheap bread and two small pats of butter. Tal started shoveling the food into his mouth. He used up the butter on two bites of bread and did not ask for more; his mind was seeing himself brilliantly performing on his motorcycle.

In silence, quickly, he finished his meal; absently he rolled onto one buttock and farted. Ute had done this herself of course, but in private. But men did things different, she supposed. She pushed her lank hair behind her ears, stood and put on her long thin maroon coat. She added a garish filmy scarf and tan cotton gloves.

Tal threw his money on the table and got up to go. Ute followed him to the door, out into the pretty falling snow and then into the adjoining doorway where he entered to climb the dimly lit stairs. He did not seem surprised or even to notice that she followed.

He entered an unlocked room from the dark hall where a pile of cartons had been thrown. Ute followed him in and paused waiting for him to turn on a light. He reached up and turned a bulb in the papered ceiling and the room was revealed to her—his room; her friend's room.

It smelled of his farts. There were several cartons of junk around the walls and under the unmade bed where there were no sheets, only several dirty loud cotton blankets. On the cheap varnished bureau was the one picture in the room; it was a school graduation photo of a plump plain girl mounted in a cardboard folder. Several bright dirty combs lay before it and a few pennies.

"AHHHHHHH!" Tal suddenly yelled, looking at his reflection in the poor mirror. He bared his teeth and smiled brilliantly at himself and again farted. He rummaged in a nearly empty drawer and brought out a ten dollar bill which he stuffed into his pocket. Ute noticed a second room, also facing out over the street, opening off the bedroom. It was filled with junk—boxes, old clothes, an old lamp; things had been tossed through the door to lie where they fell.

Tal turned out the light and left the room and Ute followed. She had planned to go to the library, for someplace to go, something to do; Tal walked beside her. Once he stopped suddenly to look at a bright clean store window full of men's clothes.

"I got all them," he said broadly, turning away. They walked on through the evening shopping crowd, the sidewalks slushy and dirty. Tal did not notice the weather; Ute was terribly cold. She said so; Tal continued walking, not replying.

They walked eight blocks to French Street and Ute turned in at the library steps. Tal followed. Ute uncertainly sought the fiction stacks and hurried to find a book—it had to be about a nurse having a romance. This was the only kind she ever read. She found one entitled *Lucy Storrow, School Nurse* and hurried to the desk to get it signed out. Pleased, she saw Tal sat waiting on a plastic bench, flipping the pages of a book he was not looking at. As she started for the door he got up and joined her, tossing his book on the seat.

"I've wrote one thousand six hundred stories," he told her, once again on the street. "But I don't do it now." They passed a line of wet parked cars and a rind of hard dirty snow along the curb.

"I wrote a poem once," Ute started to say. Tal roared out "HohoHO!" and a fat woman with a plain small boy stared at him.

Ute planned to visit Woolworth's and perhaps buy a small towel to use at the boarding house, if they didn't cost too much. She walked to Allen Avenue and turned into it; Tal went too. Ute longed for all the objects for sale in the windows—the stoves, lamps, clothes, drugstore products, books, automotive supplies, the good delicatessen food.

Woolworth's, bright, jammed with shoppers, smelling of chocolate, had long ago won Ute's heart. She knew where the linens were and they struggled along the aisles to that section.

A heavy man in dark glasses and a lumberjack's coat barred their way suddenly. "Tal. Howya doon."

"Hey-HEY!" Tal did not ever know anyone's name.

"I'm goin to a meeting tonight. Wanna come?"

"HA! Yop."

"You, too, girlie?"

"Oh—what meeting?"

"A.A. Alcoholics Anonymous. You know. Anyone welcome and all that. Serve coffee and doughnuts."

They turned back then and made their way out of the door to the street. Alcoholics Anonymous seemed to be a sinister gathering to Ute, full of people who did violent bad things because they got drunk; but it was a gathering and there would be doughnuts; she hoped she could have three . . .

The man in the glasses had a large run-down Olds parked several blocks away. They walked through the slush to it and got in, Tal and the owner in the front, Ute small and afraid in back. They drove for fifteen minutes to a side street and parked beside a small neat church on a back street. The lights of the parish house were on and people were arriving, shaking hands, calling out, slapping each other's backs. Here and there a solitary man or woman entered the door with embarrassment. The man with the dark glasses, greeted effusively by everyone, was Ted. No last names were ever used, Ted told Ute.

"You're not a boozer, are ya? No. I could tell. Well, don't ever be. Hayya doon?—" He turned to shake the hand of a grinning old man in a bright blue-green suit.

Everyone was seated and a short broad man with a wide unlined Slavic face opened the meeting. The rules and Serenity Prayer, which Ute liked, were gone through and then Leo, presiding, called on a woman named Tess to come to the front. Taking time to pile her coat neatly on the floor, remove her harlequin glasses and twitch her slacks she walked to the front of the room and immediately got a laugh saying "A closed mouth gathers no foot." She said she always put her foot in it and would again but at least she'd given them a laugh, huhn.

For twenty minutes she described her life. First there was the time before she drank; she had been poor, sick, stupid in school, boy-crazy but homely as hell. Next there was the start of her drinking, with boys who did take her out; liquor made her feel on top of the world and she got the reputation for being funny. Then came marriage to Leon, binges together when she always had to have it; their whole crowd simply met to drink themselves silly and they never knew what they'd done with who the day after...

Tess and Leon got divorced and she tried to get a job but she went to her interviews stoned at nine in the morning and no one would hire her. She had to go to welfare. Then she was sick in a hospital and nearly died from drink. Ronnie and Jeff from A.A. came to see her and to talk about A.A.

She had sat up in bed, sick as she was, and told them to get lost and go to hell.

In bad health and at the bottom, the thing that made her finally go to a meeting was getting to know the grocer on her corner—Harry. She liked him. He took her—"and jeez was I in the bag that night"—to a meeting and she'd been persuaded to tell her story and had cried and cried.

That was the beginning; with several slips she did manage to keep coming and since she liked the other members—"Well, MOST of you"—she finally was on the wagon.

Ute was fascinated. She had never had anything more than Communion wine. She wished she could belong to this friendly group.

"Baloney," she heard Tal mutter as Tess went back to her seat, wise-cracking. Tess was tall, very thin and had red hair. She winked at Ute.

Leo next called Al forward, a small sick-looking middle-aged man who had been on Death Row for years but managed to get paroled. He was hard to hear because mostly he spoke into his fist. He never tried to joke and seemed wretchedly tense.

He returned to his seat in the front row, there was brief applause and then, after everyone said the Lord's Prayer, the coffee and doughnuts were served. A plump healthy older woman cheerfully filled the cups from the kitchen, passing them through a sliding window. She urged doughnuts, of which there were at least six varieties from Dunkin Donuts, on everyone; Ute, standing alone by the window, had four. She saw Tal, also alone on the other side of the room, pound his fist into his hand forcefully, saying "Ho-ho-HO" loudly. This attracted a short plump girl to Tal's side; Ute heard Tal shout "Ah-HA" and envied the short girl. Then she saw Tal talking with many gestures; she guessed he was telling the girl about being a champ. Two other women joined them; Ute, carrying her last doughnut, chocolate with chocolate frosting, moved across the floor to stand silently listening to Tal.

Tal now said, "I worked for a real senator in Washington, D.C., for a while, but then the mayor wanted me here in Binghamton..."

Ute doubted everything Tal said but how could she know what was true; she'd never been anywhere or done anything...

128 □

After a half-hour of socializing people began to leave, cheerful and all having many friends. Ted offered Tal and Ute a ride and Ute had counted on it because now she was far from Mrs. Mott's boarding house. But Tal breezed away saying he wanted to walk; he gave no thought to Ute who said, too, that she'd walk. Ted gathered a load of others then and ground off into the night.

Ute stood briefly beside a fire hydrant nearly buried in snow, her feet in her cheap shoes and white ankle socks already very cold; then she saw that the main street was nearby and knew if she followed it—and it would be a very long walk—she could find the way to her room.

As she set out in the still falling snow, now several inches deep on the walk, she thought about her room which was nice because it was all hers; she hated the snot-colored plastic curtains, though, and the metal bed that sagged and the bare forty-watt bulb hanging down from the middle of the cracked ceiling. If she ever got up her courage to go after a job then she would move out—if she had the courage to do that; Maureen, fat, sixty, who boarded in the same house, though, was a sort of friend; she'd shared her box of Lorna Doones that time she showed her how to make up her eyes; Mrs. Mott was motherly in her mean way . . .

Ute walked fearfully on through the snowy night.

Tal went along the back streets toward a bar he knew about where he planned to tank up and talk to the other people. He remembered one guy that laughed a lot—he'd talk to him about buying his stereo and other important things. On a side street in a row of cheap sharp houses with asbestos shingles he located Bam's Bar. Bam was a fat black who poured out the gin he asked for quickly. Tal leaned one thigh up on the stool and dipped his head to his glass. In the dark interior a lot of people in booths drank and talked a little. No one for the moment was at the bar and it wasn't until Tal was almost through his second gin that the man who laughed came in shaking his jacket and hailing Bam warmly, calling him his fucking buddy.

"Fuck-you-too, fuck-you-too," Bam answered calmly.

"Ho-ho-HO!" Tal yelled, raising both arms.

"And to you too," the new customer said genially, not looking at him. He ordered a stinger and sat up hungrily at the bar watching Bam make it swiftly. Bam placed it in front of him and he drank half of it and then looked around. "You an Eskimo too?" he said, grinning, to Tal. "Here's to us Eskimos."

"Hey-HEY," Tal called out and tossed down the rest of his drink. He waved the glass at Bam who filled it again.

"I like Eskimos—all we have to do, us Eskimos, is eat and fuck."

"Phil, you're one louse," Bam said serenely, mixing a Bromo for another customer.

"I been there; a lot," Tal said, sitting sideways and cleaning his eyes. "I shot twenty—I shot fifty polar bears one winter."

"Ya did? why aintcha rich then?" Phil asked, glancing at him briefly and away.

"Om rich. I got money you can't imagine. Om buying a—another stereo tomorrow. That and a new set a suits..."

"Ah!" Phil glanced over at the booths.

"Ja ever know Om a ski champ?"

"Ya. I heard." Phil eased himself from his stool and walked to one of the booths, carrying his drink. He sat down with two other men.

Tal stayed drinking for another hour; he put away nine drinks. While he was drinking, his pride, indefinite but broad and sweet, swelled in him. These people loved him; he honored them by being in the bar.

His money was gone; light-headed he wandered to the door, opened it slowly with a vague wave to the others inside and went out into the now windy and cold night.

When an hour had passed during which he fumbled his way home, sick on the sidewalk twice, he climbed the stairs to his room knowing he would pass out there. Without turning on the light he wrenched off his trousers, jacket and shoes and dropped down on his blankets. A neon sign flashing GERBER'S in pink and orange under his window made soft colors on the ceiling as he slept.

An hour later, hot and confused, he sat up suddenly, and, wanting light, found his way across the room to the bulb and turned it. He stood tense, still confused; his head was only slightly clearer.

He saw something on the linoleum and his heart jolted—a rat? what? He forced himself closer.

It was a large turd. He gazed down at it soberly, wondering what he must do. He must put it somewhere else. What should he pick it up with; he scanned the room and saw his sister's photograph in its cardboard folder. With this he pushed, scraped and finally picked the thing up; infinitely fatigued he threw the picture and its burden into the clutter of the other room.

He switched off the light and started to go back to his bed but there was a pressure on him—something needed to be done out on the street... he hauled his trousers and shoes back on and dizzily went down the stairs, almost falling, making a lot of noise.

"SHODDup!" someone yelled.

Tal, stunned by the cold wind, staggered toward the street and started across; THEY were waiting; THEY wanted him, now, THERE...

130 □

Arnie Fink, tearing along the street on his great glittering motor-cycle to get through the green light, caught Tal's legs and the cycle threw Tal twelve yards to where he struck heavily against a telephone pole. Arnie swung in a circle and slammed to a stop on the slippery street; he stood looking down at Tal's staring eyes, all those teeth . . .

# THE NIGHT SHOOTING
# OF THE SWAN

WALKING IN the early morning mist along Route 81, Kay Trelease thought about Earl's remarks in the bar of the Red Gate Motel the night before. The fields and farms and occasional industrial buildings, the soft air, the smell of clover and hay, came to her only incidentally; she was still back in the midst of the evening preceding.

Earl had become drunk while she had only two of her favorite stingers. Finally he sprawled his torso along the bar with an arm stretched towards her; he exhorted her to stay over until the next day with him.

"Let's start out in my room right now," he pleaded. He farted slightly under the stress and went on, his brown muscular face alternating between a lovely smile and abstracted tears. Hank, the bartender with the bald head and big face, leaned back on his lower liquor shelf listening, occasionally catching Kay's eye and shaking his head.

"Oh, Earlie, you'll be sorry, fella," Hank said as Earl paused to drink some of his whiskey. "I gotta close, friends. One more, Katie?"

Kay handed over her glass and said, "Make that a double. I'm on my last lap and I'm going home to a wedding. And I'm pretty tough now, Earl and Hank, dears." She pushed back her blond hair; her healthy face was serene. Hank placed the drink in front of her and began to count the money in the till. Earl suddenly got off his stool and wove his way through the dark bar to the corridor where the men's room was, hurrying as well as he was able.

"Knew it," Hank said, looking up briefly. "Say, Kay, where'd you start this hike?"

"San Diego, early summer," she said. That had been just after the unpleasantness with Gil and the beginning of divorce proceedings. She recalled Gil's smell, combining deodorant soap and a faint whiff of sweat. She found she was empty of any thought about their beginning, some little love of a sort, Bud's birth after a year and a half.

"How'd ya get started on all these marathons?" Hank asked her, pouring himself a glass of water and drinking deeply.

"Well, by chance, it's all in Syracuse's *Herald*, tomorrow," Kay said. "Because Bill Bowman interviewed me up there. So, you get the papers, don't you?" Hank nodded and said he would look it up.

"See," she said, "It just amounts to my liking walking and wanting to travel and having no money for it. And you better believe, I've seen and heard everything, doing it." She drank briefly as Earl returned unsteadily, white and sweating. He said "You're a great woman, Katie," and slid on to his stool again. "Come on, let's let our hair down and talk."

"That's all we've been doing since supper," Kay said with a tired smile. She finished her drink as Maureen, the waitress, wearing a navy pantsuit that showed her huge bottom mercilessly, walked behind the bar to get herself a nightcap. She was big anyway; tall; she poured out half a tumbler of Southern Comfort and stood looking at Earl. She began to laugh uncontrollably and left them, her buttocks working as she retreated towards the darkened section of the bar.

Earl was watching Kay earnestly.

"I may just go with him to his room," Kay thought, looking at his face that was filled with desire. "Yes," she thought.

As she walked, the next morning, she recalled Earl lying dead asleep on the bed when she had risen, dressed and gone for some breakfast. He was still asleep when she went into the room to get her pack. A dullness, a slight depression met her when she went outside to start the last lap to Binghamton and the wedding; the view just outside was made up of the sweeping concrete of the four lanes of the road, the glaring white guard posts and the small neat vapid ranch-style development across the road.

Now the fair sweet scented morning soothed her and she thought about her son and the girl he was marrying. She remembered other reunions with her son in her past years of heroic walking and how it felt to change from a Personality to being a mother. She knew she didn't look motherly; she was too tall, too strong, too good at what she did most of the time; she wore a look of calm knowledge which had not been there when she had married Gil.

A trailer truck drew up beside her and the driver, red-haired with glasses, thin and ascetic looking, pointed down the road. Kay smiled and shook her head; the driver yelled "Okay—and go to hell!" He ground away and the quiet came down around her again as she went on; she was alone in the September heat. A line of dead elms followed a tumbled creek bed in the pasture land beside the road. A pink trailer stood in the emerging sun and the woman who owned it was putting a laundry basket into her pale rusted Studebaker. The crickets whirred and chirped; the walking made her happy.

Before she'd fallen in with Earl she had been talking to Al Essex at the motel who had been his usual bastard self trying to get the story of her divorce out of her for his crumby sheet; she had not told him much. Now she thought about the last time she had seen Gil. She had cried on the unmade bed as he methodically cleaned out his tackle box and referred at length to scripture, the plastic radio tuned to the usual gospel hour; two thin-voiced women were harmonizing on a hymn.

"You wouldn't cry if you'd stay home and listen to me," he had said, wiping the box out with wet toilet paper. His thinning hair hung over his high shiny forehead and his small hands were slow.

"It's all so damn crude. That's why I'm crying," she had said, getting up. "You get the damn divorce. God wants you to," she added, slamming a bureau drawer so that the green glass lamp over it crashed to the floor.

She couldn't let Al make copy of her sad time.

Often the press talked over her day with her and took her picture; she had sent Bud the one in Salt Lake with the fire chief, giving her autograph. Gil hated to meet Oh all the darn people she dragged home. But Bud, like her, got a kick out of them. They would sit talking late into the night and send out for pizza and beer. Gil wanted corned beef, vegetables and pudding and forbade the beer but they had it anyway. She had the A.T. and T. and the I.B.M. and could manage. She thought about Al's kinky hair and loose wet lips; then Earl's face as he slept. She knew that she would sometime meet a man she would marry. Meanwhile she had her fame, her career and Bud. She looked down at herself; she was wearing blue slacks and a pink tailored shirt with the pack riding comfortably low on her back. She wore sneakers and was tanned darkly.

As she covered the miles through the morning she wondered if Gil had met Sun. She pictured a dark stocky girl with a definite strange smell and thought of goats and arid dirt areas around shacks . . .

The familiar sound of a car slowing came to her and she turned her head. An elderly man in a felt hat in a pickup truck leaned towards her and said "Say, aren't you hot? Want a ride?"

"No, thank you," she said. But she liked him and asked him "What you got back there?" The truckload was covered with a big tarpaulin.

"Got furniture; sellin out and goin to Florida; can't take another winter up here," he said with an awkward wave. He drove off. Kay walked on, watching the junky truck till it was out of sight. The sky was clouding over and a breeze was coming up. A car containing several kids zoomed by and they all yelled "Hi, Kay!" She waved, walking steadily.

Near an intersection she approached a clot of cars and saw the flashing light of a police car. An accident; she had come across several in the past. As she came abreast of the jam she saw two smashed cars at frightening angles on the median. Three people lay near them; she walked over and looked down at them. The one nearest her was a middle-aged man with a torn scalp and useless-looking arms. A fat woman sat heavily at his head and sobbed hysterically; her leg was cut and her dress bloody. "Is he dead?" she asked generally, suddenly. Leaning over on his chest she went on sobbing; Kay saw his hand move and knew he wanted the weight lifted.

"Look, you'll feel better if you sit up and breathe deeply," Kay told her, lifting on the fat inertia of the woman who finally sat up. "Oh GAWD," she shuddered, and went on sobbing.

Kay straightened up and looked at the other two lying near. One was obviously dead with a huge abdominal gash. The other was a teen-age girl who lay quietly with broken legs and a white face, staring around her. The trooper was speaking into his mike urgently. Then he came over.

"All right, people, please go on your way," he said, holding up both hands. "Ambulances are coming. They'll be taken care of." He went to his car and got a blanket which he spread over the dead man. He looked down at Kay who was kneeling beside the young girl. "Ma'am, would you please move your car on down the road?" he said to her. She told him she was on foot; he turned and began briskly getting the cars away, standing in the middle of the concrete. Slowly the crowd dispersed.

When they had gone he picked up a large piece of metal sheared from one of the cars which he tossed on the grass. He went over to Kay and said, "You're someone I've read about, aren't you?"

"Yes. I wish I had some brandy for her," Kay said. "And for you."

Sirens sounded in the distance. "Like you to come with me as a witness if you don't mind," he said. Kay nodded as two ambulances came up and stopped. They put the victims inside and, turning up the sirens again, hurried off down the highway. Kay, the trooper and a plump young man in a basketball shirt and jeans were left in the big silence with the two wrecks. A tow truck arrived and the trooper filled in the time making out his report in his notebook. Kay sat on the warm grass and talked briefly to Ken, the other witness.

The trooper at length came over to them and said "Shall we?" soberly. He pointed to his car, went to it and got in, and Kay got in beside him. Ken followed in a Mustang covered with mud.

They drove to the troopers' headquarters down the highway about five miles, set between an apple green split-level and a huge metal barn. It was a tranquil orderly place and in it it seemed as if the accident had not happened. Kay described what she had seen and Ken gave his account of how the Buick tried to pass just when the Fairlane pulled out to pass too and said that the dead man had been thrown about thirty feet.

The trooper's name was Guy Schrader; he wrote down what they said in an even, thoughtful way and took his reports to the next room. The rain began to fall. Kay was sitting beside a green metal desk with her pack beside her waiting to leave. Guy returned and sat on the edge of the desk looking at her. He picked up a ballpoint pen and fiddled with it.

"I think I better run you down the road to the motel; raining and all," he said.

Kay looked at his calm face and dark smooth hair; she liked him, but then she always liked all the troopers.

Ken had left in a spurt of gravel. Guy said "Well, let's go". He picked up his hat and held the door for her. Kay went out and got in the car; it was now pouring. He got in beside her and at first they drove in silence.

"See many of those?" he asked, keeping at a steady fifty-eight.

"Yes, here and there; never this bad, though."

"Where are you headed?"

"Binghamton. To my son's wedding, tonight." She added that he was marrying an Indian girl. Guy thought that over and then said that was nice and he liked the Indians. He passed a gray Ford driven by an old lady who seemed afraid of the rain.

"Well, why don't I take you there?" Guy asked after a pause. "When is the thing?"

"As soon as I get there."

"You don't have to walk this last bit, do you?"

"No; I really ought to get there for the kids." Kay looked at him. "Are you off duty now?"

"Oh yuh. Now, here's Rudy's place. I'm stopping here so we can get something to eat; okay, then we'll head for town. Get there in about an hour." He turned off into the lot of an acidly green diner and they got out and hurried inside.

Eating their hamburgers they spoke of traffic and hitchhikers. Kay saw Guy looking at her appraisingly. She was used to being looked at by men and she always looked back equally frankly.

"Ever get tired?" Guy asked, picking up the check.

"Not often." She was surprised; men never asked that question; women always did.

They hurried back into the car; on the drive to the city they did not talk a great deal. He asked what sort of wedding it would be; she said she didn't know but probably very plain. "Indian, maybe," she suddenly speculated.

When they reached Binghamton she gave the address on Murray Street and they pulled up in front of a gray clapboarded house with a small yard in front. The rain had stopped; it was damp and warm. He saw her to the door and she said, realizing that she did not want him to go, "Come in and meet whoever's here."

They went in the unlocked door and Kay called "Hello!" A television was on in the room to the right of the hall and they entered. Bud, a shadow on the sofa with another shadow next to him, saw them and said "Hey, HI!"

He got up and hugged Kay. Guy and Bud shook hands; Bud turned on the lamp on the cluttered table. "Here's Sun," he said as the tall dark girl stood. She shook Kay's hand and said, simply, "Hello." While the TV show murmured on they sat down and looked each other over.

"How'd it go, Maw?" Bud asked.

"I had fun, as usual, sonny," she said, smiling. She looked at Sun. "Are you all set for the wedding now?"

"It will be tonight at the place on the river you know", Sun said. Her eyes were black and calm.

"Jerry's?"

"Yes. At six. Johnnie Wing will do it," Sun said seriously. "He's nice."

Kay remembered the young clergyman she had met one afternoon when Bud brought him home; he wore mod clothes and long hair. Jerry's she knew well, a place to get a rough good meal and to square dance; hunters stopped there but she remembered some strange types too; Joe Meany and Len Goudy came to mind, two hairy husky men who wore business suits and satin ties, and dark silent hunched women with overdone hair; Dean Pollack from the sports club, who was tall and shifty-eyed and walked with a limp; it was said he hit women and he brought fear with him; a black common-law couple, Helen and Fred, were always there and well into the booze. When Tibor wasn't there to call dances they listened to the hulking juke box by the stairs.

Jerry's was a large rambling low building with a lot of empty boxes and cartons and gear strewn around outside; at night a string of colored lights dangled from the trees and a small half-lit sign saying JERRY'S hung from a rusted pole at the macadam's edge. Jerry was the cook and owner; he wore crisp dirty white pants and shirt and Lois, his wife, large with dyed hair and a dressy blouse and skirt, tended bar. This was the club and a kind of home for the people who went there. There were few teen-agers in the crowd but married couples and couples who were living together found plenty of company. Kay and Bud had gone there with various people that came to their house through the years.

In the small room of the gray house they talked for an hour about plans for the wedding, Kay's travels and the accident. Gil was not mentioned. Kay asked Guy if he would like to come to the wedding and he said Yes.

Bud and Sun left the room to make minor changes in their dress; Kay made coffee and she and Guy drank it in the big messy kitchen. She told Guy she was impressed by the girl and he said OH yuh. He tipped back in his chair, slapped his chest idly and yawned. "Nice boy, Bud," he said. "His father dead?"

Kay explained briefly. "He won't be coming tonight," she said. "He never would have any part of Jerry's or any other bar." She guessed she could go to the wedding dressed as she was; Sun and Bud in pants; Lois; Fred and Helen; the whole crew; yes, she'd stay herself.

At quarter to six they were all in the front hall and subdued. Bud had shaved; Sun had put on a large necklace. Guy and Kay left to go in the police car and Sun and Bud followed in his Pinto. They drove swiftly to the edge of town where they got on to the River Road; the houses petered out and they drove with the windows open to the warm evening air. Jerry's sign stuck out; they turned into the lot where the usual junk, now soaked with rain, lay around.

Jerry came out on the kitchen porch and yelled "Hey-hey!", waving. They went up the splintery steps into the dining room where three dim orange lights were lit; the juke box played *Raindrops Keep Falling On My Head* loudly. Lois was having herself a short one by the bar.

"Ah!" Johnnie came through from the kitchen in a tan suit and bright tie. His hair hung to his shoulders and he had started a thin moustache.

"Jer! they're startin," Lois bawled.

Jerry came into the room blowing his nose. Kay and Guy went over by a window that faced the muddy river where Johnnie, Bud and Sun stood.

The ceremony, with the juke box shut off, took seven minutes. There was no ring. Kay looked at the two kids and wondered why she couldn't lump up a little; she found this was great. Guy had taken off his hat and stood quietly watching. Then Johnnie said they were man and wife; Guy brought his big hands together in a great clap; Fred came out of the corner and put a quarter in the machine and a rock tune hollered forth; Lois said "Free drinks—c'mon, gang," and went behind the bar.

Seated around a painted orange table with highballs in front of them they looked around the big dim room and back at each other. Bud toasted Sun; Johnnie, who seemed already to have had a few, toasted the couple; Helen drifted over and pulled up a chromium chair near Kay and toasted her trip, her whiskey breath enveloping Kay. Guy drank slowly but with pleasure.

Jerry called from his doorway they could order when they wanted to; they got him over for a drink. He sat steamily on a chair beside Guy and looked at him guiltily from time to time. The door slammed open from the parking lot and Dean Pollack came in with a shotgun slung under his arm; his eyes were a watery red and he went directly to the bar. Lois served him in silence and stood the pinch bottle near his hand. When he had had three quick ones he left the bar and went to sit near the door at his usual table with his glass and bottle. Every so often he sighted along the gun, pointing it at the open door. Guy's back was to him and he did not see this.

"Kay Trelease!" Dean yelled suddenly, seeing her. "C'mere!" As she got up and approached he yelled "AHHHHHHH! You been away a helluva long time, baby girl." As if to punctuate his thinking he sighted along the gun at her and then at the doorway.

"Hi, Dean," she said, looking down at him. "You missed the wedding."

"Wedding? oh, shit," he said, glaring at the table where the others sat. "Who? Who did that dumb thing? not Freddie and Hel?"

Kay told him, lifted her glass to him, and went back to their table. She had just seen Dean sighting again along the gun at the door and then a roar filled the room as he fired.

"Well, goddam, I got sumpn," he said, laying the gun carefully on his table and getting up. He went out and in a minute came back carrying the limp body of a swan. "God a goddamn swan," he said proudly, holding it up by one wing. "Say," he said to Guy. "Is swans around here? I ditn never see any."

For the first time Kay saw Guy smile. "There were two on the Susquehanna here; saw in the paper. Guess now there's just one."

Dean came to the table holding out the big bird. "I wanna give Kay Trelease a swan buhcuz she's a great gal and she's f-famous," he said. "Get Jer to cook it for you. Wedding roast, like." He flopped the swan down on the table and stood looking at it, swaying.

"All RIGHT. It's not going to be eaten," Kay said, standing. "I know a spot near here where it's going; where a swan should go." She gathered the swan to her with difficulty and went to the door, the swan's head hanging over her arm.

"Dammit, Kay, don't," Dean said, crossing the room after her.

Sun suddenly got up and hurried after Kay, passing Dean without a look. Together she and Kay went through the door. They paused on the porch and picked a shovel out of the clutter. Dean moved to a window to watch where they went; from his place he said, "They're just in them ferns on the edge of the lot." He watched for a good while. The rest of the group waited quietly and drank.

Finally he said with surprise, "They done it. They buried that swan."

Kay and Sun returned then; in silence they finished their drinks.

Jerry brought the dinners and, subdued now, they all ate the stewed chicken, mashed potatoes and mixed peas and carrots.

Then Bud and Sun left, going quietly out the door into the soft damp night. Guy said to Kay, "Shall we have one more and then go?"

"Let's leave now. I'm depressed."

Kay and Guy went out to the car and got in; Guy, without asking Kay's views, drove to the house on Murray and went inside with her.

"I got a favorite program on TV," he said, pushing buttons. He found the detective story and sat down contentedly. Kay, too, sat down; comfortably they became absorbed.

# THE RED HOUSE

A TERRIBLE place. Alone in a terrible place.

She stood in the musty room where faded cracked shades were pulled down over the long dirty windows; she did not want to sit down on the sagging cot where a stained khaki blanket covered the thin mattress. A locked door painted brown like the rest of the woodwork in what must have been the parlor caught her eye. She saw it would let in light and air if it could be opened.

She turned the lock and dragged on the door which opened a foot and stuck; she could smell the sour rust on the flimsy screen door; beyond was a neglected sunny hot meadow stretching a long way down to the cove. The persistent monotony of insects hummed maddeningly; this was the worst hangover she had ever endured.

A terrible place to be with a hangover; to be alone, by herself with another hangover . . .

The long drive from the city had been hell, hot, exhausting, frightening; but at the end she would reach her house, her new home, standing among spruce, granite and clear sky and water, so pure, so enduring . . . she could think. She would at last think well, and long, and she would be free.

She was nauseated and her eyes and head ached. She couldn't act; she would go mad if she went for a swim; madder yet if she walked into the fresh scented woods close to the back of the house.

She wanted to find oblivion in sleep but she was so alone; she sensed her exhausted bones inside her disgusting flesh; her brains were there, loathsome, not to be jettisoned; she was poisoned, false, filthy—perhaps, too, she remembered in a surge of nausea, pregnant . . .

She must do something.

She squeezed through the doorway, stepped down to a granite stone to find herself in the strong sunlight. Beside the door were huge sweet-smelling ferns and a tangle of alizarin rambling roses. Bees flew among the blossoms; silently a small bird swept past on its own journey somewhere. Its passage dizzied her.

She moved into the meadow and circled the house, trying to feel a sense of ownership. The red paint on it was very old and peeling; the windows, empty, had a malign repelling quality. They were set in white painted frames.

Facing the slope to the small lake and some scattered bushes was a porch; it had a weak looking railing and stood high; surrounding it on two sides was a burgeoning stand of raspberry bushes. The steps were old and splintered; she sat down on the lowest and shut her eyes.

Swept with horror as she did this she opened them and took off her chic clogs; barefoot she felt a small gratification in the air on her tortured feet.

There was no breeze; no other human; there were no clouds in the enormous impersonal sky. She could take no more Empirin yet; possibly coffee . . . she did not move. The coffee was among the random groceries she had thrown together in her apartment under her other possessions; agony to haul them out of the car.

A large water bird rose flapping from the reeds in the cove and silently, slowly, low over the water, passed into the olive shadows on the far side.

Her mouth, partly open to ease her headache, stretched wide in a silent reaction to the size and silence around her. Nothing—nothing would help. Except a night's sleep and how could she endure the coming of the great night on top of what she felt now—how fall asleep encased in herself?

Winter. The image of this place in winter suddenly came to her, calming and enlarging her; there would be the beauty of stars, snow, all so pure; she would be very different; she would feed the deer, the small animals. She did not think of what means she might have for getting to the store, five miles steeply down the mountain; she thought of snugness, safety, peace. Other people had them; now, too, she could . . .

She had shrieked, pressed, gouged, talked, handled, worked, writhed, shoved, climbed—forever. Somehow she had shoved and shrieked herself through phenomena to this spot, a goal. She must add it up—draw conclusions—leave and desist; call a halt, emerge, surmount.

Nausea clutched; she leaned to retch over the raspberries; nothing came, however, but more pain in her head.

She dragged herself through the meadow to the dirt lane where her old convertible stood and forced herself to unload it, returning slowly to the kitchen door which was open to drop everything on the floor there. At last she came across two cartons of food; she pumped first rusty water, then icy and clear, from the old pump in the iron sink. She made herself a strong cold brew with it and some Maxwell House Instant and holding the stein it was in she wandered through the five small downstairs rooms. In each the shades shut out the sun; there were pieces of second-rate dark furniture in all. Old linoleum covered the floors; the walls were unplastered, two-by-fours jutted at intervals throughout. In one room was a kerosene stove, rusted and dusty; the kitchen contained the large black iron stove, a table, shelves, one chair and the sink.

Nailed up here and there were a few oddly shaped branches; a lithographic calendar hung crookedly in the kitchen; it was dated 1931.

She ended her tour in the kitchen and sat down. On the floor at her feet was Egon's farewell present, a bottle of champagne with a wide yellow bow on it. It lay warm and repellent on its side, nauseating... she recalled the farewell party at Hamish's apartment—her own manipulating and crowded remarks, the many kisses from everyone; the crowd was faceless now though Edith and Laura were clear enough, gazing amused at her from a long way off, cool, sober, at one with life...

Egon had read something very witty from *Penthouse*—what was it; there had been the usual gallons of good liquor and some sort of supper during the evening at Maury's down the street. She could not really remember what Egon looked like now, or any of them. They were gone—but they always had been gone. She wished someone were here now, at the start—just overnight till she got a grip on herself. Perhaps she would have to stay up the whole time and simply endure... in her hypertense state now she felt the weight and growth-effort of everything nearby—the trees, bushes, grass, flowers, birds; she felt the weight of the lake's water; she was gravity personified.

All the things she had wanted, obtained, dealt with; all the efforts, every bit of conversation crowded her now and suffocated. The coffee made her ill. She ought to go upstairs and open a window; she could not. What might she find—a skeleton; certainly; certainly a skeleton. She tried to see herself as a character in a book—a long rich fine subtle and powerful story...

No. Nothing. I'm without. Outside. Ill. Alone and it's horrible. What have I done?

I ought to leave. Why not...

Her exhaustion was total; she wept into her lap. In the past she had inspired and bolstered herself at trying times by conjuring with single evocative words: history; peace; the sea... Now these did not work.

She heard something; immediately it seemed good; what is that—an automobile approaching—nearer, nearer...

Someone is here. Oh, you, she said shudderingly, fearfully, hopefully: who? She stood and moved to look out of the door. She saw a neat dark red car coming to a halt, parking beside hers.

A slim man in jacket, tie and dark slacks got out slowly. He stood looking for a minute over at the house. Then he strolled towards the kitchen door.

Oriental. By god he's Chinese or something—now what.

She heard his shoes in the grass and then a light voice saying "Pleess?" She stepped to the doorway and said hello. She had not spoken to anyone all day, she realized. She actually could still communicate.

"I am Dr. Kim. May I walk to the water?"

"Certainly." She watched him go past the corner of the house and out of sight; she went to the front room and jerked the shade to one side to watch him. Saved. Oh dear Oriental, you're my darling . . . she saw him stop by a bush and finger a leaf, then descend to the shore. He stood, hands in pockets, turning his head to look at it all.

"Oh you Kim-kid, come and save Super-Prune . . ." She suddenly recalled the champagne and went swiftly to the messy kitchen to plunge it in cold water. Wryly she observed all her old pattern fly into action. But he won't want Super-Prune after the lovely quiet shore. Maybe he's an *ominosity*. To be fled from.

But she searched her gear for a second container and threw her coffee out the back door. She found she could tolerate the thought of a cigarette and located the fresh carton under the lettuce and flour. And she knew in the infinite scheme of things she was a phony.

. . . but just to get me through these few hours, she pleaded firmly with the Great No-One.

After fifteen minutes she again heard steps and a knocking. She went to the door; Dr. Kim was smiling widely and made as if to come up the step. She held the door for him.

"You are—who?"

"Bijou Bloom."

"This is your house?"

"Yes, as of one hour ago." Bijou saw the dry spiky short black hair and slanted black eyes, the spotless clothes. "You're ahead of me—I haven't been to the shore yet."

She gestured at the champagne. "Would you celebrate in a sort of messy housewarming with me—do you like champagne?"

"Ah. Yesss—very happy thought." Dr. Kim moved to the sink and lifted the bottle out. "I shall discork it, yesss?" He did so neatly. Bijou held the stein and a red tumbler and he filled each. She handed him the stein in a rush of good feeling, sure that a bit of wine would subdue her sick feelings.

"Well—let's go outdoors and sit on the steps out front." She led the way. Dr. Kim courteously waited for her to choose the spot she wished to occupy and then lowered himself to the step.

"I should like to be up there flying in a plane," he said, looking off into the sky. "Do you care to fly?"

"Oh, yes."

"I must of course have lessons." He drank. "You should not smoke, you know." He regarded her cigarette. "I have never." He looked peacefully down the meadow. "You will live here alone, Miss Bloom?"

"I plan to, yes." She continued to smoke. The champagne, or the thought of it, was making her feel better. She liked this man. "Where do you practice?"

"Nowhere yet. I am just come here, from Korea. I shall make much money and return to my bride."

"You're just married?"

"No. Parents have chosen. When I return." He took a small sip. "Now I look around me, everywhere; I shall work later."

"Do you miss Korea?"

"No. I like, here; like, everywhere." He turned interestedly to her. "Hoboken? you have been?"

"Ah, yes. Dreadful."

"Oh, no. It I like. Is really hell, yes? But one must see all. I have had fine hot dog in Hoboken." He smiled widely. "I do like the hot dog."

"I do see, yes," Bijou said, nodding. "If I were hungry and ate one in Hoboken, I'd like it."

"You should have man; here is fine for man." He looked around appreciatively. Bijou thought he was offering himself but he added, "Farmer, yes? I myself must have the city, machines, all that. I am very strange in Korea, they say." He drank again and looked at her keenly. "You will be alone here?"

"Yes."

"Not good. No. Too young." He shook his head decisively. "A good farmer, so. A nice, a nice-looking farmer, strong." He looked again towards the water where a merganser was leading her three ducklings in a swim. "You are rich?"

"Ahahaha. No. But up here I won't need much."

"And you will occupy yourself how?"

"I expect to fix up my house, paint it, have a garden—oh, two, vegetable and flowers and herbs. To begin with."

"Good, good. The gentle life. And you will walk and swim. Good."

"I've always wanted this kind of place. My one objection here is there's no fireplace. But that's minor, I'll have the great big old stove. Probably sleep in the kitchen in cold weather."

"You cook well, perhaps?"

"I will; I promised myself that." Bijou swallowed largely of her champagne. The future ballooned attractively now. She looked at his small neat hands clasped around his small knee. She had never been attracted by small men. "Next time you come I'll make you a real New England dinner with roast chicken and corn and blueberry pie. How's that sound?"

"I shall be happy, yes. Next summer, I vacation here, nearby. Or, perhaps, fly here in plane. I could land—no, I could not land here—though, on water, yes . . ." He smiled, pleased; there were no problems for him.

An orange butterfly alighted on Bijou's foot and stayed briefly. The hay smelled lovely; her sickness had passed.

"You aren't drinking—you don't really like champagne?"

"Ah, I drink very slowly, and not very much—I do not like to be affected too much. There is too much else to do and also to look at." He sipped a little. "Ah, yes, it tastes very well." Then he set his stein down and stood. "But I must drive away now. I must find a place to rest; I have driven from Boston." He looked down at her, smiled widely once more and descended the steps. "I shall reappear, next summer for your good meal, Miss Bloom." He bowed slightly and moved away through the hay to his car.

She watched him go with a feeling of loss; she drank the last of her glassful and went to the kitchen with his stein which she planned to finish. She heard his car driving away.

Silence.

She walked through the house slowly, holding the stein and pulling up the dry old shades. Once again in the parlor she was working on the last window and was startled as she released the cracked shade to see someone looking in, very close to the house.

It was a big fat woman in a dirty light green pantsuit; her face was mottled and her gray hair kinky, long and also dirty. As she saw the shade rise she grinned and showed a set of upper false teeth. She waded around to the door and squalled "Hey!"

Bijou met her and together they wrenched the door open wide enough to admit the woman.

"Say," she panted. "I ain't never been inside here. Never could see nothin lookin through them windas neither." She put her hands on her fat hips and walked through the rooms satisfying her curiosity. Bijou followed her, smelling fat and kerosene on her.

"Say. This wine?" The woman lifted the bottle and looked at it against the light to see how much was left.

"Pour yourself some, lady," Bijou said, picking up the red glass; she held it while the woman dumped champagne in it. She gulped avidly and then grinned, seating herself on the chair with her large thighs spread.

"I'm May. May Russo. I'm yer neighbor. Live up in them woods. I heard them cars. No one ever comes here so I thought I'd walk on over." May stared at Bijou, looking over her figure, clothes and face. "Visitin?"

"No, I bought this place. I'm living here."

"Look kinda thin fer the work." May wiped her large nose with the back of her hand.

"Oh, I'm very tough," Bijou said, leaning on the stove. She found she welcomed the old slut who helped her shut away her hangover.

"Say, gimme smore," May said, holding out her glass. Her hand shook slightly. "I got me a nice trailer off over towards Snells'."

"Snells'?"

"Them's got the green bungalow onto Rowt one-two-nine. Right next ta the sand pit." May swallowed more wine and scratched her armpit. "Say, this all ya brought?" She leaned over with difficulty and searched loosely through a carton.

"More's being shipped by my friend," Bijou said, thinking of Egon, trim, brown, urbane, seeing to her furniture and clothes. Suddenly she longed for him. Perhaps he would drive up. She'd invite him—

"Oh, I got a real nice trailer. You got to come eat with me some-time . . . right through them woods, hon. I'll have some pizza and—ya like gin? that; and some—oh, lotsa nice stuff, just the two of us. My husband—that turd—went off. Just went off. Howdya like that. Turd." May finished her champagne and drained the rest of the bottle into her glass. The room had darkened suddenly; Bijou saw the sky was a dark bruise color. A storm was coming. She mentioned this to May who, fortified, entertained and not busy, laughed and said Oh, she'd stick around till it was over. She ditn mind no rain.

"Say, what's the upstairs like? bet it's hot." She got up and went looking for the stairs.

They were shoddy, they shook, leading up from the front room. Bijou followed the large green rump to the very hot second floor where two rooms, filled with cartons, old magazines, and some mildewed old clothes, baked under the sloping roof. Squirrels had nested everywhere. The floorboards had been painted gray and had inch-wide cracks between them; she could see down to the floor below. Each room had two small windows at each end, nailed shut.

"Ya gonna live here alone?" May asked in a worried way. "Them hunters—them ya gotta look out fer. I sure do. Lock everything."

Rain began to fall on the roof over their heads; soon it was torrential and leaked down on the clutter and on them.

"Let's go down," Bijou said, suddenly utterly fatigued. She descended and went to the kitchen; she could hear May going through the boxes. "Kin I have soma them magazines?" she squalled through the floor.

"Sure," Bijou called back, making herself another cup of cold coffee. She sat down to drink it, looking out at the soaking meadow. May was silent, evidently having found something to read.

There was no sound but the rain and gusts of wind bending the trees in the nearby dark woods.

Bijou could not think past this moment solid with ugliness; she saw that the earth here did not belong to her . . .

As the storm continued Bijou tried to interest herself in taking her things from the cartons and perhaps lighting a friendly fire in the stove; after a short search she found there was no wood. She gave up. Eventually she moved to the sagging cot in the parlor, lay down and gave way to memories, now, of the city.

May, silently having her steamy being upstairs, did not make a sound but her personality mingled depressingly with the storm.

The wild beauty of the country was still there somewhere, Bijou thought despairingly.

# THE BULLHORN

THE TALL bare trees rocked in the March wind against a dark sky as Dan Pettengill walked up Storch Road on his way home from Senior Woodworking at school. His pea jacket pocket bulged where he had put the lignum vitae armadillo he was working on and had almost finished; he wanted to show it around now; Mr. Rand at the school had loved it as he did and spent a lot of time with him describing wood carvings he had made; he'd even invited Dan to come to his house to look at them.

The wind was cold and fresh; the noise it made almost drowned out the call of the chickadees but Dan could hear them and a flicker, too. The weeds by the dirt road were orange and puce; dead goldenrod was everywhere and the last of the snow filled crevices in the shale rock. There was a slight touch of the sweet smell of spring and because of this Dan thought he would take the longer cut through the woods so he could enjoy more of it. This would take him past the shack where the strange man lived with all his cats; Dan was used to him, Carl Mowat, and thought he might like to see his carving.

He turned off Storch into the lane going up through Steffan's woods; there was less wind but he could see the tree tops waving wildly and hear it more here. The ground was spongy and there was more snow; Dan wore his Sears boots and was comfortable.

He walked for a quarter of an hour along the lane, noticing prints of small animals in the snow and in one open patch some arbutus starting. He found he was hungry; when he reached home on the creek he could fry up some eggs.

Now ahead of him he could see, through the trees, Carl's shack, partly obscured by a thicket of sumach and raspberry. Smoke rose from the tilted chimney; Carl was there.

As Dan came out of the woods he saw a car parked on a slant in the rutted lane; it was the State Police. Dan went to the car and looked in;

it might be Leo's. A woman sat in the front seat with her arms folded over her large stomach. She was fairly old, Dan thought; in her thirties. He did not recognize her.

"Is this Leo's car?" he asked her.

She leaned over and rolled the window down on his side. "What? Oh, yeah," she answered. Her face was white and smooth like a cake of soap. She had dry brown hair pushed back over her ears; she wore no makeup. She was unattractive, Dan thought.

"Leo inside?"

"You damn well bet he is," she said violently.

Dan turned towards the shack; he went to it and knocked. There was a subdued conversation in progress; no one came to the door. He knocked louder; the door was wrenched open by Leo, large in his state trooper uniform. Dan had never seen his brother in action till this moment.

"Whayya want?" Leo said. Obviously he didn't want to be bothered with Dan just now.

"I came to see Carl," Dan said. "Got something I thought he'd like to see." He yanked the carving from his pocket. A warm pleasant smell of wood smoke and kerosene came through the door.

"Well, you can't come in now," Leo said, glancing behind him into the room where a tall thin dirty man sat by a table. Dan knew the man was in trouble and knew what kind.

"Okay." Dan turned away; Leo shut the door.

"Say," the woman yelled to him. "You know that guy?"

"I know both of them," Dan said, going over to the car.

"Is he nuts like they say?" she leaned across the seat, her dusty dark blue coat and cotton dress stretched across her belly.

"Seems all right to me when I go there," Dan said. One of Carl's cats rubbed against his leg; he looked down; three young kittens were with her. "My ma went to school with Carl and she says he was all right then." He stooped and picked up a kitten. "Like cats?" he asked her, holding it so she could take it.

"God, no," she said, drawing back. "Get that thing away from me. Carl done this to me," she said, laying an impatient hand on her stomach.

"Why, where do you live?" Dan asked her.

"In town. He come in for some groceries a couple times down near where I live—down to Loblaw's—I met'm at Gerber's Grill. I go there for a beer sometimes, you know." She stopped talking and gazed out ahead of her through the windshield at a sere ochre field rimmed with the tossing trees.

Dan knew Chatham well enough to know where Gerber's was and knew it was a lousy stretch of town.

"Well, cut'n ya tell, yourself?" he asked her.

"Everybody's nuts," she said, still staring unseeing at the field.

Dan looked away from her into the back seat of his brother's car, still stroking the kitten. He saw a bullhorn on the back seat; wondering if Leo'd planned to use it on Carl, he said, "Can't ya go in there?"

"Hell, I dowanna go in," the woman said, yanking her coat closer around herself. "Goddamn men," she said quietly. Her mouth jerked into ugly crying and the tears weren't even the clear drops Dan was used to when his mother or Helen, his sister, cried; he realized they both cried a lot and he was used to it. His mother cried every time she thought about her dead husband; Helen cried when she couldn't have things, which she seemed to feel bad about practically every day.

The kitten mewed frantically and began to claw him; he put it down. "I gotta go home," he said. The weeping woman didn't even look at him.

Dan went on down the lane to Route 131 which would take him to Red Kill, the creek where he lived. He felt very sorry he couldn't show the carving to Carl; he realized too he'd wanted to go in and get some more of the good smell. His own house smelled sweet from all the air fresheners his mother bought and sprayed around; they smelled awful.

He went, now downhill, along the macadam in the wind which seemed to be getting up to storm force; the dry hay in the field beside the road lay almost flat; the clouds raced and a few drops of rain smacked his face. The birds were blown off their courses; he wondered why they tried in this weather.

As he approached his home he thought about the bullhorn and it being used on Carl. Carl must have some sort of gun. He'd go on down to Red's and discuss it with him after he ate.

The dirt driveway off Route 131 leading to his mother's house started with a rough bridge across the kill and led along it for about a half mile. He passed Cuddy's where Ed did the body work and then he passed the Jews' house where they had the Lincoln. It stood beside the bright new brick, shining and low. Someone was standing looking out the window; maybe it was Diane but he couldn't tell. Cuddys and Goldsteins and his own family all did a lot of looking out the windows.

Now he went along the stretch where there wasn't any room for houses; beyond that he could see the swollen bare apple green of his house with the pumpkin trim. The lane leading to it became narrow because theirs was the last house.

He crossed the muddy March-wet patch that would have been lawn and went up the two splintery wooden unpainted steps to the front door; from there he went into the kitchen at the side and found Helen eating marshmallow cookies; she was writing on lined paper. Food was everywhere in the stuffed hot steamy kitchen; half-used loaves of brightly wrapped bread, cartons of dusty empties, a half full bottle of his mother's Milk of Magnesia; boxes of crackers, packages of sandwich cookies, cans of Carnation, all open; there were many cellophane bags of bright cheap candy, all partly used up; there were two large size cans of Spaghetti Os standing on the table where Helen sat beside two cartons of king size Pall Malls. A pile of dirty clothes overflowed two bent cartons by the table. On the salmon pink paint of the wall by the stove a rattlesnake skin was nailed up near a network of cords and wires attaching to a pink shaded boudoir lamp, which was on, and a green plastic cracked radio was near the sink. The milk company's calendar hung on another wall where there was also a framed picture of a too-smiling Helen, tinted; she was wearing her graduation things.

Dan opened the refrigerator door and got out a half-empty carton of small eggs and busied himself frying five. Helen, not looking up, said "What rhymes with pretty?"

"Shitty," he said. Helen was writing some more greeting card verse; it was all she did now that Artistic Card took the first one two months ago and paid her five dollars. Dan hated the verses she wrote; he knew, however, that she'd immediately read to him what she'd produced that day. He hurried his cooking all he could.

"Aw. No." She concentrated. "What about kitty?" She thought and wrote something, making flourishes in pencil.

Dan lifted the eggs from the pan and put them on a white plate with a black and mustard floral design around the edge; he sat at the table next to a large green overflowing ashtray and ate them quickly. He was thinking about the bullhorn and Carl. Leo would be in for his dinner soon and he could try to get the story then.

"Dan—cmere," his mother squalled from the next room.

Dan went from the kitchen to the small cluttered room where his mother, fat in a flowered pink and black house dress, was sunk in an overstuffed chair covered with a black and gold throw. A small dusty television set was tuned to a quiz show.

"Leo's gone over to Crazy Carl's," she said, helping herself to Cheezits from a bag on a chair pulled over beside her. A large cat that had sick eyes sat malignantly on a pile of comics on the linoleum floor.

"I seen him there," Dan said, pulling off his jacket. "Some woman was in his car gonna have a baby."

"Gonna have a crazy baby," his mother said contentedly.

"I like Carl," Dan said, taking a fist full of Cheezits. "Lookit." He pulled his carving from his jacket pocket.

"Huhn," his mother said, glancing at it but not taking it. "The hell's that?" Dan told her and also about Mr. Rand. His mother was only interested in Crazy Carl. "Tser name," she asked him.

"Don't know. She cried," Dan said. "Guess she boozes it up."

"Ah!" his mother squalled triumphantly. "See why I say don't git the habit, you kids. I seen ya come outta Bus' bar, you and Red and that Bernie—that Bernie's always there boozin—I seen im layin along the road more'n once. Now see what ya get into. Get the girls fat, swhat."

The cat lay down uncomfortably. His mother had more crackers.

The back door crashed; Leo came through the kitchen to them. He kept his trooper's hat on; Dan knew he was stuck on himself in that hat.

"Got the woman with ya," Dan's mother asked, hauling herself out of her chair to go look out of the window.

"No."

Leo sat down on a plastic hassock. His gun bulged at his hip. He was big but not yet fat. He had a bland big face, small blue eyes and Dan's dark hair. They were not alike.

"What were you doin at Carl's," he asked Dan.

"Cuttin through. To show him this," Dan said, holding out the armadillo. Leo took it and studied it briefly. But he only said, "Ought to keep away from Carl. Just took him to town. Jail overnight. Nearly done rape, according to Cora. That's the woman."

"Was she cryin yet?" his mother asked avidly. "She pregnant, hahn?"

"Oh yuh," Leo said, putting the carving down and cleaning his nails. "Took her home. Bawled the whole way. What a dump. Down by Gerber's, East Main. All the tramps live around there."

"Boy you guys see everythin," his mother said, her small eyes hotly alive. "Well. Got to get them Sphaghetti Os hot." She smoothed her hands over her flowing hips and went out to the kitchen.

"Spaghetti again," Leo said in disgust, at last taking his hat off and putting it on a divan loaded with rough dry laundry, a gray and maroon towel folded on top. A pair of hip boots stood beside it.

Dan put his jacket back on and went out. As he passed Leo's car he again saw the bullhorn in the back. He wanted it; opening the rear door he took it out, slammed the door and went down the lane with it to show Red.

He had to walk down 131 to get to the trailer where Red lived. It was still raining and the wind tore at him.

"Hmmmmm," he said experimentally into the horn. Nothing happened; he looked for a switch and figured out how it worked. "Ahhhh!" he said and found the sound wonderfully loud. He walked for five minutes until he came to the depression in the field where the aqua trailer stood, desolate in the rain.

He stood outside and speaking into the horn said "Red, come out with your hands up—we know you're in there."

The door opened with a crash and Red stood in the doorway. At first he looked scared; seeing Dan, he began to laugh; he came over to Dan and reached for the horn. "SHIT!" he yelled into it feelingly. "FUCK YOU!" He turned to Dan and said "I ADORE you!" Dan hit him on the arm and they roared with laughter till they staggered.

"Let's have some fun with Bernie if he's down to Bus' place," Dan said, taking back the horn.

"Yah," Red said enthusiastically; they set out down the hill toward Bus', taking turns muttering into the horn, laughing hoarsely and hitting each other.

"Got any money?" Red said into the horn as the rain increased.

"Yuss, a buck, you shithead," Dan said, into the horn. A car passed in a rush, spraying them with water.

In ten minutes they came to Bus', a low cinder block building in among some second growth trees with neon Schlitz and Budweiser signs in the steamy windows. They went through burdock and briar underbrush to hold their hands by their faces, looking for Bernie at the bar.

"There he is," Dan said. "Lookit, he's gittin drunk." Red looked and said "Gimme the horn." He got back through the weeds and stood in the road. "Come on out, Bernie Shapley—we know you're in there—come on out with your hands up!" Red laughed delightedly. "Get the hell out here!" He and Dan moved towards the doorway. Dan took the horn and said "Lemme. I don't guess he heardja."

Into the horn he said "We gotcha this time, Shapley. Come out with your hands up!"

The door suddenly jerked open and Bernie started out, a shotgun in his dirty hands. He fired immediately at the two boys, who fell slowly in the wet road. Bernie yelled something and four men ran past him from the bar. Bus with his white hair plastered to his flat head shoved past them and grabbed the gun. He went over to Red who was nearest and who moved a little. "Bernie," Red said. "We was kiddin." He began to cry.

"This one's dead," a man in a hunting jacket said, stooping over Dan. It was pouring rain now. "Jesus."

"Get em inside," Bus said, pulling on Red's arms. A man in overalls and sweatshirt took Red's legs and they took him inside and laid him on the floor next to the Arcola heater. The other men brought Dan inside and put him down. Dazed, Bernie, a stocky man with

154 □

rimless glasses, came over. "How'd they know what I done," he said, sitting down on the nearest chair.

"What didja do," Bus asked him, looking up from the floor where he was kneeling next to Red trying to stop the bleeding. "You damn fool." He stared at Bernie.

Bernie's mouth broke as he started to cry. "I got drunk again, y'know, the other day—I done somethin bad but I don't know jis what—" He sobbed and his nose began to run. "Oh Jesus."

Red, white as a sheet, groaned. "Bernie, we was kiddin," he said, trying to look up at him. Red's hair was stuck to his forehead and a large spot of blood grew on his shirtfront.

"No, I done somethin bad but I DUNNO WHAT IT WAS!" Bernie yelled. He grabbed his hair in a frenzy and gasped.

"Call Leo," Bus said then as Red's eyes grew fixed. "They're both dead." He dragged himself to his feet.

# THE CORNER

VICTOR ENTWHISTLE pushed open the heavy glass door of the hospital and entered the hot, medicine-and-urine-smelling air of the vestibule. Then came indirect lighting and some seated visitors in the smart colored plastic chairs in alcoves which gave to the scene a look of leisure and peace but the tall spinster at the information booth eyed his face coldly when he gave his name and asked for Mrs. Wilma Abbott. Every time he had come here for the last three months—in fact every other day he had come—the receptionist had given him the same look. In the business he was used to meeting all kinds and thought of himself as always holding up his end, but the hospital made him feel vulnerable.

"You can go up now," the tall woman said, turning her back. Victor saw that her hips were wide and recognized the same shape Wilma had in her peach corset. Wilma had asked if the corset looked all right; he had assured her it was fine. He had hated it.

The green-tinted elevator, large enough to accommodate a hospital bed, rose smoothly to the third floor. The doors slid back and he stepped out onto the black marbleized floor. The smells were strong and particularized; urine outside the old man's room, cheap cologne near the room the jivey teen-ager had, ether, food, sterilized linen. A student nurse was removing trays and did not look at him.

He stopped outside Room 347-C; the door was ajar. "Wilma?" he asked.

"Come in," a weak voice said. He entered, pushing the door open. Wilma lay on her back, large and flaccid, her hennaed hair a coarse ruching around her flat gray face. She looked at him, not speaking or smiling. He took off his hat and coat, dropped them on the arm chair and pulled up a straight chair to the bedside. He asked, for the millionth time, it seemed, "Well, how are you?"

"Awful," Wilma murmured down her bosom, her eyes staring at the foot of the bed. She belched. "I got awful gas. I told Doctor about it but as usual he didn't listen, just turned his back."

"You'll be out soon," Victor said helplessly, reaching a thick hand over to pat her arm lying under the bedclothes.

"Oh, don't—I hurt," Wilma wailed. She belched again and spat into a wadded towel. "You don't know what it's like to be sick. You never been in a hospital," she went on weakly. Tears rose in her eyes and ran down her cheeks. Victor, short and solid, cleaned an ear with his little finger nail, staring at her, with nothing to say.

"Say," he came up with. "Howja like those flowers I sent yesterday? Two dozen," he added.

"They give me a headache. I give 'em to the night nurse," Wilma said.

A pause. Wilma sighed and then began to look uneasy. "Say, hon, get me the bedpan—Doctor says I shouldn't wait when I gotta go. Over there on the stand," she ordered, partially raising herself to point. Suddenly, with something to do, she seemed happy. As Victor approached she shoved the covers back. "Now help me on," she ordered, hauling at her short nightgown. She revealed hugely fat, white, dimpled thighs. Victor tried not to look at them but she insisted that he raise her until she was poised on the pan, her back supported by her pillows. Victor sat down again, just inches from where the white fat hung over the edge of the pan, and in misery looked at his Masonic ring while she made a little water.

"Okay, hon, take it away," Wilma said almost gaily; her tone was reminiscent of Wilma out in the park twelve years ago when she was quite a chick and Victor was enjoying cheating on his wife. He thought about the wife, now happily running a refreshment stand in Florida. How clean that seemed. Sitting here beside Wilma was like riding her around on his back all day and all night too. He felt soiled and trapped as he moved the pan to the table. Their long liaison ceased to have meaning; cozy evenings with Wilma and whiskey and the big twin pair of lamps at the ends of the curved emerald green sofa turned on warmly, supper frizzling in the small doodad kitchen, the door locked against his wife and her brother—those times were gone.

"Well," he said, clapping his wide hands on his meaty knees. "Guess I'll run along." He looked at her for some reaction; there was none; her eyes were closed and her flat hair looked terrible. Quietly he got his hat and coat; he wondered what he should do about the bedpan but gave up tiredly. "Goodnight, Wilma," he said.

He went out, pulling the door shut behind him. At that moment the doctor arrived; he was also short, wore a white coat, had a high sloping forehead and rimless glasses. Coarsely his thick lips turned down at the corners as he shook his head and gestured with his thumb at Wilma's door.

O, mouthed Victor, and followed the doctor's form with frightened eyes as the doctor went into the room.

He stopped dazedly at the nurse's station and gave his home number and that of Gerber's Grill.

Numbly Victor went down the softly lit, populated corridor, seeing no one, hauling on his heavy coat which he buttoned prematurely waiting for the elevator.

"We had to take it all out," he shudderingly heard a voice say assuredly behind him.

"Yup, yup. But he'll die, of course," another voice said.

"I know it," the first voice said as the elevator doors opened.

The conversation continued on that level to the first floor; Victor, shaken and sick, went across the lobby as quickly as his short legs would take him. No sense of the dramatic, the cosmic, or poetry came to him now to save him. Only one thing loomed on the horizon to aid him; a taxi outside the door was empty and he hailed it. "Gerber's," he said sharply and was wrenched back against the seat by the swift acceleration of the cab. Outdoors people walked, talked, shopped and ate as usual, but still Victor was not comforted. Only the thought of the dim, roomy bar and grill on the corner of Hector and Helen Streets brought him a little solace; they sped along the dirty winter streets, past neon signs, apartments over shoe stores, the station, and at last arrived at Gerber's with its brown and brick front and a dim sign in the window lit to say BUDWEISER.

Victor paid the cabdriver and hurried with an elevation of spirits across the sidewalk; Al Fortuni was sure to be there, five-thirty; Torch Boggs; maybe Cora would fuss over him tonight; inside the door he pulled off his coat and hat, hung them beside the others on the rack, and went to the bar. Anticipating the glow the cocktails would give him he was smiling broadly and looking for someone's back to clap. Doug, the bartender, glanced up and said, "Hya. Manhattan, son?"

"Yes," Victor said, edging on to a stool. He sat with his hands folded on the bar while the anticipatory glow built up in him.

"'Yar," Doug said and delicately placed the glowing drink before him.

"Thanks," Victor said, and drank. At that moment a vision of Wilma's loathsome white flanks on the bedpan shot into his mind. His one-time love, Wilma, about to die, and he loathed her. Panic-stricken he saw his unfaithful fat face in the dark mirror opposite him; automatically he gulped a large swallow, knowing the sweet, lovable change would be in the bottom of about his second drink.

Meantime, Wilma was dying, perhaps dead—he wondered if he should return to the hospital; but he could not. He could not face her, the room, the short doctor with the thick lips turning down in scorn at Wilma, at death. He could not go back.

Two railroad men behind him, eating oyster stew and having no liquor, were discussing peas.

"How do they get them all the same size" the big one in the cap asked.

"Nothing I like better'n a dish of 'em cold right out a the ice box," the other said. "Just like cider, by gum."

*By gum. What a kid's expression. Shit,* Victor said bravely to his glass. *Everybody eat shit, like I'm doin.* The conversation about peas was over. Victor signalled Doug for another drink. It was getting to him, the liquor; he wondered where Cora was; a hearty type; made a man feel big.

The drink came. His reflection in the mirror looked interesting, yes; a fine type; might be better in uniform; he began to imagine what fine, tight-lipped things he might say to LBJ if he happened to stroll in; and it could happen, too:

*"Say, sir, what's the drink specialty here?"*

*"Why, sir, mine's always a Manhattan. Let me."*

*The drink is obtained in silence; all watch as Victor ministers to the president. No undue talk; Victor knows a tired man when he sees one.*

*In silence they polish off two each.*

*"Thank you, my friend, for your understanding," LBJ says to him, in departing, with a keen look on his face as he memorizes this new friend. "I do thank you." Exit.*

*Victor pays, of course.*

Victor had forgotten Wilma. Cora came up rubbing her bosom in a friendly way against Victor. Unfortunately Victor, when last there and tight, had told her about Wilma so of course she asked about her.

The liquor had given Victor the power and glory he had so lacked on leaving the hospital. It gave him a sense of importance in Cora's beautiful mascara-covered eyes to say "Dying; dying."

"Aw," Cora said, hugging him. "Can I getcha a bowl of stew, Vicky?" Solicitous.

"No, no. Thanks," Victor said. Strong; thin; brave and keeping his troubles close to his chest.

"Well, duck, ya gotta have sunthin," she persisted; a mother.

"Later. With you." Victor eyed her face in the mirror. "When do you get off?" He was surprised. He hadn't seen this coming. Wilma is dying and you go after a piece, right off.

"Okay, Cory?" Look nonchalant over her head at the clock, though for no reason. Not going anywhere. Don't want to. Can't *bear* to.

"Now, Vic, you know my boy comes for me at eleven!" She patted his face. "Lemme get ya sunthin."

"Doug!" Victor bellowed, to be funny. "One more." He looked down at Cora from his stool. "Forget it, little one." *Let her go, into the night; I'll stay here alone and eat shit.* He knew if he had food now it would blot out the fine effect of the drink.

The phone rang in the booth by the monkey bar. Doug answered. "Who? Oh year. 'Minute." He stepped out. "Vic. For you."

Victor walked lightly to the booth, leaving the door open. A man of affairs. Probably Lloyd at the store about something he couldn't figure out.

"Yes?"

A woman's nasal impersonal voice at the other end of the line said "Mr. Victor E. Entwhistle?"

"Yes," Victor said.

"This is Mangone Hospital. I have to tell you that Mrs. Wilma Abbott just died, I'm sorry."

"Oh," Victor sighed. He was suddenly sober. "I'll be right over."

"Oh, no need tonight—tomorrow morning will do fine. You are Mr. Victor Entwhistle; I mean, I didn't expect a—a—bar—" she ground to a halt.

"Well. Thank you, Ma'am," Victor almost whispered, and rang off. He must see Cora. Now. She was in the kitchen and he went to the door.

"Cora?"

"*Yes*, honey!" she responded, smiling and coming right up to him.

"She's—she's dead." Victor could think of nothing else to say. Again he thought of the bedpan and felt ill.

"Jeez, honest a God, I'm sorry," Cora said, patting his arm. "Now, I'm gonna get you a nice bowl of chowder and a BLT for you, and Doug'll give you a drink, free," she added with a stretched grin.

"Gee, Cora," Victor said as she pushed him to a seat. The bustle, the solicitude warmed him; Cora made him think of kitchens, and coffee, and roasts, and maybe a bit of slap and tickle at first. . . .

Ah, well, he sighed, tired out as Doug brought him the drink—a double—old friends are best. He drank deep.

Cora would come around, one day—they had a lot in common. At least, they had Gerber's.

160 □

# LIMA BEANS

"I LIKE boiled rice or steamed..." the monotonous voice was going on.

Bebe shook out a frayed dish towel, good linen once, a hostess present from Dutzi Leeming about ten years before. She took off her horn-rimmed glasses and left the sink, her gaze going over the head of the unwelcome speaker to look at the first falling flakes dropping past the telephone pole outside.

"*You* like rice, Bebe?" the voice insisted.

"Oh. Yes." Bebe forced herself to look at Theresa and answer her. Dear lord, she thought, how can I stand this.

"And you know what I like too," the voice went on. "Beeb?"

"What?"

"Pizza." Theresa waited, her crippled hands in her cotton lap, thin and rather dirty. "I love pizza. Noreen and Bobbie and I always went for pizza Fridays." She sat, looking bright-eyed at Bebe who was going through the shelves making out a list. It hurt her to see the meagerness of the assortment, remembering the plenty of her girlhood home where a large cold room was filled with hams, bacon, cheeses—what a fine thing, right now, to have a Provolone sandwich and cider—condiments, flour, butter....

"And with the pizza, ya know what, Beeb?" Theresa waited to catch Bebe's eye.

"*What*, Tessie?" Bebe replied, looking into an empty box of raisins.

"We always had orange soda. It was good."

Bebe heard Theresa clatter the head of her cane against the worn wood of the rocker she sat in and thought, relieved, oh, she's going somewhere.

Theresa stood with difficulty, a small sad figure, bent with arthritis, but not very old and with the fierce fires of life glowing in her light eyes. "I ga go the bathroom," she announced, puffing as she made her stumping way to the door.

Bebe finished her grocery list, economizing on each item, choosing canned rather than frozen food, cold cuts and strong cheese instead of chops and Camembert. Tormenting her was the thought of the Saturday and Sunday lying before her, with Tessie. Once again she aligned her present situation—divorced, or rather, deserted—a working woman, her companion her crippled cousin who she had invited to come and live with her in a terrible Christmas loneliness one year not long ago—with the sweet look of the pasture beyond her window in Vermont in summer with Bart, a new bride, everything within reach.

She stood a long moment motionless by the shelves, a package of apricots unnoticed in her hands. Quickly, then, she gathered her list, went to her bedroom, unplugged the Arco heater and threw on her coat and gloves in a frenzy, wanting to be gone before Tessie appeared with an account of her movement.

She jerked the recalcitrant door with the frayed scrim curtain shut after her. The sharp cold was fresh and she felt a slight improvement in her lot as she stepped along on the new snow. She glanced back once at her half of the shabby house where a new maple was struggling at the curb in a forest of parking meters, traffic signs and telephone poles. Ugly, it was; her heart sank again. And Tessie thinks its heaven, Bebe thought dully.

Her walk to the store on Nesbitt Street took her past the court house, a yellow brick, huge building with broad dirty steps and no windows. A photographer loitered outside and a drab group of men in gray and black stood part-way up the steps. Bebe suddenly thought of the article she had read the night before in a news magazine saying it was almost a duty for people, people like her, to go to courts and attend trials.

She stopped by the photographer, an egg-faced man with a small mean moustache. "What's happening here today?" she asked him.

"Oh, some guy beat up a woman," the man said.

"Thank you," Bebe said and looked up the steps at the men. They were uninteresting; she almost went along on her errand. Then Tessie's boring conversation and drab habits caught her up short; anything but returning to her small quarters and the conversation of Tessie; she went up the steps to the great doors of the building and moved along the corridors inside to where she could see a sign saying COURT-ROOM. There was a row of sturdy ugly bright varnished chairs outside; the door was open.

She went in and a man in some sort of uniform looked questioningly at her. "May I—watch?" she asked, her manner a mere ghost of her early assured self of years ago. She thought as she went down a row of empty seats and settled herself of television trials and the types who were seen as spectators and she had always thought of them as sensation seekers. *What am I, then?* she thought; and a grim voice from within her answered NOTHING. She knew if she were by some chance shown on a television drama the camera would mercilessly pick up the puffiness of forty-four under her eyes, the hollows in her pale cheeks, her old permanent, her bargain hat—of feathers, but still a bargain—and her old tweed coat. Perhaps it would show strength; more likely, though, she thought tiredly, it would point up her mean thoughts about Tessie, bitterness towards Bart, longing for a gentle poignant monied life. She settled her feet more comfortably on the floor, lifted her head to remove the sag from under her chin, and looked around.

Bleakly she pushed back her coat and waited as clerks and police came and went; how safe they seemed. She waited for the main participants to come in and felt conspicuous. Three men came and sat in front of her, one in a black satin basketball jacket that read THE MAMBOS in script on the back. Another had a fat neck and new haircut beneath his new narrow brimmed too-small hat which he left on. The third was an old man who smelled of liniment, rather pleasantly. Bebe began to be glad she had come and felt a glow of pride in herself as a citizen doing her duty. She thought of many ways she could support her community and her spirits rose, although actually she was too tired when she came home from the office to do anything but get supper for Tessie and herself and fall into bed with an Ian Fleming.

There was noise of a crowd approaching in the corridor. Several men walked in very fast and stood in pairs and threes with papers and briefcases, talking, tapping the furniture or with hands in pockets; she wondered where the principals were, and the judge.

Suddenly they were there. A small dark man took his seat at the bench with a small stir as a few of those who happened to be seated rose briefly. He leaned back and waited. Then through the side door came Bart with another man; oh yes, she knew it was Bart though he looked heavier, his face was fuller; his hairline had not receded; yes, it was Bart. He wore a tweed jacket with double vents and he looked serious.

A moment later, through the same door, came a slim woman in a gray suit with a single fur thrown gracefully around her neck. She wore no hat and her hair was thick and rolled into an attractive French twist. She wore red gloves and carried a small gray suede purse. But it was her face that caught the eye: it was thoughtful but not stern, wise and quite serene. Bebe wondered who she was and what Bart was doing there.

The business of the court being opened was passed through quickly enough and the man with Bart, now seated, stepped forward and addressed the judge. Bebe gathered that two weeks before Bart had struck, several times, the woman in the gray suit, while very drunk. Bebe watched Bart's back but could see no signs of uneasiness. The lawyer explained Bart's reason for beating her—Susan—he said Bart insisted she was behaving just like his ex-wife. Bebe froze. How he must have disliked her—and she had always felt so righteous.

Bart and Susan were not married but, it appeared, they had been intending to be. It was brought forth that Bart almost never drank much, he regretted what he had done, he intended still to marry Susan if she would have him, but now this all seemed to preclude that.

Bebe saw Bart rub his face nervously once but throughout most of the exposition he sat up graceful, large and poised and she saw him look frequently at Susan. Susan was somewhat agitated at first but as things went on, a smile began to play around her lips and on two occasions a peal of pretty laughter broke from her. She continued to smile as her lawyer described how Bart had thrown a statuette of Julius Caesar, or one of the Caesars, at her; it missed her. Bart and she looked across the room at each other and both smiled.

"Now, Miss Parsons," Bart's lawyer was saying to her, "You do not appear to bear a grudge nor do you appear to be taking all this very hard. What is your present attitude toward Mr. Bart Searles?"

Poised and lovely, Susan stood up, smiling broadly; she turned from the lawyer to Bart and said "Bart, let's leave; this is all so silly; I apologize." She stood waiting.

Bart then stood, graceful and relaxed and also smiling the attractive smile Bebe remembered so well. In a deep voice he said "Susan, I'll never do it again, and specially will I not throw Caesar at you. Let's go buy a couple of non-alcoholic martinis and take the bench with us—" He turned charmingly towards the judge who was smiling broadly.

"All right. Case dismissed," the judge said as he rose and turned away, waving a benevolent hand at them. Bebe watched in an agony of envy as Bart and Susan made their way towards each other through the rows of empty chairs; they did not embrace as they met but the radiance on their faces stabbed Bebe. They went out quickly, not looking back.

Bebe was suddenly aware that everyone was leaving except two policemen; she pulled her coat around her and stood. She felt exhausted. For something to do to bring herself back to reality, she groped in her purse; her grocery list met her eye. She took it out and, scanning it, made her way into the corridor. The overhead fluorescent lights glared whitely, the place smelled of steam, a few anonymous men and a janitor loitered. She did not even have the price of a martini, let alone someone to drink it with. Stunned she went down the long flight of outside steps in the gentle snow.

She turned her steps toward Nesbitt Street and by the time she reached Palfrey's Market she had collected herself enough to go to the canned vegetable department and choose the bargain in lima beans, three for a dollar.

# THE WARDEN

THOMAS OSBURN found his mind clear, racing, though he had just left his single bed half an hour before he usually did—it was only five thirty.

The fog as usual lay in the marsh behind his yellow ranch-style house and no car passed on the road. It was silent totally as he stood for a minute on the front stoop outside. Across the road the new earth where a house was to be built lay in orange heaps, damp, heavy.

—Well, something to eat, he thought, going in again in his clean T-shirt and rumpled brown pajama pants. He never turned on a light in the morning, carefully saving electricity; electricity—his mind veered powerfully away from the thought.

Today John Spivak would die—at precisely ten this morning. Die how? How terrible was it?

He went into the kitchen and automatically prepared his tea, eggs and bacon. The job had to be done and he had to give the word. At ten. He knew the man should die; he had killed his wife and baby; not insane; a mature young fellow; had been laughing often at his trial, they said; he should die.

Thomas felt unprepared. He was known to be efficient and practical, got things done well and quickly; no fuss; he moved into the center of disturbances at his prison, short, calm, cold, a man of few words but they were always to the point; he would brook no argument.

He recalled a few faces from the day before: Jud, red, tall, as cold as himself; Larry, fat, dark, white-skinned, looking contemptuous; Thomas had returned the contempt with the ease of practice. And the two old men, wise, clean, telling him their decision; he replying briefly No.

He had left them after seven minutes and ordered their guards to watch it and to fire on anything threatening; anything. He had done it well and then gone on to three fine conferences in his green office, a good lunch with the Sheriff, on trays, also in his office, and a busy afternoon reviewing cases for parole, alone. No one, he had found, was eligible. His secretary, Mavis, middleaged and plain, concurred as he dictated a letter to the Board.

—The world doesn't need THEM, she had said as she heaved her fat rear from the neat secretarial chair the budget had finally afforded her.

He had worked, fresh, ready, practical, on the prison budget until seven when all was neatly finished and filed by him in the olive cabinets. Cool, in control, he had switched off the bright ceiling light, visited his small clean bathroom and locked his door.

No one knew that he drove to a certain row house in Gunnageville then. No one was going to know; why should they? He was Warden, in control; the woman's low-voiced pleading pleased him, made him feel powerful. He had seen his reflection in a mirror on her wall as he sat, relaxed, in her cheap parlor; he had cooly liked his full-fleshed figure seated with crossed legs in an armchair with a Bicentennial patterned throw on it; his bare dark eyes surrounded with their usual mauve behind his clean glasses always noted carefully what he saw and he used it briefly, then forgot it. His receding hairline was neat and his hair short. The longer hair on the sheriff and other men his own age was too like that of the prisoners.

The woman had not cried but would have gotten no further with him if she had. She had raised the fellow; let her now be silent and pay for it.

He set out stainless steel knife, fork and spoon, a nice china plate, cup and saucer, water glass; he held with drinking plenty of water. The food, however, when he had cooked it, repelled him; he could not eat. He drank the tea and two glasses of water and went to sit in front of his small television set for the early news. He wanted some mention of the execution and yet he did not.

He was no killer, no Hitler; he gave moderately when asked for donations for the various diseases and had never struck anyone. . . .

No—he had struck, once. During the war his one buddy, a man named Alston Japp, had twitted him about his neatness; Thomas had thrown a paper clip at Alston and then had moved closer to slap him once cruelly in the face.

Japp had deserved it; Japp had judged him, and badly.

He, Thomas, was no killer; under no circumstances would he kill, he was sure. Even in the war he had not killed; he had been used in the stores solely. He had hated the Germans, yes, but everyone always had.

He sat preoccupied in the new large armchair, not seeing the television. He did not hear the car turn into his drive and was only aroused from his speculation on the effects of electrocution on the brain by the gentle door chime.

The woman stood at his door, white, set, wearing the same wrinkled cheap dress and green sweater of the day before.

—Yes?

—I gotta talk to you.

—My dear madam, we have talked.

—Mister, I done it. . . .

—You did—what?

—I killed um. LaVerne and the kid. I done it.

—Madam, it was shown categorically at the trial that your son did it. Now. You know that.

—NO. I done it and a lot else—lemme come in—please lemme come in. She began to cry, retching and beating her fists on her thin thighs.

—No, madam. You are to return home. Now. You must allow justice to be done. He stepped back to close the door; she threw herself inside, striking her shoulder bruisingly against the jamb; she was shrieking, coughing:—Mister, please—I done it. I like doin that—everything in the paper bad I done—I done it ALL. . . .

She stood sobbing, tears raining down her white sagging cheeks.

—I shall call the matron at the jail to come and remove you. She will get you home.

He went to the gold princess phone on a table by the picture window and put in the call:—Immediately; two of you; I don't care who you get. Get over here.

He hung up.

—Sit down; I must get dressed.

He left the room to do this, paying no attention to the woman's sobs, screams. He stayed in his room cutting his nails until he heard the door chime once more.

A short wiry woman and a youth in the dirty white of a kitchen worker entered, went to the woman now sitting staring at nothing, and lifted her to her feet. —Come on. Come ON.

They led her, silent, to the door and out to a black state car in the drive. They ground away; silence again enveloped the house, the road, the world.

Thomas tidily went outside, found the car keys in place in the woman's battered white car; he locked it and then backed his own car, a red Impala, clean and purring, into the drive. It was too early to go to work but he did not want to be alone. He locked his front door and drove off to his office. The drive to the correctional facility eased him slightly and he walked through the brightly lit corridor feeling better.

But there was no work that needed to be done; nothing. He had finished everything the day before.

He filled a paper cup with water and poured it on Mavis' philodendron. He sat at his desk looking at the phone; he could make some calls. But to whom? He had no friend he chatted idly with; there was no loose end left in connection with the execution to settle; the staff and the people in the sheriff's office were all cold efficient men like himself; he sat looking rigidly around his office. . . .

Then he had a wonderful idea: the empty space along one wall would nicely accommodate a neat leather-type sofa. He visualized one such in gold with perhaps chrome legs, placed there.

He noted it was now nearly nine o'clock and he could call the store and get someone out to discuss the project with.

He filled the next ten minutes sorting the steel paperclips in the desk drawer from the copper ones and was just through at nine.

With buoyancy and dispatch he talked to a Mr. Madsmer who agreed to come right out and consult with him. Waiting for this meeting Thomas saw a brochure on farm insurance in the waste basket, retrieved it and read it meticulously.

Madsmer, a willowy effeminate man in a pink leisure suit and with long blond hair, arrived promptly and entered into a vivid discussion about the couch, the exciting possibilities for drapes, lamps, an attractive waste basket, a hutch for liquor—No?—well, for coffee; Thomas, exercising his usual decisiveness, brief and yet careful, spent some minutes adding up costs, asking about the chance for a discount; the hour passed quickly.

At five minutes to ten a knock came on the door; one of the older guards, Ben Hatch, had come to invite him to witness the execution. Swiftly Thomas said No, you carry on—I'm tied up here with Mr., Uh. Well, go ahead, sir.

He turned back to Madsmer who had been describing the large books of samples he could bring out.

For the next twenty minutes Thomas gave his attention fully to the novel thought that the filing cabinets could be covered with material matching the drapes, and a handsome mural, possibly of Jefferson's home, could be applied to the wall over the new couch. . . .

# KRUEGER'S ISLAND

IN THE early morning mist rising from the Hudson River a thrush called; drops fell from the trees.

Renate, sitting on the edge of the mussed double bed in her old short nightgown, lit a cigarette in the stillness. It was only six o'clock. Paul lay on his back, naked; his body, heavy, fat, even, was mostly covered with dark springy hair; his face, bearded and darkbrowed and without his horn-rimmed glasses, looked innocent, plain, mysterious. . . .

She stared at him, remembering the wet lovemaking during the night, the soaked sheet, his huge weight spearing her, the long rage and struggle as they worked at their love.

She liked him. She liked their nightly workout and the heavy summer night air, their sagging bed, their quiet days alone in the shacky cottage on this island, found so by chance; perhaps she liked best the rainy spells when they lit a kerosene lamp and she put together their spotty, often oily, meals, fried, smelling beautiful, giving them lovely rolling energy, for him in his occasional furious writing—a third novel—for her the energy to work on a poem or a long letter abroad to her old friends in Ireland, and Scotland, and to Lorraine in Florence.

Renate, appearing temperate, mysterious, dark, had a beautiful body. She had met Paul when they both worked at New York University, each teaching on the lower levels of the Department of English.

The day promised to be fair, light sun shone into the room and brought out unexpected beauty in a sick green bureau under the open window that had no curtains.

Renate, still holding her cigarette, went into the darker larger living room and through the screen door to stand on the step; the green smell and the calling of the thrush filled her; she was frightened at the happiness she felt. She progressed to the grassy patch and on into the open woods. Pines lined the shore; she walked between two and went into the cold water where the mist still hung here and there.

Standing knee-deep on the stony bottom she finished her cigarette and dropped it into the water. She decided to commit herself to the river and lowered herself up to her neck. At first it was terribly cold; then she found that it soothed, enlarged.

A barge appeared around the point a distance down river, low and itself dull in color but heaped with furiously yellow sulphur. The sight thrilled her and the stones pressing her legs became, it seemed, warm. The water was like glass. The barge moved toward her simply and slowly. A song sparrow sang in the meadowsweet.

Renate suddenly desired Paul, inside her, here, now, in the water. She stood and waded to the shore and ran back to their bedroom window.

—Paul. PAUL.

Paul cast himself upright in the bed, saw her and got up.

—Come with me.

He joined her on the grass, warm and sticky. She led him to the water and he walked heavily into it beside her; he understood; he joined her in waist-deep water and found her ready, easy, quiet.

—My god, I didn't see that.

—It's been on its way since I came out.

The barge was near; they could see three men at the rail observing them.

—Ey. Cha doin there?

—Morning.

The man who had spoken, very tall and thin, wearing an undershirt and brown pants, wrenched them off and dove in.

He swam clumsily toward them and then stood up; his bush of graying hair was not wet. He walked in to the shore, naked, bringing his pathetic undersized organ into view. He sat down on a patch of pine needles and said, "Do it again, huhn?"

—Do what?

—Well, what you was doin.

—I'm cold, Paul.

—Oh, I'm for it again. Come on. . . .

Paul put his arm around Renate and led her back into the water.

—What are you DOING?

—Satyr. . . .

Paul made love for a much longer time; Renate endured, now colder and wondering. She looked over at the man on the shore who was standing now watching with a dazed look on his homely long face. His body was redly sunburned on shoulders and arms; the rest was pearly and concave.

Renate, now again wildly excited, found herself thinking Why not, for the poor guy. —Let's do it on the pine needles, luv. . . .

They splashed hastily to shore and fell on to the pine needles directly beside the man. The barge had stopped nearby and the two other men stared avidly. Paul yanked Renate's nightgown off and they coupled hotly, now in a patch of early sun. They now found themselves full of new ideas and daring; they slowed to enjoy the effects on themselves and on the men.

After half hour Paul and Renate lay back, separated, their eyes closed.

—Ey, drop yer cock and grab yer socks—we gotta git goin, Walt.

The man on the barge who spoke was small and wiry, wearing a navy blue dirty suit jacket over his undershirt and baggy gray trousers.

Walt got up and licked his dry lips. —We come up and down every two days. I'll be back again then, okay?

He waded out and swam back to the barge.

—Ja make it, Walt? Goddammit I can't swim.

—We'll be here, all right, Paul called out to them. He closed his eyes again, slept.

Renate sat up and watched the sulphur load vanish up river. Now, she thought, we're a gang—it'll always have to be a gang. Their nights alone would only be the bread, without the caviar; so, how much traffic was there on the river, passing this close; not much. . . .

We adapted, she thought with pleasure.

◁ ▷

During the two following days Paul and Renate did not talk much to each other; in passing one might briefly stroke the other; the nights were spent side by side in the bed and they did not crave to make love; nor did they sleep much. The long still beautiful nights moved hesitantly past. They heard rustling in the trees and ferns, acorns fell occasionally on the roof. A toughness developed in them, a worldly approach to everything; they did no writing; they could not get in the small car and drive off for groceries and whiskey. The weather was damp and sunny; they sat separately out of doors examining their feet, hands. . . .

Paul, leaning against the cottage in the shade, loved this stillness, quiet. He felt complete, fine, noble. He liked what they had done so publicly and longed for a repeat. He loved his wife, he found, more—but differently, like a pet, a clever pet.

Renate, at the shore in the misty hot sun, sweated and felt a raging nervousness. Perverted, now, were they? No. It made them all happy; that was good. Good. And yet she had no desire to do it again; she wanted Paul alone, to be hers, privately. The sight of their messy bed beside which she had stood a bottle containing wood lilies drew her. She was homesick for Paul and the bed.

They had, had they not, a small orgy. She pondered what they had done, she and Paul, under the three pairs of eyes; she felt excited again; if music could be played now she would be unbearably lacking in control... ah. Perhaps if she put the Elgar on their changer she could induce Paul to come to her, very soon.

She put on her shirt and went to the cottage. In the cluttered crowded living room she located the record and turned on the player very loud. She pulled off her clothes and lay down on the cool sweat-smelling bed, waiting for Paul. The sun shone hotly into the bedroom; it was stifling. A large boat threw its wake against the shore; then, silence except for the birds enervated by the nooning.

The record ended; Paul had not come.

Cheated, embarrassed, she rose and went into the kitchen, naked. She could see Paul's feet out in front of him where he sat.

—Luv?

—Yuh?

—Ch doing?

He got up and came into the kitchen where he poured the last of the whiskey into a cup and stood, abstracted, leaning on the old stove.

—Hot isn't it?

She busied herself making two cheese sandwiches, hardly aware of her nakedness. Paul, carrying his drink, went out again, slipping his hand carelessly down her back as he passed her.

The screen door slammed.

Silence.

Renate left the food, no longer interested, and put her clothes back on. Suddenly there was nothing to do. She was not sleepy and could not even nap. She realized she and Paul in their now separate ways were simply marking time until the barge returned; tomorrow, she thought. She decided to play herself a vast concert and get the time past somehow.

She stacked Verdi, Telemann, Mozart, Schubert, Felix Martin and James Loach in a pile on the player and returned to lie on the bed and listen. Occasionally she heard Paul's footsteps in the brush outside as he slowly paced.

During the night a wild storm rose; at dawn they saw it would last far into the day. They lay on their bed listening to the thrashing branches and hissing water. They ate nothing and did not get up.

About eleven-thirty they heard a hoarse cry from the river; it was the barge, big, dark in the slanting rain; the sulphur had been unloaded and now the cargo was lumber held in place with large chains.

As they emerged on the shore Walt was swimming toward them clumsily; he was followed by the two other men in a small rowboat badly tossed by the waves and the wind. The barge swung heavily at anchor.

Awkwardly the two men in the boat beached it and climbed out, both carrying whiskey. Obviously they had had a lot already; in a minute they were as naked as Walt. The rain pelted down.

Renate took a bottle and drank deeply from it; she was soaked, cold and not in the least ready. As she drank she looked with loathing at the third man, short, grossly fat like jelly; his sex was huge and red. The small thin man drank deeply too, to ready himself. He moved near Paul and shared his bottle, eyeing Paul's physique and each of the others. Renate, helpless, found herself thinking of her apartment in New York where, dry and inspired, listening to the city outside, she had written about making love with the cool picture of Lawrence facing her across the room. . . .

Soon they were all drunken in the rain, sitting near each other; someone laughed. A train passed on the bluff.

—Ahhhhh BOY! Paul yelled and grabbed Renate. He took her roughly; she gasped.

The three men watched hungrily; then the fat man threw himself next to Renate and fastened his mouth on her breast desperately, clutching her. He and then the thin man made swift inexpert violent love to her, Walt now standing hugging his elbows.

Then the fat man turned to Paul and began to maul him. Paul said "Hey," and got up. Renate squirmed loose with difficulty and ran to Walt to stand defiantly. She picked up an empty bottle and raised it.

—Ah, honey, the fat man said, groping his way to his feet.

—Leave. Go. Git, she said. She dropped the bottle and ran through the woods to the cottage. They heard the door slam.

—Well, you studs, come on, the wiry man said, climbing into the boat he had shoved loose, his dripping clothes slung over his shoulder.

—Come ON, goddammit, he yelled at the other two who were unwilling to leave.

They reclaimed their clothes and clumsily got into the boat and fought their way the short distance to the barge.

Paul stood sodden and spent in the gray storm, looking after them when they finally got the barge under way again. As they moved off the fat man gave Paul the finger; Paul heard the laughter rise to coughing and hoots; cold, empty, unfortunate and alone he went slowly back to the cottage.

# THE SUDDEN

WHAT WIND blew at that ancient hour, the late earliness when she awoke to gasp on her pillow and recount to herself old children's tales, tales for the old now, she reproved herself with desperate compunction and dust-irritating semblance of humor, to rout the vision of the two chicken legs and the tall twins ever growing, growing threateningly out of her attempted rest on the hard ship's pillow. What wind in the empty goading night wrapped the ship in its grasp and frightened the smoke stack, slew the sparks that plunged into the rapid black ocean. Where can I go for peace, she throttled in her tight throat; on the land she called home the night visions came to harangue and throw her, to embitter her subtle mind with their unreasoning movements part of her had separated from her life as valuable to be considered later; and these drove her looking with horrified closed eyes at the true stuff of life.

Taxis, she thought, opening her blue staring eyes. I'll think of them, going along the Meuse, going to see Frederick ... dear handsome pirate, wearing the cloth ... Her glance went from the pale shapes in the room to her bedside clock with its bright jabber of numbers; it was the beginning of her struggle for sanity during the endless night; the hours presented countless raucous laughs, explicit posturings and chance acts, clear as daylight, clear as reverence in a postulant, clear as the postulant's small bright eyes, she thought sullenly, woodenly, resisting the strong honorable thing of resting back on her pillow that smelled of disinfectant, watching with her famous sang-froid the culled antics of a huge world of which she had seen and known the whole.

Tenderly she adjusted her long narrow bones, her apricot scented body of whose strength and the tedium of being beautiful she knew as a long list of achievements and oh, the work demanded of such a one, she knew, she could tell to the few the very few who counted anywhere what she gave forth, spun from a mind seated in flesh but wedded to the airy, beating, dear, dirty, ah, the filth, weight of the going on, the achievement that was hers . . .

Only her crushed buttocks, the ugliness of the withered, the slain, the depressing old, betrayed her form as she once glanced at herself in the long gold bath mirror at Whyte, her home of roses, the scent of witch hazel and milk, the healer of her counted measured friends who came, she knew, to look upon perfection and the unthroed loose clasp she had on what they saw as her lover, life. The envy, she thought upon her pillow with fatigue . . . ah for one who did not envy me . . . how I would envy her or him . . . a vision sprang hotly before her closed eyes of a bride mouthing horribly at a black door . . . how like something, she thought . . . giving way to a ribbon of tensely changing notes in color of a swirling passage, all of which she knew would never repeat itself, so minutely had she seen and heard, so sucked at the total face of a blasted endless world . . . in the middle of a touch of nausea, while a black man flexed small muscles and someone ate slyly, she slept, exhausted by her own appetite for peace, the peace, she thought, of youth, when god existed and tomorrow held oneself, along with the secure expectation of perfect newness . . .

The gray air stood thickly in her stateroom at the hour of her early awakening. Without her visions she could forage in her alertness and the dry smell of hard objects at rest for a plan. Always she made a possible pathway through the eighteen hours of an untried day with the flattening out of her mind of any formula; because one day has held a cargo of one particular sort was, she knew with the apprehending of the total sophisticate, no reason for another day to be its mate, its match, its solution, reason or reckoner. Nothing connects the days but me, she thought with the casualness of the busy, the living, over the operator upon her own weaknesses, the thorough master of the beautiful negative in life.

She swept the clean harsh covers from her and stood immediately; immediately she saw the letter on the dressing table. Her arched feet crossed the fine carpet, the blue of a faded violet, the blue of old veins. It did not matter to her that she had stolen, taken illicitly, that which was another's; her knowledge demanded fuel, a new fine fact, a lessening of others. The letter was not hers; the young girl who had dropped it on the stairs on the way to dinner the evening before would not know the sort of eye, an eye of total understanding, destined to read it; coldly she took it from its cheap envelope and spread its thick contents under her cool hands. Looking down, a beautiful and old woman in a flowing robe, she read.

Love letters sent to her were to her a simple statement of her own actual existence, which for a moment or two each day she doubted as she strained to hear the silence above it all and, hearing it, attempted to refuse that silence as too great, too light, too airless to endure. So she enjoyed the letters and those that were edged with cynicism she treasured in a painted box with a key; but she never took them out; she knew them, and the men, ah, she knew them and all the chords they could play she knew and throbbed with avidity at their attempts to step up on to her one dais where intangibly a genie, a vast cordon, an air, a gaunt lack of license put down the man; so she never took a lover, never married. Was not she married to a stupor of life-gathering; how can a golden notebook marry, how can a vivid eye copulate or admit the pressures of the body happening to coincide with her drive, her mania for experience in her mind which had been her only heart?

The letter was in pencil and made straight statements about the physical possibilities for the lovers; the mode of passion here suggested contained a variety of such wealth that she read with more than her usual total concentration, pressing the paper until her fingertips turned white. The room lurched and she turned white-hot with a confusion unknown to her. The man in question could have been a sailor or a mad servant, but she had to honor the pure intent of this man to achieve in the greatest heat his one desire. When she had read the many pages she turned her eyes to her image in the long mirror, looking at her face, her body, for expression of the heat she felt, the complement in glass to the newness of the one thing she had not known, a desire so great that she felt a signal must be visible on her magnificent surface.

Will I dress... will I speak again and if so shall I say the thoughts... shall I run to the nearest handsome ancient with a lovely note, inviting... will I fail now that I have a world to give, at last... who can heal me now that I am open to the hot wind... no one can heal...

She stood looking at herself, not seeing, luring any man with a prehensile will that tore at clothes, panted in a slime of sweat, writhed in exquisite discomfort and disunion, with knowledge of the distance of a man in union, of the closeness of a bedded converse while it was drowned out by the slamming of hearts' doors, the sweeping of them open... all that the author of the letter, some one who never thought any other thoughts, had set forth for his woman, she willed to be hers in the face of a world, a long continuum, of perfect turning from all male advances of this kind, of other orienting.

In her stone appraisal of the tall old figure in the vast mirror she saw no past but only the present, the void of her empty cabin, the flagellating pulse of desire in the dancing motes of morning dust. A chill of fright grew around her as she forged another person at that moment, radiantly woman, gasping and grasping at that new great presence, the man she could have, could wring herself around, grinding in their mutual pestle morning, day and afternoons of a truly painted wandering, ever new fervor, delayed forever until now.

The chill, the ice around her grew as her awareness of the shape in the mirror taunted, looked with a haughty prick, the mire of her complexity evident in her knowing eyes, her cool stance, her poise, command and a staring control.

She had turned this mien upon her chances; she had passed all the gates to fathom a dour uncomfortable neglecting world, exacting admiration and achieving an adoration of all things she was. No man could warm this kind tower, adamantly faithful until now to complexity's glow, fire, tender smoke, beginning newly every step, every thought.

. . . I have had a faith and had a shape to conceal it, steal it gracefully from another, a faith too varied for a man to follow when he wanted, demanded solely, me. Bad evil rested in my neat heart, she thought; I housed it with a broad tenderness and thought that brave, delightful and of wideness; my judgments lent permission to all to sin with grace or hard blows if only they have a fresh intentness, not the old blunt garbage used by nobodies.

Empty the day hung in the cabin; she turned from the mirror with appalled finality, saying a deep goodbye to the infinity she had just shared with it.

She sat down on the lounge waiting for her maid with her tense punctilio, her nailed service, to bring her coffee. Her own death began today and would come quickly, she knew certainly, placing her graceful foot as brace for a sudden weakness.

As an old mind-ravished woman she saw as a hope, with her still living intellect that planned paragraphs even now for no further listener—she felt she could not speak again—a certain accessible poetry in nothingness.

# WHITE CANDLES

I WAS running; into the flagrant blacks, rusts, grays of the flats of space in and beyond the black-trunked grove I ran; the white wind whistled in my throat; it rasped, tore, gave, continued to let me breathe; a white light, perhaps in my tortured head, perhaps from a lost star, shone from above into the deep night where I ran, I ran.

My pursuers came closer. I could hear air slap and revolve around their muscular knees, the black trousers on their powerful legs, the tight strong chests and shoulders on them; a white shirt would blaze briefly in the light from above, a frightening white eye would look at me as I ran infinitely swiftly, totally committed to the act of speeding past the dead, the threatening dead jutting tripping heavy seething bottomless earth. Grass whipped, vortices formed around the bodies of my pursuers; no voice was heard of theirs or mine as the pursuit, in cold pure horrifying beauty, was performed in the colored infinitely personal stand of stone-hard black boles with their black limbs stretching into the large night.

Those who pursued were young and big and ran with the speed of a cheetah, the muscular strength of a rhinoceros, the sureness of any cliché. The night loved and abetted them, for them rosy and alluring, for them tightly knit into their closed and damned-happy lives.

Ahead of me, coming in from the right, a smooth-faced boy with black hair, impenetrable, then wearing a look of malign joy at knowing he would catch me.

With a new speed I ran faster, covering the ground in grating lashing strides, wearing myself out, forgetting everything I had learned in the steam, the wheeling complexity of story that was my life; the crowd of boys crossed their shadows with those of the trees and the nuances belonging to them and to the trees, running possessed, dangerous, quite liquid in the beautiful dumb landscape.

The stone houses rose ahead of me, the labyrinth my haven to be reached, the shut look of night windows my assurance no one would tell they had seen me in a deep forgetting alley, a shed, any one house.

Totally thrilled in the dying spasm of the last spurt, vital in the wide stillness, horror in my glands raiding the last of my woman's strength, I lost my pursuers as I cunningly ran and then walked in a sort of calm into the depth of the stone town.

Then into my house where the smell of lilacs and roses met my flayed nostrils; the insecurity that had been down around my hair subsided, left; still breathing fast but wildly alive I stood beside the window looking into the garden as dawn came down freshly no-color to rest on the world I never knew well enough yet knew I loved. And had I learned during my flight; and had I been made more than a moving thing in the hazardous quitting staring night; was I a small container of fear only because of chase, because of encounter, because death fleered, clapped, jeered, wound life into that tight spinning coil, sent boys to rend night and continuity . . .

I touched the pear, the peach on the sill by the open window, smelling them; knew the night had wrested continuum from off my shoulders as an impersonal barber would cut my hair, deftly, easily, carelessly; I had received a gift from the night, a punctuation so great as to be deserving of honor at some rife dignified altar thumbing its nose at security, wearing one incredibly rare scented flower on its clean surface.

Letters had come; they lay on the table; taking them to my large bed by another casement from which I could see the lavender mountains with their white and pink rock summits and taking off my clothes I lay down to read. Hunger did not strike; the night seemed to have taken the need away as another gift; an altar to no hunger, altars everywhere; I hung my hand calmly over the side of the bed thinking about altars I would erect: to plump oozes of life in its food, flesh, laughter, especially laughter; to my friends my words a steel and birch altar with my thanks to something somewhere; to the singing notes of the wind in rigging off Ireland particularly, to the singing notes of a train, that fortress of welcome home, to the singing notes of a small morning hen just looking, walking; to the small audience I have met and not all known, revealing with a certain strength their nakedness as one is shown an engine either in early or highly wrought model, but I, a woman, cannot fathom engines though I can invent them; and to a great ancient cultivated impersonal kindness that winds the receiver in a beautiful blanket of otherness, feeling deserving and cherished, the best product...

These altars stood restfully at the back of my mind as I read one by one the letters from David, Harold, Felix, Morgan... all materialized in their various selves in the morning room as I read; their worlds, the world settled in attitudes filling my thoughts just emptied by the running and the smoke and fire of life rested on me on my bed. The memory of the delights of lust arrived with these reminders and I was torn with longing for the departed; but they would all come back; each assured me of this, remembering the mystical-temporal room intemperately filled, or at a walking pace filled; they did not forget.

Only one thought rose to prod their rich images from immediacy: when, then, if they came back, could I run in the boundless thrill of a night like the one past; they could not give this; but then I counted their innumerable bignesses, their variety, their power, their roughness to be smoothed, their varied eyes to be answered with quality and quantity by mine with a reflection so that they could see; and I stayed quiet, and waited...

But later, as the stars were coming again and the wind rose, I heard a susurration, a scuff, a bitter snicker, the indecision of boring children and smelled the perfume of the boys; I was not surprised that night by a summons to come and run, run again, for the boys so that they could forget: forget the coming no-plot, their unseen unknown manhood and all the altars...

Knowing their need, and for the wonderful game and terror, the white shrilling terror of it all because one of us might die, I dressed, I opened the door, I descended the steps into their milling disquieted smelling midst, and vanished ahead of them in the large darkness where the town ended.

# ON THE AUTHOR

Jackie Seiden

EMILY KATHARINE HARRIS was born in Ithaca, New York. A graduate of Radcliffe College and The Philadelphia Museum School of Art, she has done extensive work in poetry, prose fiction and painting. Her stories and poems have appeared in many journals here and abroad. Her poems are represented in Walter Lowenfels' anthology, *In a Time of Revolution*, and in the Dremen Press' *Anthology of Women Poets*. Four volumes of her poems have been published. Her paintings have been represented in art exhibitions at The National Gallery of Art in Washington, D. C., the Everson Museum in Syracuse, New York, and in many others on the eastern seaboard. With her husband, Richard Hill, the author lives in Binghamton, New York, where she writes, paints and teaches in the Poetry Studio at Roberson Center for the Arts and Sciences. She has written two novels, *A Tree of Hearts* and *The Far Festival*, and is currently working on a third.